DIRTY
FOR ME

DIRTY
FOR ME

Jackie Ashenden

KENSINGTON BOOKS
www.kensingtonbooks.com

KENSINGTON BOOKS are published by

Kensington Publishing Corp.
119 West 40th Street
New York, NY 10018

All Kensington titles, imprints, and distributed lines are available at special quantity discounts for bulk purchases for sales promotion, premiums, fund-raising, educational, or institutional use.

Special book excerpts or customized printings can also be created to fit specific needs. For details, write or phone the office of the Kensington Sales Manager: Kensington Publishing Corp., 119 West 40th Street, New York, NY 10018. Attn. Sales Department. Phone: 1-800-221-2647.

Kensington and the K logo Reg. U.S. Pat. & TM Off.

eISBN-13: 978-1-4967-0391-0
eISBN-10: 1-4967-0391-X
First Kensington Electronic Edition: August 2016

ISBN-13: 978-1-4967-0390-3
ISBN-10: 1-4967-0390-1
First Kensington Trade Paperback Printing: August 2016

10 9 8 7 6 5 4 3

Printed in the United States of America

To Ms. Street, my fourth-form English teacher.
You were the first one to tell me
I could write and that's why I'm here.

Acknowledgments

I would like to thank my editor, Martin Biro, for his fabulous editing. My agent, Helen Breitwieser, for getting the Royals into print. Maisey Yates, for holding my hand while writing this book. Megan Crane, for saying "the story with the scene in the car? THAT scene?" And to Nicole Helm, for reading and thinking it was hot.

You, gentleman and ladies, all rock.

Chapter 1

"Here?" Tamara Lennox turned around to give her friend Rose an incredulous look as they got out of the taxi. "Really?"

Rose's brown eyes glittered in the neon-painted darkness of the Detroit night. She was looking at the building in front them, a big, broken-down warehouse, its brick walls thick with graffiti and some of the windows smashed and boarded up. A narrow doorway led into the building, a small sign above that read ROYAL ROAD GYM—the only signal they'd reached the right place.

"Yeah." Rose gave her a naughty grin. "Really."

"Great," Tamara muttered.

She liked Rose, she really did. She hadn't made many friends at Lennox Investments where she'd been interning for the past six months, because she hadn't had time to make any. She'd been concentrating too hard on work. Yet Rose had brushed aside all her refusals, approaching friendship with Tamara the way she approached everything—aggressively. Yeah, Rose was great. But there were times when Tamara really questioned the other woman's judgment.

Such as now, as they stood on the sidewalk in the middle of one of Detroit's shadier neighborhoods, on a hot Wednesday night, and all because Rose had heard about the even hotter instructor who taught women's self-defense classes.

Tamara let out a breath, staring at the shitty-looking building ahead of them. Well, she couldn't say she was surprised. Rose wasn't serious about much except when it came to men. And she was deadly serious about men.

Her friend narrowed her gaze at Tamara, giving her outfit a disapproving glance. "You should be joining in, you know."

Tamara pulled a face. Obviously the soft, dark blue designer jeans and white cashmere blend T-shirt she'd gotten on a Barneys shopping trip the last time she'd been in New York visiting Robert weren't exactly appropriate self-defense wear. But then she wasn't the one taking the classes.

"Moral support only," Tamara said, closing her fingers around the strap of her Louis Vuitton purse. "I told you. That's the only reason I'm here." Starting to feel a little bit too downtown and out of place, she carefully turned the distinctive monogram on the flap of her purse inward so it was less conspicuous.

"And I appreciate it, Tam, you know I do." Rose turned toward the gym doorway. "But what are you going to do for an hour? I don't think waiting on the sidewalk would work around here."

That went without saying. Here and there, Tamara could see signs of revitalization: a new building a couple of blocks away, the looming spike of a crane signaling construction, a cleaned-up old building with bright new signs flashing in the windows. But there were also too many boarded-up doorways, broken-up sidewalks, and seedy-looking sex shops to make a woman feel safe waiting around at night by herself.

A strange little thrill crawled down her spine, a prowling restlessness pacing under her skin.

She couldn't say why she'd come with Rose tonight, because she had a lot of work she had to get through and Royal Road wasn't exactly a top tourist destination. She wasn't too keen on the thought of learning self-defense either. Getting hot and sweaty with a bunch of strangers didn't thrill her and she avoided gym classes for precisely that reason.

Yet as soon as her friend had mentioned it, something had shivered through her, that restlessness. It had been dogging her for weeks now and where it had come from she didn't know. But she'd suddenly felt a little suffocated by her apartment. Like the walls were closing in. Like she needed to get out, feel some of that vibrant Detroit energy run through her like a current. Recharge herself.

She'd been working too hard.

Perhaps she should have tried to dress down a little more. Then again, it wasn't like she was swanning around in a cocktail dress. It was only jeans and a tee.

"I've got my phone." Tamara patted her purse. "I'll catch up on some work e-mails."

Rose shook her head. "You're way too dedicated, man."

Of course she was. She had to be. If she wanted a permanent position at Lennox Investments she had to work twice as hard as anyone else because her dad owned it. And she did want a permanent position. She hadn't worked her butt off at Stanford for nothing.

"I'm behind," she said. "It's no big deal."

"Okay, okay. Fine. But if that man in there is as hot as the girls in HR were saying, you might be finding your own way home, know what I mean?"

Tamara rolled her eyes. That was pretty much a given when going out with Rose. "So why did you drag me down here then?"

"Hey, I'm thinking of you, too, okay? Maybe the dude's got a friend or something."

"I have a boyfriend already, Rose. I don't know how many times I've told you that."

"What? That guy in New York? Whom we've never even seen?"

"Yes. That guy in New York." Tamara tried to keep the exasperation out of her voice. It wasn't the first time she'd had this conversation with Rose. "And you've never seen him because he's in New York."

Rose waved a hand. "Whatever. Just trying to help a girl out." She turned and started heading toward the doorway.

Tamara shook her head and followed Rose inside the building, stepping into the hallway.

It was just about as rundown as the exterior, narrow and dark, the floorboards dented and dirty. There was also a smell, of sweat and unwashed towels, and something else unpleasant Tamara couldn't identify. She wrinkled her nose at it. Why the hell couldn't Rose have found a hot guy giving self-defense classes somewhere else? Like at one of the cleaner, brighter gyms in her area? Why did it have to be in one of Detroit's meaner neighborhoods?

Rose pushed open a door that read GYM and Tamara let out a silent sigh of relief.

Light flooded a massive open space with concrete block walls and some exercise machines scattered around. There were a couple of punching bags hanging from the high ceiling and a boxing ring down one end, a water cooler and a bank of shelves with various different exercise gear stored on it standing near a wall.

Well, it wasn't at all like the polished, boutique gyms she was used to, and that sweaty, musty smell was still hanging around distastefully, but at least there was light.

Tamara looked around, hoping to find a chair or a bench or at least something to sit down on where she could wait.

Alas, there was nothing but the bare, dirty wooden floor.

A group of around ten women were already gathered in a circle near the ring, their eyes fixed on the man standing in the middle of the group, who turned as Rose and Tamara entered.

"Holy shit," Rose breathed. "The HR girls weren't kidding."

Eyes the color of polished steel swept them a glance, sharp as a sword blade. "You here for the self-defense class?" The man's voice was husky, gritty like fine sand, a kind of energy running through it. Like Detroit itself, always moving, changing. Full of punchy vitality and a stubborn determination.

And for some reason it made Tamara's breath catch.

"Uh, yeah." Rose was already walking forward, dumping her purse near the shelves. "Sorry about that. Traffic was a nightmare."

Tamara couldn't stop staring at the instructor. God, he was beautiful. His face was all perfect lines, straight nose and hard jaw, high cheekbones, a long, gorgeous mouth. And yet marring all that perfection were the stitches through one dark, winged eyebrow, the bruise along one side of that classical jawline. A half-healed cut marring the perfect shape of his lower lip.

A shiver brushed over her skin, though she couldn't fathom why. Since when had she ever gotten off on scars?

The women shifted around him, an unfocused blur as the circle parted and he came toward them, moving with the lethal, fluid grace of a leopard.

Her heart began to pick up speed.

There was something about him, as if the restless energy in his voice moved along the surface of his skin, too. A barely leashed violence that pulsed in the air around him like electricity from a live wire. He almost crackled with it.

That, combined with the marks on his face made him . . . disturbing in a way she didn't quite understand. She found herself rooted to the spot as he came closer, his strange, glittering silver gaze catching hers, a blade running straight through her.

This is what you've been searching for. What you didn't even realize you wanted.

The thought registered dimly in her brain, a strange fear gathering in the pit of her stomach.

Weird. Why would she have been searching for him? She didn't even know the guy. And besides, how could a man in a tight-fitting, faded black tee and black sweatpants be threatening?

Yet . . . somehow, he was. Projecting violence and darkness and danger like a storm front, switching something primitive in her brain into fight-or-flight mode.

She held the strap of her purse in a death grip.

He stopped abruptly in front of them and when his gaze switched from her to Rose, it felt like she'd been released from heavy chains.

"Traffic?" he demanded. "At this time of night?"

Rose, who was never cowed, blinked. "Um . . . Yeah."

"Bullshit. For future reference, if you're gonna be late, I don't wanna see you. Understand me?"

Rose all but shuffled her feet like a teenager. "Sorry. I didn't—"

"What's your name?"

"Rose."

"Rose, I'm Ezekiel West. You can call me Zee. Now get your ass in the circle."

Without a single protest, Rose did as she was told. Which was unheard of, if you knew Rose.

Zee switched his gaze back to Tamara and again the air seemed to thin around her, the ground unsteady under her feet. "What about you?" He swept a look down her body, his cut lip curling as he took in her preppy jeans and T-shirt. "You here for the class or what?"

"No," Tamara said carefully, forcing her voice to work. "I'm just waiting for my friend."

His gaze came back to hers. And for a moment it felt like he could see right inside her. Right down to her bones, to her soul.

It made the fear turn over inside her, panic closing long fingers around her throat.

What the hell? He can't see inside you, idiot. Pull yourself together.

What was wrong with her? This guy was seriously freaking her out for some reason she didn't understand, and she did not appreciate it one bit.

"Uh-huh." He was still staring at her, the electricity radiating from him, crackling over her skin. Burning right through her clothes. Holy crap . . . "No one comes into my gym to do nothing," he said flatly. "Either you get involved or you get out."

Arrogant bastard. She was used to arrogance from Robert's friends, or from some of the people in the social circles her family moved in. But certainly not from some guy in sweatpants with bruises all over his face, in a shitty part of town.

Still, it wouldn't do to be rude. A Lennox was never rude.

"I'm sorry," she said coolly, "but I'm not dressed for the class. And I'm certainly not waiting outside in the dark."

He continued to stare, the sheer intensity of his focus unnerving.

Resisting the urge to lick her dry lips, she tried a polite smile instead. "Do you have anywhere I can sit?"

He said nothing for what seemed like a very long time. Then, with an abruptness that was only just short of rude, he turned away. "Nothing but the ground, pretty girl," he said carelessly over his shoulder.

It was not a compliment, that much she knew.

Tamara gritted her teeth and looked around for somewhere that maybe had less dirt on it than where she was standing. There wasn't anywhere.

So she sat gingerly on the floorboards, her back against the concrete wall, her purse held tight to her side. Her heart still beating hard and fast.

Crazy. This was crazy. It just made no sense at all.

She'd never met a man—anyone—she'd had such an instant and strong reaction to, and why it was this guy causing her such a chemical imbalance she had no idea. For God's sake, Robert was just as good-looking yet she'd never even felt that way about *him*. And he was her damn boyfriend.

The concrete was rough against her back, no doubt snagging on the fine cashmere of her tee, but Tamara ignored it as she got her phone out of her purse and began going through her e-mails.

Another one from her mother, long and full of the usual boring society gossip.

Zee's husky, gritty voice drifted in the big empty space of the gym and Tamara couldn't help herself, looking up from her phone screen to see what was going on.

He was demonstrating some move or other, at first fast and fluid, then slowing it right down so the women could see each separate movement.

She couldn't take her eyes off him. It was as if he'd taken that restless, violent energy and channeled it into a series of precise shifts of his body. A hold. A pivot. A kick. A turn. All of it measured and controlled. All of it powerful.

He must be a professional fighter. Martial arts or whatever.

God, she shouldn't have been looking. She'd always abhorred violence and she was inclined to go with her instincts on this one. If her gut said the guy was bad news, he probably was. And boy was this one bad news.

Yet she still didn't look away. Couldn't.

His T-shirt was starting to stick to his body in the heat of the gym, outlining the hard, cut muscles beneath. Broad shoulders and narrow hips, his skin tanned and smooth and . . . inked. There were what looked like flames extending from under the sleeve of his tee, licking around the powerful muscles of his right upper arm. On his left the coils of what looked to be a serpent.

Well, of course he had tattoos. Didn't all professional fighters have them? They weren't her thing at all so why she was staring at them?

Zee had stopped in the middle of the circle, still talking, running an absent hand over black hair shorn close to his skull. The women were clearly all enthralled, including Rose, who didn't even glance in Tamara's direction.

Tamara wrenched her gaze away and concentrated her attention on her phone.

No. No more looking. She had work to do and she wasn't going to be distracted.

An interminable time later, the buzz of chatter rose and when she glanced up, she saw the group of women were starting to break up. A few of them were gathered around Zee and the looks on their faces were openly avid. Rose—unsurprisingly—was one of them. The rest had drifted over to the pile of purses near the water cooler, talking among themselves as they started gathering up their belongings.

Tamara got to her feet, brushing off the dust and hoping there were no permanent stains on her jeans. Her butt was numb from sitting on the floor and quite frankly she couldn't wait to get back to her downtown apartment and finish the spreadsheet she'd been working on, then get started on the presentation Scott, her asshole boss, had told her to put together. Focus on her path to success; that was the key.

And maybe not the hot self-defense instructor.

No. Especially not him.

Soon enough, Rose went to get her purse, slinging it over her shoulder as she came over to where Tamara stood. Her cheeks were pink, her forehead sheened with sweat, and she was looking a little sheepish. "Hey, a couple of the others are going to a new club that's just opened near here and I thought I'd go along. Do you mind? Or you know, if you want to come . . ."

This wasn't entirely unexpected behavior from Rose and Tamara tried not to feel annoyed, but irritation sat in her gut all the same. Fantastic. So not only had she had to sit for an hour on a dusty gym floor, fighting the almost overwhelming urge to keep glancing at Zee, but now she was being ditched in favor of a club.

This evening was getting better and better.

"Thanks for the offer, but no. I've got a spreadsheet I need to finish." She forced a smile on her face. "Besides, I don't want to get in the way of . . ." She directed a glance toward Zee. "You know . . ."

Rose pulled a face. "Zee apparently doesn't do the chicks in his classes, or so Katie over there tells me. So if I want to hook up tonight, it's the club or nothing."

"You really have to hook up tonight?"

Rose gave her an incredulous look. "Is that really a serious question? I haven't gotten laid in, like, two weeks. A girl has needs." A naughty grin spread over her face. "Oh and I hear this club is a serious bad-boy magnet and you know how I love a bad boy."

Yes, Tamara knew that very well indeed since Rose had no problem sharing blow-by-blow descriptions of her various conquests. "How are you going to get home then?"

"Don't worry about me. I'll be with Katie and the others. I'll organize my own ride."

Excellent. So she was going to have to find a taxi herself, was she? Trying not to think about the broken-up sidewalks and abandoned buildings outside, Tamara clutched her purse tightly. "Fine. Well . . . have a good evening, I guess."

Her friend lifted a suggestive eyebrow. "Hey, no reason you can't get lucky. Especially since you're not actually taking his class and all."

Tamara pulled a face. "Boyfriend, remember?"

Rose blinked. "But tall, dark, and tattooed. And a body like you wouldn't believe. Perhaps you can work something out with your guy in New York? A get-out-of-jail-free card?"

Tamara shook her head. Her relationship with Robert was long-distance, but they'd never talked about seeing other people. At least he hadn't and neither had she, mainly for the simple reason that she'd never met anyone else she wanted. She'd assumed the same of him.

But what if that's not the case? What if he's been sleeping around?

It was a shock to realize that the thought didn't really bother her all that much.

Disturbed, she ignored it. "Tattoos are not the be-all and end-all, believe it or not."

Rose only snorted.

The small group of women began to head toward the gym's exit, one of them gesturing at Rose to follow.

"You're going to be okay going home?" her friend asked belatedly as she turned toward the group.

Tamara got the feeling that "no" wouldn't be what Rose wanted to hear and since it wasn't worth making a fuss about, she only smiled. "Of course. I'll get a cab home. You go and enjoy yourself, okay?"

Rose grinned back, gave her a thumbs-up, then vanished through the gym's exit along with the others.

Tamara took a deep breath and then started after them.

No, she wasn't going to turn around and see where Zee had gotten to.

No, she didn't need to see him one last time.

The hallway was as dark and as dingy as it had been on the way in and she *really* wasn't looking forward to going out there by herself and finding a taxi, but maybe she'd get lucky.

Then abruptly, the door behind her banged open again. "Hey," a deep, rough, and gritty masculine voice said. "Where the fuck do you think you're going?"

She stilled, her heartbeat fast and furious. "I'm leaving, what does it look like?"

"You're not going with the others?"

"Not tonight."

"You gonna get a taxi?"

"What is this? Twenty questions?" She didn't turn, just started walking. "But yes, I'm getting a taxi."

"Where to?" It was not a polite request. It was a demand.

A ripple of anger moved through her, though she didn't really know why. Repressing it, she stopped and turned around to see Zee standing in the doorway, one tanned and tattooed arm resting against the doorframe, those uncanny silver eyes fixed on her.

Something hot stirred in her blood. A shifting, hungry, unfamiliar thing.

It irritated her.

Lifting her chin, Tamara gave him the ice queen stare she'd perfected during her college years, the one that had cowed and discouraged many an unwelcome advance. "Where do you think? I'm going home, if you must know. Not that it's any of your business."

"You don't wanna be standing out on the sidewalk for a taxi in this neighborhood." His gaze never left hers. "Pretty little rich girl like you wouldn't last long."

Pretty little rich girl. How patronizing.

You're only pissed because he's right. Standing out on the sidewalk here would *be a stupid idea.*

Her fingers moved restlessly on the strap of her purse. For some reason, she really didn't want him to see her uncertainty. "Thanks for the concern, but I'm sure I'll be fine."

Zee leaned against the doorframe. "You're a little lamb, pretty girl," he said casually. "And there are wolves in this neighborhood who would eat you for breakfast. So I guess that depends. Do you wanna be breakfast or do you wanna be alive?"

Her spine stiffened. She was no one's breakfast and she wasn't a lamb. He had no idea.

Careful. Keep it under control.

She forced down her annoyance. "Don't you have something else to do? Someone's butt to kick?"

His smile was white in the dim light of the hallway. "You should have taken my class. Then I wouldn't need to worry about you standing out there on the sidewalk by yourself."

"Yes, well, I'm sorry, but I'm not taking any classes right now. And you don't need to worry about me. Like I said, I'll be fine."

There was a moment when she thought he was going to drop it. Where she expected him to do what any of the other guys she knew would do, which was to shrug their shoulders and back away, leaving her alone.

But he didn't. He just looked at her and she felt the air between them get dense and thick, humming with static like the atmosphere before a particularly violent thunderstorm. Then, with a sharp movement, he stepped into the hallway, the gym door slamming shut behind him.

It happened so fast that even hours later, she still couldn't figure out quite how he'd managed it.

One moment they were facing each other in the dim hallway. The next she was up against the wall and he was standing in front of her, caging her, his palms flat on the dingy plaster on either side of her head.

Tamara stared at him, shock forcing all the air from her lungs.

His eyes gleamed, cold and sharp as razors from beneath thick black lashes. "You shouldn't come here if you can't handle yourself, baby."

She blinked, still unable to process quite what was happening. The heat coming off him was incredible and he smelled of hot metal, oil, and clean, male sweat. And something else, a spice she couldn't quite identify.

Her mouth dried, her heart battering itself against the cage of her ribs, that strange knot of sensation in her gut gathering excruciatingly tight.

For God's sake, pull yourself together. He's just another man being an asshole.

Yes, good point. After the problems she'd been having with Scott at work, she was getting really sick of men being assholes.

She swallowed. "Perhaps you should have thought of that when you decided to have women's self-defense classes at night, in a shady part of town."

"The classes aren't for the likes of you. They're for women here, not fucking sightseers."

Her heartbeat was now like a drum in her head. She could barely hear anything over the sound of it. "Look," she said, trying to keep her voice level. "I just want to go home. So back the hell off."

He smiled. "Make me."

The blonde's lovely eyes were wide and he could see fear in them, staring back at him. But that was good because fear would save her. Being afraid was a healthy survival mechanism and if there was one thing he tried to teach women in his classes it was to listen to their fears.

Don't be a hero. Stay alive.

His classes weren't intended for rich bitches from downtown looking for a bit of rough. They had their own protection built in, along with their wealth and privilege. Except of course when they came down here on their own like lambs to the slaughter, all helpless and unknowing. Thinking they could just wander outside and wait for a taxi in their fancy-fucking-ass designer clothing and monogrammed purses.

Christ, they pissed him off, especially women like this one. So fucking beautiful. Deep golden hair in a high ponytail and smooth, soft-looking golden skin. She had dark eyes for a blonde, lovely and deep, the kind a man could lose himself in.

And she smelled . . . Jesus, he didn't know what kind of perfume she wore, but it was expensive and it smelled like a garden after a rainstorm, sweet and sensual and heavy. It was delicious.

You're not pissed off. You're turned on.

Yeah, well, he couldn't deny he'd felt the charge of attraction almost as soon as she'd walked in with her friend, long-legged and delicate as a butterfly, staring at him with those dark, guarded eyes as if he were a dangerous dog.

An inexplicable attraction.

He'd spent the whole class only half paying attention to what he was trying to teach, the rest turning over in his head just what it was about the rich-bitch blonde that held him absolutely riveted. Because it wasn't like he had a shortage. He had ring bunnies and fight groupies lining up outside his bedroom door most nights and all of them were just as beautiful as this woman. She wasn't anything special.

So why have you got her bailed up against the wall?

Stupid fucking question. He was being a prick and intimidating her to prove his point, which was a dick move, but in his experience it generally worked.

Her chin lifted, jutting determinedly. "Make you do what?"

Fuck, her voice was pretty too, winding around him, softness with a faintly rough edge, like raw silk. "Make me back off. If you can do it, I'll let you leave on your own."

What he should be doing was just letting her leave and to hell with her. Yet as soon as he'd noticed her exit the gym on her own, he knew he couldn't let her go, not without at least seeing if she was okay. He had enough on his conscience already.

Her gold-tipped lashes swept down. Beneath the pristine white of her T-shirt, her breasts rose and fell fast and hard, the pulse at the base of her throat frantic. Oh yeah, she was afraid, though she was doing her best to hide it.

He nearly felt sorry for her. Until her knee rose, catching him off guard as it aimed directly for his crotch. Sneaky girl.

Blocking her easily enough with one arm, he slid his hand beneath her upraised thigh, catching it and holding on tight.

The hiss of her indrawn breath echoed in the silence of the hallway and he could feel the heat of her through the denim of her jeans, her muscles trembling beneath his palm. The fear was still there in her eyes, but beneath that he could see a flicker of anger. Good. Anger helped. As long as you remained in control of it, of course.

He raised an eyebrow at her. "Now what?"

Her mouth flattened. "Now you let me go."

"You haven't made me back off yet."

Again those soft, lush lashes of hers swept down, veiling her gaze. "I'm not your student. I don't know how to do that."

"Then stop fucking around. You can't handle yourself, admit it."

Her body had gone rigid, the flush rising in her skin evident even in the dim light of the hallway. "Do you always harass women who come to your classes like this?"

Actually, he didn't. Not unless they wanted to be harassed and some of them certainly did, not that he ever took them up on the offer. He had a firm rule about not messing around with his students and he never broke it. Besides, the women who came to his classes tended to be vulnerable and vulnerable women weren't his type.

So why are you touching her? Remember, asshole. When you screw around with girls like her, they tend to get broken.

Exactly. Girls like this one were meant for rich fucks in fancy downtown offices, with fancy downtown apartments. Porsches in the garage and country club memberships. Not for guys like him with violence in their pasts, who fought most nights just to let off steam and got their hands dirty working as mechanics in garages during the day.

Yet still, he didn't let her go. She was all warmth and expensive softness, like the fancy material of her T-shirt, like a luxury he couldn't afford. And Christ, it had been so fucking long since he'd allowed himself any luxuries. "Not usually. I make exceptions for pretty girls hanging around in places they shouldn't."

She muttered something under her breath. "Okay, you win. Clearly I can't fight you off. Now can you please let me the hell go?"

He didn't really want to, which was a worry, but he forced his fingers to release her, stepping back to give her some space. "If you'd taken my class you would have known what to do. I give tips on the right way to knee a guy in the balls."

She'd pushed herself away from the wall and was smoothing down her T-shirt, her other hand still clutching her ridiculous designer purse. "Thank you, but no thank you," she said in a crisp, scrupulously polite voice. "I keep telling you, I'm not here for the classes."

"Why not?"

She stopped smoothing. "Because I don't agree with using violence as a means to defend myself, that's why."

Jesus. He wanted to laugh, nearly did. That kind of attitude was nice for the people who could afford it, shitty for the people who couldn't. "So what would you have done if I'd been seriously trying to hurt you just now? Cut me to death with some sharp words?"

Something shifted in her dark eyes. "But you didn't hurt me. I was fine."

"That's not the point."

"What's it to you anyway?"

"You got a problem with me not wanting to see a woman get hurt?"

She looked away at that. "No. Of course not."

There was a strange, tense sort of silence.

Fuck, what *was* it about her? Was it the fact she wasn't falling all over herself to get in his pants? Or was it the air of expensive privilege around her that made him want to smash through it and show her what the real world was all about? Or was it because he just wanted to touch something soft and beautiful for a change?

Oh, hell no. You can't do that. Remember?

Yeah. He did. And really, he should be getting back to the gym and stop wasting time proving whatever the fuck he was trying to prove to this woman. People like her never got it anyway.

Yet he didn't move. "What's your name?" he asked, because he realized he didn't know.

She gave him a wary look. "Tamara. Tamara Lennox."

"Okay, Tamara Lennox. Two things. One, you're not gonna find a taxi because they don't come down this end of the city at night. And two, if you walk out of here right now, despite my warnings, you're on your own. Got it?"

One fair eyebrow arched. "I think I got it. And I have a phone. I'll call a company."

Let her go. She thinks she can handle it? Let her. She's no concern of yours.

Zee fought down the automatic denial. He'd been there, done that with a woman before and it had all turned to shit. He wasn't doing it again.

"Suit yourself," he said.

Giving him a last wary look, Tamara Lennox turned gracefully on her heel and headed down the hallway to the exit.

He watched her all the way and tried not to wonder if he'd just made a big mistake.

Chapter 2

Tamara stepped onto the cracked pavement outside and instantly wished she'd decided to go with Rose to the club instead of insisting on going home.

The night was hot and there were a few more people around than there had been before. A gang of youths laughed and catcalled outside a liquor store across the street, while at the seedy-looking bar a bit farther down a drunk had collapsed onto the pavement.

A group of young women in short skirts, tattoos, and piercings approached, giving Tamara some scornful looks and yelling a few obscene comments as they passed by.

She ignored them, too caught up in the fact that her heartbeat was racing and parts of her skin felt burned, like she'd pressed up against a hot oven door. And that she was almost shaking with anger.

And the worst part of all was that she didn't even know why.

Yes, you do.

Okay, so it was Zee. It was the fact that he'd been an asshole and caging her against that wall had been an egregious invasion of her personal space. But she was normally way cooler at handling stuff like that. For example, she'd been expertly dealing with her boss being a giant bastard for the past six months now, yet even he hadn't managed to get her as wound up as Zee had in five seconds flat.

It's not just anger you're feeling.

She swallowed, wanting to deny it to herself, yet knowing she couldn't. Because the effect his physical presence had on her was still echoing through her body. She could still feel the intensity of the heat that had radiated from him. Still smell the scent of oil and sweat, and that unforgettable spice. And when she closed her eyes, she could still see his looking back. A clear, perfect gray with a darker charcoal around the edges, like tarnished silver. . . .

Taking a deep, shaky breath, she held it. Then let it out.

Damn. She couldn't feel attracted to him. She already had a boyfriend, and even besides that, why on earth would she be attracted to anyone who shoved her up against a wall and dared her to try to move him? Okay, so he might be incredible to look at, but he had scars all over his face and tattoos all over his body. And she'd never gone for the bad-boy look.

So why are you still thinking about him? Come on, you've been so restless, wanting something like this to happen. . . .

Tamara shut down that thought hard. Nothing was going to happen, Zee was the very opposite of her type and she shouldn't be feeling any of this stuff for him. She needed to get a handle on herself, lock it all down.

Not exactly the right behavior for a Lennox, after all.

Yet . . . her thigh burned from where he'd held it. And she could almost feel the imprint of each finger even through the denim of her jeans. The sheer strength of that grip and the speed with which he'd moved . . .

Robert had never held her like that. He had always been very restrained and respectful. And he certainly had never made her feel that tight, half-scared, half-excited feeling.

She swallowed. Why the hell was she thinking about Robert? And why was she comparing him with Zee? Okay, she was *really* insane now and she should definitely be paying attention to her surroundings, not thinking about stupid Zee.

She took another look around.

The youths across the street were shouting about something, and one of them had his head turned in her direction. Down the sidewalk to her right, the door to a building opened with a crash and a group of guys burst out of it, all laughing hysterically.

A deep sense of unease settled in her gut.

Zee hadn't been wrong. Hanging around here on her own was a really bad idea. In her designer gear, she looked exactly like what she was: a poor little rich girl stuck in the wrong part of town. She should have worn something more inconspicuous, except she'd thought she *was* wearing something inconspicuous. Which was stupid in retrospect. Grosse Point jeans and a T-shirt was obviously going to be different from Royal Road jeans and a T-shirt.

She shouldn't have insisted she was fine. She shouldn't have let him get to her.

Forcing away the gathering panic in her gut, she scrabbled in her purse for her phone. Time to call a cab company and see if someone could come and pick her up. Yet when she pressed the button on the phone to turn it on, the screen lit up briefly, then went dark.

Shit. She was out of power. All that sitting around in the gym checking her e-mail must have drained the last of her battery. What the hell was she supposed to do now?

"Still here, pretty girl?"

Tamara turned sharply to see Zee closing the gym door behind him, then locking it.

A peculiar relief gripped her. He was an asshole and she *really* didn't want to ask him for help, but it was either that or she continued standing here like an idiot, putting herself at risk of being some wolf's breakfast. And she didn't want that. She had things to do.

"Oh hey," she said, hoping she didn't sound as scared as she feared she did. "I was going to ring the cab company, but . . . well . . ." She waved the phone at him. "I ran out of power. I don't suppose I could borrow yours, could I?"

Zee glanced at the phone, then gave her a long, silent look that made her feel like she was five years old.

"Okay, so you were right," she said, now both annoyed *and* afraid. "Standing out on the sidewalk here *was* a really silly idea. But I'm trying to take care of it and I could really use your help."

A smile that looked suspiciously smug curved his mouth. Then he turned away from the gym door, already starting down the sidewalk. "Come on," he said. "We're gonna have to go by the garage to get my car."

"Wait, what?" Tamara stumbled after him, unwilling to let him vanish into the darkness and leave her stranded. "What do you mean get your car?"

He glanced over his shoulder. "I'll need it if I'm gonna give you a ride home."

"A ride home?" An inexplicable thrill went through her. A thrill she forced away. "I don't need a ride home. Just let me borrow your phone and I'll call a cab."

Zee shook his head. "Like I told you, cabs don't come down here after dark. So unless you're planning on standing on the sidewalk all night, you're gonna have to go with me."

Tamara hesitated. She really didn't want to go with him. She didn't know him from Adam and apart from anything else, the thought of being stuck in a small space such as a car with him for any length of time was . . . *exciting?*

No, not exciting. Definitely not exciting.

"Make up your mind, pretty girl." Zee was already turning,

heading down the sidewalk again. "Not gonna wait forever for you to decide. I got shit to do tonight."

Well, it wasn't like she had a choice. If she didn't go now, she'd be stuck here and being stuck here was a very bad idea.

Swallowing her trepidation or whatever the hell it was, Tamara followed him wordlessly, having to walk quickly to keep up with his long stride. Thank God she'd gone for trainers instead of heels.

He didn't speak as he walked or glance over his shoulder to make sure she was behind him and that suited her just fine. She definitely didn't want to talk to him, not that she would know what to say. It wasn't like they would have had much in common anyway.

Eventually he stopped outside a big metal roller door near the corner of the block, the words BLACK'S VINTAGE REPAIR AND RESTORATION spray-painted artistically on the front of it. There was a small door at the side, which he pushed open, jerking his head at her to indicate she was to go in first.

After a slight hesitation, Tamara did so, walking into a huge garage space brightly lit by fluorescent lighting along the ceiling. There were motorcycles everywhere, with parts neatly arranged along workshop counters that ran the length of the walls on either side of her. Banks of metal shelves full of tools and paint and other mechanical paraphernalia stood near one of the counters, beside a massive row of grimy windows. Some of the panes were cracked, others replaced with different colored glass, and it looked like it would let in a lot of light during the day. Right now, neon flashed across the glass, and through some of the open windows, the sounds of a raucous summer night filtered in.

God, it was hot. Her T-shirt was already starting to stick to her back.

Sparks abruptly lit an area off to her right, where an old-looking motorcycle was up on a stand. A powerfully built man in faded blue overalls stood bent over it, a welding torch in his hand. Beyond that was parked a huge, black muscle car, the garage lighting gleaming over the glossy paintwork.

Zee's car, no question.

Another movement caught her eye, the sound of a light female voice filling the quiet as the welding torch shut off. A woman sat on the worktop, legs dangling. She had black curly hair caught in a ponytail on top of her head and glasses on the end of her nose, and she wore frayed denim shorts, a black tank, and motorcycle boots.

Footsteps sounded and Tamara looked up to see another woman coming down a set of metal stairs that led up to what looked like an office. This woman's long hair was loose over her shoulders and dyed a brilliant electric blue. She wore the tiniest denim miniskirt Tamara had ever seen, a black T-shirt, black platform boots, and a studded metal belt. The bright colors of a full-sleeve tattoo covered one of her arms and a silver ring gleamed in her nose. "I ordered," the woman said as she came down the stairs. "Zee's not eating with us tonight is he? 'Cause if he is, he's going to be hungry."

"I'm not," Zee said as he stepped past Tamara. "I've got a fight later tonight."

Everyone turned in the direction of Zee's voice and Tamara braced herself.

"Who the hell is this?" The blue-haired woman had stopped on the stairs, her dark eyes narrowing suspiciously.

"This is Tamara." Zee moved over to the black car. "She was at my class. I'm giving her a ride home."

"I thought you didn't fuck the women in your classes?"

"Rachel." The man in the blue overalls put back the welding mask he wore over his face, his voice deep, and rough, and a touch reproving. He was tall as Zee and as broad, but older and more heavily muscled. His features were roughly handsome, his nose crooked, as if it had been broken at one time or another. Black stubble lined his strong jaw, while shaggy black hair curled over his collar. If Zee was the lithely muscled martial artist, this man was the heavyweight boxer. "Hey, Tamara," the man said, giving her an easy, friendly smile.

Tamara gave him a tight smile back. "Hi."

"I'm Gideon and this is Zoe." He jerked his head toward the younger woman perched on the bench. "Oh and ignore Rachel. She's pretty much rude to everyone."

Rachel folded her arms, scowling.

"Hey." Zoe lifted a hand. There was a smile on her face, but the big golden eyes behind her glasses were guarded.

Tamara felt her expression become fixed. She felt like she'd just crashed a small, exclusive, and intimate party, where everyone knew everyone else and strangers were definitely not welcome.

"I just need to grab the car," Zee said, pulling his keys from the pocket of his sweats.

"Sure." Gideon put down the welding torch. "Want me to get the door?"

"Yeah, thanks." Zee glanced at Tamara. "Come on, get in."

The two other women were gazing at her speculatively as she made her way across the garage to where the big black car stood. She tried to ignore them and the awkward tension that had suddenly pulled tight in the garage as she pulled open the passenger door and climbed in.

The car had black leather seats and smelled of polish and oil. Kind of like Zee, now that she thought about it. Did that mean he worked here? Obviously he knew the people and they seemed like friends. Perhaps one of the women was his girlfriend? Then again, the blue-haired woman, Rachel, had said something about him not screwing the women in his classes, so maybe not.

Zee got in the other side as the grinding rattle of the roller door being drawn up echoed through the space. He stuck a key in the ignition, turned it, and the car's engine started in a low, smooth rumble.

"What's your address?" he asked as the car slid out of the garage.

She didn't want to tell him all of a sudden. If he knew where she lived, that meant he could find her again. And she didn't want him finding her again.

What makes you think he'd even want to?

Well, he might not. But then again, he was a total stranger. She knew nothing about him other than the fact he could move fast and could probably kill her before she was even aware of being in danger. Which made it far better to be safe than sorry.

She gave him Rose's Midtown address instead. She could easily take a taxi from there to her own apartment.

Zee pulled out into the traffic while Tamara tried to pretend the heavy, tense silence that filled the car didn't exist. Their encounter in the hallway was all too fresh in her head, not to mention her own reaction to it, and she didn't want it there. She didn't want to talk either, didn't want to interact with him in any way. All she wanted was for the car journey to be over, to be in her own apartment, with his disturbing presence out of her life.

"You're really pissed with me, aren't you?"

The husky rumble of his voice, not to mention his observation, sent a little pulse of shock through her. How the hell had he picked up on that? "No, I'm not," she managed, at least sounding relatively calm.

"Bullshit. You're fucking mad as hell."

She held her purse on her lap, her fingers tight on the leather. "What makes you say that?"

"Because you're holding yourself all tense and your knuckles are white."

Tamara flashed him a glance. He wasn't looking at her, his gaze firmly out the front windshield. "I'm not."

"Sure you are. You've got a death grip on that purse of yours and you're sitting in that seat like if you move it's going to eat you alive." His head turned, his eyes a gleam of silver. "Or maybe it's me you're worried about. People usually get mad when they're afraid."

He's not wrong. It is him *you're worried about. Though not for the reasons he thinks . . .*

She gave a laugh that didn't sound as natural as she hoped. "Why would I be afraid of you?"

"I shoved you up against a wall. Tried to make you fight me. You were afraid, pretty girl, don't try to deny it."

Her jaw was tight with denial anyway, even though of course he was telling the truth. She had been afraid, just like she was afraid now. But she didn't really want to think about why that might be.

Or is it him you're worried about? Maybe it's yourself you need to watch.

Tamara refused the thought. "Well, what do you expect?" she said. "You're a complete stranger. I don't know you from a bar of soap. And one minute you're offering me a lift home, the next you're shoving me against walls."

"I'm not apologizing for it."

"You should. Being an asshole isn't a good way to drum up business."

His head turned again, his gaze sharp, gleaming. One corner of his long, beautiful mouth curved. "Calling me names now? Shouldn't you be minding your manners?"

She gritted her teeth. Yes, that's exactly what she should be doing. Her parents had brought her up better than that and as her mother had always told her, manners went a long way.

All she had to do was ignore the fact that the scent of him kept making her feel hot and restless. Rein in her awareness of the powerful muscle of his thigh inches away from hers. Of the long-fingered, blunt-tipped hands on the steering wheel.

No, damn—no looking at his hands.

"You're right," she said stiffly. "That wasn't polite. I apologize."

He laughed and the sound trailed down her spine like a velvet-covered finger. "You're just fucking with me now. I've been called worse, believe me."

"I'm sure." Despite herself, her gaze was drawn inexorably back to his hands on the steering wheel, hypnotized by those long, scarred fingers.

"I wasn't drumming up business anyway," he went on, seemingly not picking up her *don't talk to me* vibes. "I was only proving a point."

"By being threatening and intimidating?"

"Yeah. You needed to feel how vulnerable you are."

"Right, so I would know how stupid I was?" She tore her gaze resolutely away from his hands. "If so, point made."

"It's not about you being stupid. It's about being able to protect yourself."

"I can protect myself just fine."

"Like you did back in that hallway? That's why you accepted my ride, right? Because you could protect yourself and weren't afraid standing around out there on the sidewalk by yourself."

Anger roiled in her gut. She didn't want to have this conversation with him. It picked at an old scab, one that was painful. One that had been healing very well on its own. "Violence is not the answer."

"You think it's about violence?" He gave her another searing glance. "Pretty girl, it's about control."

She stared at him like he was insane. Well, whatever. He wasn't wrong. People who spouted all that anti-violence bullshit generally had no appreciation of the realities of life. It was all violence as far as he was concerned and pretending otherwise was just putting your fucking head in the sand.

What mattered was the control. In life, in the fight. Control of your actions, your decisions, your emotions. Every damn thing you did. Because once you lost control of yourself, you were fucking meat. He'd learned that lesson very early on.

That's what he enjoyed about his fights. They were a carefully controlled burn-off, allowing him to let a little of the darkness inside him out, in a place where everyone knew the rules. Where there were no surprises. You either won or you lost, there was nothing in between.

Because you couldn't fight the darkness. Everyone had it, everyone. Possibly even her.

But then what would she know? She was fucking money from head to toe. She reeked of it. Polished and perfect, she probably had never had to fight for anything in her whole damn life.

Christ, why was he pushing her again? If she didn't want to join the class, she didn't want to. He sure as shit wasn't going to force her.

What he was going to do was take her home—if the address she'd given him was indeed her home and he suspected it probably wasn't. Then he'd go back down to Gino's for this evening's fight, let off some of the steam that had been building up inside him.

Silence fell inside the car. She didn't ask him any more questions, withdrawing into herself, hiding behind the walls he'd seen in her cool, dark eyes.

If she'd been a different woman he might have found that intriguing. But she wasn't a different woman. She was the kind he'd never touch, not in a million years. Not after what had happened to Madison.

Christ, if he wanted pussy there'd be plenty of it at the fight anyway. The girls there never asked for his number afterward. They were as happy to fuck and run as he was.

They were drawing up to the address she'd given him, some nice-looking Midtown brick building with a café at street level and apartments up top. The gentrification had well and truly happened here, nothing like the first stages that were going on down in Royal Road, his own neighborhood. There were a few things that had been revived, an old warehouse—much like his shitty gym—that was now a nightclub. An abandoned row of stores that had been converted into a restaurant and café. The old building housing Rachel's tattoo studio that she was looking to turn the rest of into an art gallery. Yeah, it was happening all right. Part of why he'd stayed in Detroit when common sense should have told him to get out and get as far away from the city as possible. Because, fuck, if Detroit could rebuild itself, come out good as new, then so could he.

Slowly he drew the Trans Am up beside the curb and stopped.

She began to fiddle with her seatbelt. "Thank you. I appreciate the trouble you took to—"

"I know this isn't your real apartment," he interrupted, not wanting to hear all her polite bullshit. "So I'll wait here until the taxi to take you home arrives."

Her hands paused a moment. Then she looked at him, her gaze unexpectedly direct. "Why are you doing this? I mean don't get me wrong, it's very nice of you, but I'm sure you don't give every woman you meet a ride home. Why me?"

So, she didn't protest about the apartment thing. This really wasn't her place. For some reason her clear lack of trust rankled, even though he hadn't given her any reason to trust him.

"Why not you?" Zee leaned back in his seat. "Or don't you think you're worth protecting?"

Color rose in her cheeks, but she didn't look away. "You're perfectly happy ferrying complete strangers around then?"

Women didn't normally ask him questions like this one did. The girls who hung around the ring wanting fighters were looking for hard muscles and rough sex, not anything more. And he was fine with that. He didn't want anyone trying to get to know him, trying to see past the curtain. He hadn't spent a good ten years putting his past behind him and turning himself into someone else for nothing.

This woman though . . . There was a challenge in her question, even if she didn't realize it herself. And the fighter in him wanted to answer it.

Bad move, man. Leave her alone.

He could smell her though, that expensive heavy, sensual scent. And he remembered the feel of her, the tense muscle of her thigh as he'd held it. She looked all class, sophisticated and cool, like fucking caviar wouldn't melt in her mouth. But she hadn't felt cool. Her body had been so goddamn hot it had nearly burned him alive.

She was still looking at him, watching him, so pretty and perfect in her designer clothes.

You know what happened last time you had a good girl.

A deeply buried grief shifted inside him, the edges of it sharp even after all those years.

"Get out," he said shortly, because those edges still had the power to cut him right down to the bone. "And don't let me see you wandering around Royal Road again, especially if you have no idea how to get yourself safely home. Christ, girls like you . . . You're a fucking liability."

Anger flared in her eyes. "Oh, don't worry." Her voice was stiff, cold. "I have no intention of going there ever again, believe me." She fumbled again with the seatbelt. The thing had always been tricky to open and she clearly wasn't having much luck with it.

He cursed. "Hang on. Let me undo that for you."

"No, it's okay. I can—"

Ignoring her, he leaned over to unfasten the clasp for her.

And then realized his mistake.

The scent of her hit him like a punch to the jaw, the drowned-flower smell now overlain with something else. Something like . . . musk. And damn, she was so hot. All the tugging she'd been doing had pulled the belt even tighter, which meant he was going to have to half lean over her in order to get it free.

She pressed herself into the seat as he did so, as if she were trying to escape out the back of it, and he could hear the sound of her breathing. Short, hard pants. And she was trembling. As if she was terrified.

He looked at her, unable to help himself.

But it wasn't fear in her gaze.

It was something else.

Chapter 3

She didn't know what the hell was happening to her. One minute she was furious, desperate to get out of the car and slam the door in Zee's arrogant, scarred face. The next she was fighting for breath as that hard, muscular body of his leaned over her to get at her seatbelt. And it wasn't anger lighting a fire in her blood, but a deep, dark hunger that had seemingly sprung out of nowhere.

Nowhere? Really?

Okay, not nowhere. The attraction to him had been pretty much instant the moment she'd seen him in the gym. But she'd thought she could ignore it, that she could keep it under control the way she kept everything else under control.

Yet now he was looking at her with those tarnished silver eyes of his, like blades so sharp there was no pain as they slid under her skin. And she didn't know why that made her so afraid, because it wasn't like the truth about herself was imprinted on her soul or anything. Sure, the eight years she'd spent applying herself, aiming hard for success, wasn't nearly enough, but once she'd gotten a place at her father's firm, once she'd realized the potential her parents had seen in her, then maybe it would be.

But Zee didn't know that. Zee couldn't see that. So why did the way he looked at her make her want to throw up her hands and shield herself?

"What?" she demanded, her voice hoarse, hating the strange desperation clawing up inside her. Hating the way she felt so vulnerable, especially in front of a complete stranger. God, how she loathed feeling so out of control.

He said nothing, only looked at her. He wasn't touching her anywhere, but he had one hand on the side of the seat near her thigh, the other reaching across her to pull at the belt on the doorframe. And he was so freaking close, his face inches from hers.

"Stop looking at me." She couldn't get a breath. Why couldn't she get a breath?

"You're not scared." It wasn't a question, more of a flat statement.

"What? What's that got to do with anything?"

"You're trembling."

Oh crap. So she was. "Because you're leaning over me like an asshole. Unfasten the damn seatbelt and let me get out." She tried to stop the little tremors shaking her, but it was impossible.

His gaze dipped, settling on her mouth for a moment before moving down, and in its wake she felt a wave of heat prickle all over her skin. Like he'd moved his hand over her, stroking her. Her nipples were getting hard, pressing against the fabric of her T-shirt, a hollow kind of ache gathering way down low inside her.

"I don't think that's why you're trembling." His gritty, husky voice was even rougher.

He was going to touch her. Oh God, he was going to touch her. And if he did . . .

You will burn.

"I have a boyfriend," she blurted out, the words shaky.

His gaze lifted to hers again and, quite frankly, that wasn't any better than when he'd been looking at her body. "Do you? He not look after you well enough?"

"Of course he does." Robert looked after her very well. The last time they were in New York, he'd brought her roses and taken her out for dinner.

"Pretty girl"—Zee's silver gaze searched hers—"your nipples are hard and you're shaking. And I'm gonna take a wild guess here that it's not him you're thinking about right now."

She could feel her cheeks blazing, embarrassment ricocheting through her. But she didn't want to give him the satisfaction of being right so she didn't look away. "How would you know? You know nothing about me."

"No, it's true. I don't. But I know when a woman's wet for me. And you are, Tamara Lennox, I can smell it."

Oh hell.

Tamara shut her eyes, as if by not seeing him, she could somehow pretend he wasn't there. But the crude words were resonating inside her, calling to a hidden part of her, a dark part she'd thought she'd excised a long time ago.

And he was so close, so very, very close. The underside of his wrist nearly brushing her thigh. The wide stretch of his chest inches from hers, the black cotton of his T-shirt molding to his body so she could almost see the hard muscle beneath it. The dark, wicked spice of his scent. The way he was leaning over her, looking down at her, intimidating her. . . . No, intimidating wasn't quite the right word. More like . . . overwhelming her with the sheer force of presence. And with the dirty, dirty things coming from his dirty, dirty mouth.

"I don't want you," she said, as if by saying it aloud that would make it true.

"Yes, you do." There was heat in his voice, lazy and soft. "Boyfriend or not, I think you're dying for me."

"I don't *want* to." She opened her eyes, staring straight back into his.

He hadn't moved, yet it felt as if he was even closer now. Inescapable. Overwhelming.

Bizarrely, all she could think about was Robert saying goodbye to her at the airport, about how she'd waited for his usual kiss, but he hadn't given her one. And she'd felt . . . relieved.

"I don't wanna want you either," Zee said. "But the way you smell is making me crazy."

"S-so let me out." Dammit, she hated that stutter. "Let me out and we never have to see each other again."

He didn't reply immediately, the silence becoming hotter, thicker.

Then he said, "Or, we could give each other a little relief first. Then you get out like you said and we never have to see each other again."

A little relief . . .

God, yes.

She sucked in a breath. "Did you miss the part where I said I had a boyfriend?"

"I don't give a shit about your boyfriend. Do you want me to fuck you? Yes or no?"

Such a crude word for it and yet now that he'd said it, she couldn't get it out of her head. Getting in the backseat with him, having his hands on her, having him inside her . . . A hard, violent, scarred stranger, taking her roughly.

It was wrong and it was dirty, and most importantly of all, it was out of control. And it pretty much went against everything she'd been trying to do for the past eight years.

You want it. You want him.

The expression on his face was tight, his eyes all lit up with the same kind of hunger that was turning her inside out. A hunger she'd never seen in Robert's eyes, not once. Her boyfriend didn't look at her like this, like he wanted to eat her alive.

Even the last time they'd had sex it had been . . . perfunctory, for lack of a better word. And that too had made her glad, though at the time, she hadn't been able to put a finger on why.

Because you didn't want anything more from him. You never have.

She was conscious of a certain shock moving through her. She'd met Robert at a party given by her parents and they'd introduced her to him. They'd encouraged her to date him and she had because he was in all ways perfect for her and they liked him.

But he'd never been her choice.

When was the last time you made a choice about anything?

"It's your choice," Zee said, uncannily echoing the insidious thought lurking in her brain. "But you'd better choose soon. I'm usually a patient man, but I'm kinda not feeling it right now."

Her body ached like it hadn't been touched in years, her heart beating wild and fast in her chest. And she was scared. Not of him, she knew that now, but of herself. Of what she wanted. Of the restlessness pacing about inside her soul, a need to reach out and grab hold of the energy that crackled around him, take it for herself.

The need to not, for once, keep it under control.

You'd never have to see him again.

Tamara swallowed. "Make me," she said, consciously imitating his earlier words to her.

Something flared bright in his eyes, the challenge she'd flung at him being accepted.

Then he lifted his hand from her seat belt and took her chin in his hand. The touch of his skin on hers was a shock that drove the breath from her body, made her go still in her seat. Then he turned her head to the side with a firm pressure. She trembled, unable to stop, staring out through the driver's-side window as he kept her head turned, every single cell of her body awake and aware.

Zee bent and she felt his breath whisper over her skin, the heat searing. Then she felt the brush of his lips and the firm pressure of his teeth closing around the tendons of her neck.

She jerked against the restraint of her seatbelt, a sharp sob escaping her as a burst of sensation overloaded every nerve ending she had. And just before the bite crossed the border from pleasure into pain, he eased back, his tongue licking over her skin, rough as a cat's.

Tamara shuddered, her breathing wild, his fingers holding her head to the side.

"Last chance to change your mind," he murmured against her throat. "Before I take us somewhere more private."

She shook her head, unable to speak. Because she wasn't going to change her mind. It was too late for that.

Zee said nothing, releasing her chin and moving back to sit in his seat. He started the car again, pulling away from the curb, and five minutes later he'd found a dark little alley to park in.

Tamara tried not to think too much as he turned off the engine, then leaned over and casually pulled open the clasp of her seatbelt. But a raw and quite frankly terrifying excitement had her in its grip, and she didn't know what to do with herself.

"Get in the back," Zee ordered, his voice full of rough heat.

And she did, awkwardly and without grace in all likelihood, twisting until she was sitting in the backseat, waiting for him.

Then he was in the back too, his arm catching her around the waist and hauling her over to sit in his lap, her back to his chest, so she was facing the driver's seat.

God, he was so hot, the feel of his body under hers hard and strong and powerful.

"Don't wanna make this obvious," he murmured, his arm tightening around her waist. "So let's pretend you're just sitting there, waiting for someone."

She tried to nod, but then his mouth brushed over the back of her neck, sensitive skin left bare by her ponytail, at the same time as his hand moved to the button of her jeans, deftly undoing it. Grabbing the tab of her zipper and jerking it down.

"I've never done this before," she heard herself say in a high, breathy voice, the words coming out of her before she could stop them. "With someone I don't know."

"Well, I have." His hand was resting on her stomach now. "Don't worry. I'll make it real good, I promise."

Maybe the fact that this was obviously not new to him should have bothered her. But it didn't. If anything, it was a reassurance that at least someone here knew what they were doing because she sure as hell didn't. And clearly she didn't. Two hours ago she'd only just met him and had disliked him intensely. Now here she was, in the back of his car and she was letting him screw her.

She could barely believe it was happening, let alone that she'd agreed to it.

But then his hand moved, pushing down beneath the waistband of her panties and all thought, all her nervousness and doubt, vanished utterly.

His fingers found her clit, brushing gently over it, and she stiffened as jolt of intense pleasure knifed straight through her. "Oh . . . God . . ." Her hands gripped on tight to the hard muscles of his thighs beneath her. She felt like she was burning up, like she was sitting on an open flame.

His hand moved again, his fingers easing down over her aching flesh, finding the entrance to her body and pushing inside. And a hoarse noise escaped her, a choked sob, pleasure like a bonfire building high.

"I knew it." His mouth brushed her neck again, his fingers easing out of her, then pushing back in again. "I fucking knew you'd be wet for me."

Her hips were moving helplessly against his hand, and she didn't feel awkward or nervous anymore. She felt desperate.

"Hold on to the seat in front of you and lean forward."

She obeyed without thought, trembling all over again as he removed his hand from between her legs, then shoved her jeans down, taking her panties with them. There was another pause, the sound of fabric shifting. His breathing was harsh in her ear as the crackle of foil filled the car.

"Lift up." The words were bitten off and taut.

She did so, shuddering. And then his hand was back, sliding over the bare skin of her butt and beneath her, between her thighs, spreading her, while the other hand rested on her hip, urging her back down onto him.

A long, low moan tore itself from her throat, the press of his cock stretching her wide. Because he was big and she was so damn close to the edge. She gripped tight to the seat in front of her, pressing her forehead against the headrest, and closed her eyes, her breathing wild.

"Ah . . . that's good." His voice was rough and raw, his hands on her hips now, holding her painfully tight, his cock buried deep inside her. "So fucking good."

His hips flexed as if he was testing the fit of her and she groaned at the friction, so close to coming already all it would take was another movement like that and she would go over. "Zee . . ." His name a broken whisper. "Don't. I'm nearly . . ."

He ignored her, flexing his hips again, and this time she did come, the orgasm crashing over her without warning, a rush of blinding pleasure that had lights bursting behind her eyes.

"Now," he said, his voice dark, gritty, and hot through the roar in her head. "Let's do this properly."

And his hands tightened on her hips and he held her there as he began to thrust in earnest, hard and sure and deep, each one shoving her forward against the seat in front of her, making her cry out, her knuckles white on the leather. Because it was almost too much. Almost too intense.

Every part of this was wrong. The sounds of his flesh sliding into her and the rough, growling noises he made as he thrust. The raw ache in her pussy and the exquisite friction of his cock. The way her forehead kept being pushed roughly into the seat in front and the thick, musky smell of sex.

All of it was wrong and dirty and so not what Tamara Lennox of the Michigan Lennoxes would be doing.

And for some reason she couldn't fathom, that made it perfect. Utterly perfect.

Her hands spread out on the leather and she began to shove back against him, meeting his thrusts with her own. He laughed, a low, dark sound that had heat prickling all over her again, her sex clenching tight around him. "Fuck, yeah. You like that, don't you?"

"I can't . . . I don't . . ."

He leaned forward, reaching for one of her hands where it clutched at the seat and pulling it away. Then he pushed it down between her thighs, guiding her fingers to where he was seated deep inside her, hot and hard as steel. "Feel that, pretty girl? Feel me there?"

Her own wetness was against her fingers and she could feel where her flesh met his, and some dim part of her was telling her to pull away. But she couldn't because his hand was over hers and he was holding her there. And somehow that was exactly what she wanted.

He kept her hand there as he moved, so she could feel him as he thrust. Then he guided her fingers to her clit and pressed them down. "Touch yourself," he whispered roughly in her ear. "I want you coming all over my cock in the next five seconds."

It took her about ten, but by then neither of them was counting.

As the second climax roared through her, Tamara had to bury her face in the leather of the seat in front of her to stop herself from screaming. And then, a few seconds later, she found herself being hauled back against Zee's body as he turned his mouth into her neck, biting down as his thrusts became harder, wilder, out of control.

And when he came she could feel the vibration of his roar against her skin, the echo of it moving deeper, imprinting into her flesh like the grooves in a record.

For long moments afterward, neither of them moved, their breathing slowing. And Tamara let herself lean back against him like she was lying on a rock that had been heated all day by the sun, for whole seconds not thinking of anything at all.

It was he who broke the silence finally, his voice like a shock of cold water. "I should get you home."

Home. Yes, that's right. She been desperate to get home, hadn't she?

"Okay. Sounds good." Her voice was husky, as if she'd been screaming a lot.

His hands were at her hips again, shifting her, and then came the awkward process of putting her clothing back in place and putting herself back together. Pretending like the sex hadn't just broken her open for reasons she couldn't explain even to herself.

As they got back into the front seat and he started the car, he said, "Tell me your address, Tamara. Your real address. I'm not letting you wait on the side of the road for a cab."

There didn't seem much point in holding back now, so she gave it to him. And a silent ten minutes later they were pulling up outside her apartment building.

She wanted to say something then, but what could she say? After that? They weren't going to see each other again anyway, right?

So she settled for, "Thanks, Zee."

And got out before he could reply.

As she walked up the steps to the front door of her building, she didn't look back.

But she heard the sound of the engine as he drove away.

* * *

Zee drove home, his head ringing like a bell and his body aching for more.

He carefully didn't think about anything as he parked the Trans Am near the shitty old warehouse he'd bought dirt cheap a couple years back with some of his fight winnings.

The ground floor housed the gym that he'd outfitted himself and let the teenage outreach center use free of charge whenever they needed it. Often that meant giving martial arts classes and he liked doing that. Giving back to the center that had taken him in as a fucked-up seventeen-year-old running from his past.

Upstairs was his apartment, which he kept very basically furnished because he liked it clean and clutter-free. It was easier to keep his mind clear without a lot of junk around, helped him focus on the future without the past constantly trying to draw him back. Not that he'd had that problem in a while, but tonight . . .

Zee went into his bare lounge area, sitting down on the edge of the worn leather couch Rachel had found for him in a yard sale. He put his head in his hands.

He'd sworn to himself he wouldn't touch her, that she wasn't his type. And what the fuck had he done? He'd screwed her in the back of his Trans Am.

Shutting his eyes, he stared into the blackness behind his lids.

What was wrong with him? Normally he had no problem keeping his dick in his pants when he wanted to. Yet Tamara had totally messed with his head. Not only was she exactly the kind of girl he swore he'd never get involved with again, but she also had a fucking boyfriend into the bargain.

He didn't like complications. He didn't like surprises. And that was both.

Christ, he should have stopped there, but he hadn't. Because he hadn't given a crap about her goddamn boyfriend or the fact that she probably came from a rich family like Madison had. He'd smelled her in the air, felt her against his body, and he'd wanted her.

And when he'd looked into those cool, dark eyes of hers, he'd realized they weren't so cool anymore.

Women wanted him all the time. They saw him in the ring, liked his moves, his tattoos, his muscles, and they weren't shy about letting him know. So it had been a while since he'd had to chase anyone, a while since he'd had to seduce anyone. And fuck, he couldn't deny there was a hell of a thrill to it. Leaning over her, dirtying up those pretty ears of hers with a few words, watching the heat bloom in her eyes. Watching that cool, expensive woman disappear under the raw burn of desire.

Desire for him.

Yeah, he'd gotten a kick out of that. It was always a thrill to make a woman like her want what she shouldn't have. Make her ignore her boyfriend, her better judgment, and no doubt all those rich-girl scruples of hers, for a quick fuck in the backseat of his car.

Which made him a prick and not at all what the last few years of his life had been about. He was supposed to be locking the darkness inside him away, turning himself into a decent guy, not letting it out and seducing poor little rich girls in his car.

In the backseat, making her scream, balls deep in the wet heat of her. Rough and raw and hot. And that had been pretty damn intense all on its own. But then she'd lifted her hips and shoved herself back on him, meeting his thrusts like a fucking champion.

He'd felt the same adrenaline rush as if he'd been in a fight and when he'd come, he hadn't been able to stop himself from pulling her back against him, sinking his teeth into her shoulder. Jesus. He didn't know what the hell he was doing with that kind of thing. He kept roughness for the ring; it didn't creep out anywhere else. Or at least it shouldn't.

Good thing you're not seeing her again then, right?

Zee let out a breath. Yeah, a very good thing, which meant he shouldn't be getting all wound up about it. He'd slept with plenty of women before, and sure, he had a few rules about that, which he'd thrown out the window spectacularly tonight. But there was no point letting one in particular mess with his head.

So he'd fucked a nice girl in the back of his Trans Am and he'd been a little rough. They'd both got a couple of orgasms out of it, no biggie. And he wasn't going to see her again, so what the hell was he angsting about?

He shouldn't be thinking about this shit anyway. He had the martial arts program he was running through the outreach center to go over, which was good, because focusing on the kids was a great way to keep his own behavior in check. Plus he had a fight coming up in a couple of hours. Sex was a great way to let off steam, no question, but some time in the ring with an opponent was better. The rules were clearer, all parties able to defend themselves well enough, and when it was over, it was over.

Zee dropped his hands from his face and stared at the floor a moment longer. Then he pushed himself to his feet and went to the bedroom to prepare.

And he did not think again about Tamara Lennox.

Chapter 4

He was coming for her. Again. And this time she knew he wouldn't stop.

She raised her hand and the gun was there.

She fired.

The shot echoed and echoed and echoed. Getting louder and louder and louder. And she screamed as he fell, because she knew he wasn't getting up again. . . .

Tamara woke up, her heart hammering, the sheets tangled around her.

God, she hadn't had a nightmare like that for years.

She looked blearily at the clock on the nightstand. Five A.M. Wonderful.

Letting out a breath, she lay back down and stared at the ceiling, trying to get her heartbeat under control. How weird to get a nightmare again after all this time. They'd gradually tailed off six years ago and she'd thought they'd gone for good, but apparently not.

What had set this one off?

Are you sure you don't know?

A memory suddenly unreeled. Of her in the backseat of a car, a man's hands on her hips, his cock buried inside her. Of her, screaming into the leather of the seat in front of her. Teeth closing on her neck. . . .

Zee.

Tamara groaned and rolled over, pushing her hot face into the pillow, a wave of embarrassment and heat sweeping through her.

Keep it under control, her parents had always told her, and for the past eight years that's exactly what she'd been doing. But she hadn't last night. She hadn't kept anything under control last night. She'd ignored her boyfriend, her family name, her job, her need for success. Everything that made her Tamara Lennox.

She'd ignored it all for the sake of sex in the backseat of a car with a tattooed bad boy from the wrong side of town.

Shame joined the heat and the embarrassment. What the *hell* had she been thinking? She was better than that, wasn't she? After all, as her parents had kept pointing out to her, she had to be.

Tamara sighed, then rolled over onto her back again. Okay, so she'd made a mistake, but she wasn't going to beat herself up about it. What she had to do was keep on the way she always did, moving forward, not looking back. Her career was her future and so was Robert, and that's what she needed to concentrate on.

That and not making any more mistakes.

She slid out of bed and stalked into the bathroom. Running the shower on cold got rid of any lingering cobwebs from the nightmare, not to mention the lingering heat from the memories of being in Zee's car.

Running through her daily schedule as per usual also helped.

She was nearly at the end of her internship and she really needed to pull out the stops if she wanted a permanent position in the firm. Her father certainly wouldn't give her a free ride, which meant she was going to have to suck up big-time to

Scott, her horrible boss. Who, unfortunately, had it in for her for some inexplicable reason.

It could be because she was the big boss's daughter, but more likely it was because he'd asked her out when she'd first started working at Lennox Investments and she'd refused him. Since then he'd been a pain in the ass to deal with, on her back about everything, and that wasn't even taking into account the way he looked at her, making her feel a bit dirty—and not in a good way.

Not in a Zee way, right?

Tamara shut off the water. Hard.

No, she was not going to think about him or what they'd done together last night. That was over and done with, and she needed to move on.

Stepping out of the shower, she dried herself off and then went into the bedroom to get dressed. But it wasn't until she was putting on her makeup that she saw the bite mark on her neck.

Oh hell. Presumably that had come from Zee.

"Great," she muttered under her breath, examining the mark. "You bastard."

How the hell was she going to deal with that? She couldn't go into work with a damn hickey.

Quickly she changed her top, going for a blouse in soft, black silk with a high collar that hid most of the damage, and using a bit of concealer to cover the rest. It wasn't perfect, but at least no one could see it. If they didn't look too hard.

Half an hour later, having stopped at her favorite café to get her morning latte, she walked into the offices of Lennox Investments, hoping for once that she'd gotten there before Scott so she could have at least an hour of uninterrupted peace in which to get some work done.

No such luck.

He tended to be an early starter and was already in his office by the time she arrived.

She tried to slink by his doorway on her way to her cubicle, but as she passed, he called out, "Hey, where's mine?"

Dammit.

She stopped and turned. He was looking pointedly at her latte.

"Good morning." She gave him a forced smile. "I didn't think you'd be here or I would have gotten you one."

He leaned back in his chair and put his hands behind his head. Scott was a handsome guy and knew it too, in his mid-thirties, tall and dark, with blue eyes that were always looking at her with varying degrees of suspicion. "Well, maybe I'll just have to send you out to get another."

"Uh, sure. Just let me go put down my—"

"In a minute. I need to talk to you for a second."

Oh, great. What was it now?

Keeping a polite smile plastered to her face, Tamara came into his office and closed the door behind her, before moving over to the chair by his desk and sitting down. "What did you want to talk about?"

Scott put his hands on the arms of his chair and pushed out of it, letting out a long breath as he came around the desk to perch on the edge of it, looking down at her. His usual primitive dominance display.

He liked putting her down and making things difficult for her.

She liked annoying him by taking everything he threw at her and making it no problem at all.

Except you kind of liked Zee's primitive dominance display.

Tamara shoved the thought from her head and widened her smile.

"So," Scott said, clasping his hands over his knees. "I've got a project going on that I need someone to put in some extra time on. It's going to mean lots of late nights, but I really think it would be beneficial for you experience-wise. You'd get a lot out of it."

Tamara held on to her cooling coffee tightly. *I think this would be beneficial for you experience-wise* was usually code for *I'm determined to make your life hell, bitch.* At least it was in Scott-the-bastard language.

She held the smile, trying not to think of all the other work she had on currently that she could barely fit in as it was, let alone taking more on. "That sounds great. And when you mean late nights you mean . . ."

"Exactly what it says on the box. It'll be a couple of nights a week, I would think. At least until the backlog is done." His cold blue eyes watched her, gauging her like a snake watching a mouse.

Tamara made sure he saw nothing but utter delight at the prospect. "I think I can manage that. In fact, it sounds like a wonderful opportunity to get myself noticed."

"If you can manage it, of course. The top brass do like a hard worker, it's true." His smile had begun to take on a sharp edge. "You've done wonderfully so far, but that means the pressure's going to be on if you want one of those positions, especially given the quality of the other candidates in the running."

Unfortunately, he wasn't wrong. Competition for the limited number of Lennox positions was fierce and there were other interns who were just as hungry for it as she was. And none of them had the bad luck to be the boss's daughter. Or to have wretched Scott watching every move she made, just waiting for her to make a slip and screw up her chances.

Tamara's face ached from smiling, but she kept it up. "Oh, I'm sure I can handle it."

"Can you?" Scott's own smile had vanished. "I guess you'd better. I'm sure you haven't forgotten that I have to make my recommendations at the end of the month. That's two weeks from now."

Oh no, she hadn't forgotten. That was burned into her brain. Because if she didn't get a good recommendation from Scott, she wouldn't be considered for the position, which wasn't an option.

She had to get a job at Lennox. Her parents were counting on her to achieve and after all the support they'd given her in the aftermath of Will's death, she couldn't let them down.

"I remember." Tamara gripped her cold coffee tightly. "Don't worry."

"I'm not worrying. That's your job." Scott slipped off the desk. Then he abruptly stopped, his gaze dipping, narrowing.

And a wave of cold washed over her. Because he was staring at her neck, right where Zee's bite was.

Dammit. She didn't want him asking questions about that, because he would, she just knew it. And she had no answers to give him, no excuses to make. Everyone over the age of sixteen knew what a hickey looked like, for God's sake; she couldn't explain it away as something else.

She couldn't even say Robert had put it there since Scott was very much aware that Robert was in New York.

A mark on her neck wasn't any of Scott's business of course, but that wouldn't stop him from making an issue of it if he thought it would disadvantage her. *Especially* if it would disadvantage her. . . .

With a sharp, decisive movement, Tamara stood up, continuing to smile brightly. "Well, I'll just go get that coffee you wanted. Espresso, two sugars, right?"

Slowly, Scott's gaze came back to hers, suspicion glinting in the depths of his eyes. "Yes, that's right."

"Great. See you in five."

Then, turning on her heel, her heart pounding, she left his office before he could say a word.

She managed to avoid Scott the rest of the morning, burying herself in work, so by the time lunch came around, she'd almost forgotten about the night before. Then, as she was grabbing a quick coffee in the small kitchenette that serviced her floor, she ran into Rose.

Her friend was looking remarkably bright-eyed after a night spent clubbing. She even had the gall to give Tamara a sympathetic look. "Whoa, you look tired. You got home okay last night?"

"I did." Tamara leaned against the kitchenette counter, watching as Rose shook a packet of sugar into her coffee. "And you don't look tired. What happened with the club?"

"Actually I didn't end up staying out all that late."

This was news. Rose had the stamina of an ox and liked to prove it whenever she could. "I don't believe you," Tamara said flatly.

Her friend laughed. "Yeah, I know, but strange as it may sound, it's true. I think it was Zee's class that did it. I just came away from it feeling so . . . empowered." She stirred her coffee, flicking Tamara a glance. "Like . . . in control of things. And the other girls all felt the same way." She put down the spoon, turned, and leaned back against the counter, holding her coffee mug. "We went to that club afterward and when we got there I got so busy talking with the others about the class, I didn't even feel like hooking up with anyone. I kind of forgot about it."

Tamara blinked. Rose forgetting about hooking up was unheard of. It was also a little strange that her friend, the biggest man-eater out there, had gone out looking to go home with someone and hadn't, while Tamara had gone out *not* looking to go home with anyone and had.

Which you are not going to think about.

That restless, edgy feeling curled in her gut. Dangerous . . .

She picked up her coffee from the counter. Work, that's clearly what she needed.

Rose's gaze had narrowed in the direction of her neck. "Hey, is that what I think it is?"

Tamara groaned inwardly. Trust Rose to pick up on the damn hickey. Resisting the urge to pull her collar higher to hide it, she turned toward the door. "It's nothing."

"The hell it isn't. Spill, Lennox. Did something happen last night?"

"No."

"Bull. Get an unexpected visit from your boyfriend, maybe?"

Guilt turned over inside her, a small sharp thing. Would Robert even care she'd been with Zee?

No. He wouldn't. And you know it.

"Wouldn't you like to know?" she said, tossing Rose a secretive smile over her shoulder as she headed for the doorway.

"Oh come on now," Rose said disgustedly from behind her. "You have to tell me. Was it Zee? Did you hook up with him last night after we'd gone?"

But Tamara only laughed and kept walking.

No one would ever find out about Zee. No one. And maybe, if she was lucky, she'd even forget about it permanently herself.

"Hold still. This is going to hurt."

Zee let out a breath and waited patiently in one of the garage's office chairs while Zoe began the process of sewing up the ragged cut on his eyebrow. She was wrong. It didn't hurt. Or at least, he'd long since ceased to feel stuff like that.

There was a disapproving look on her delicate face. "You shouldn't be doing stitches yourself, not when you can't sew for shit."

"The Band-Aid didn't work and you know I can't go the ER. I had to stop it bleeding somehow."

She snorted. "You should have called me."

"It was three in the morning, Zoe. I'm not waking you up in the middle of the night." Especially not when all it needed was a couple of stitches. Though she had a point when she'd said he couldn't sew for shit. He couldn't.

"You're going to scar."

Zee lifted a shoulder. "Scarring is the least of my problems." And what was a little scar in any case? He'd had worse. Anyway, the fight had been a good one, leaving him pleasantly hollowed out and empty. Calmer.

"You're looking very pleased with yourself," Zoe commented as she neatly drew tight another stitch.

"Am I?"

"Uh-huh. Not thinking about that chick you took home last night?"

A flash of unexpected and very unwelcome heat went through him at the mention of Tamara.

That was the other great thing about the fight: He hadn't thought of her once since.

Damn Zoe.

"Her? She turned up at the class with a friend." He shifted in his seat, earning him another stern look. "Her friend went off to that new club, Anonymous, and she didn't want to go. So I offered her a ride."

Zoe pulled tight a stitch, then leaned in for another, the needle sliding under his skin. Fuck, he felt that one. "Generous of you."

"Yeah, well, girls like her don't normally turn up for those classes. And she was dressed up in all that designer shit. Couldn't leave her waiting around on the curb for a taxi. She'd have been eaten alive."

Zoe nodded. Both of them knew the truth of that. Royal Road might be among Detroit's up-and-coming neighborhoods, but it wasn't there yet. It could get dangerous at night, especially if you weren't a local or didn't know what you were doing.

The clang of the downstairs door echoed through the garage and Zee didn't miss the sudden, bright flash that crossed Zoe's face as she tied off the last stitch.

Gideon was clearly back.

Zee didn't know quite what was going on with those two, but it was majorly obvious to everyone that Zoe had a giant crush on Gideon. Kind of wrong when he was her foster brother. Then again, it wasn't any wonder. Zee didn't know their background—Gideon never spoke of it and Zee never asked—but apparently Zoe had been fostered into the same family as Gideon. She was quite a bit younger than him and when he'd aged out of the system they'd stayed in touch. Then something had happened and Zoe had run away and Gideon had somehow rescued her, which, if you knew Gideon, was pretty much par for the course since the guy had a white knight complex a mile wide. Whatever had happened, the result was a bad case of hero worship on Zoe's part that Gideon was completely blind to.

It was kind of cute.

Zee met her gaze and watched the color rise under her smooth, light brown skin. She turned away sharply, fiddling with the medical kit she'd gotten out to stitch Zee up with.

Yeah, she had it bad all right. Damn shame, especially when Zee was pretty certain Gideon would never, ever see her as a woman. Hell, Gideon didn't much like it when *other* people saw her as a woman.

Footsteps came up the stairs, the door opening to admit the guy himself.

"Christ," he said, taking one look at Zee's face. "Good fight then?"

"I won, so yeah." There was another office chair on casters nearby. With a lazy movement of his foot, Zee sent it rolling across the floor to the other man.

Zoe finished packing away the medical kit, turning as Gideon grabbed the chair and sat down. Her arms were folded across her chest, a crease between her brows. "So? Is it true?"

Zee raised the non-stitched eyebrow in Gideon's direction. "Levi." Gideon blew out a breath. "Just been visiting him."

Levi was the fourth member of the little makeshift family Gideon had drawn together ten years ago, back when they'd all been lonely, unwanted teens at the Royal Road teen drop-in center.

He was currently in jail, doing time for manslaughter.

They tried not to mention Levi when Rachel was around, since the whole reason Levi was doing time was because of a mistake she'd made eight years ago, when she'd been young and stupid. Levi had protected her from an assault and in the process had accidentally killed the guy who'd been assaulting her.

He'd been away for eight years, but since he'd been a model prisoner his lawyer had managed to get his sentence reduced. It looked like he was going to be getting out pretty soon.

"And?" Zoe prompted. "What did he say, Gideon?"

The other man leaned back, pushing a hand through his shaggy black hair. Then he grinned. "So impatient, little one."

"Oh come on!"

"Okay, okay. Yes, he's getting out. Another month tops."

The beginnings of a hopeful smile turned Zoe's mouth. "Seriously? That's it? Another month?"

"Yeah. I told him he could stay with me while he gets himself back on his feet."

Zee could feel his own grin happening. They'd all been gutted when the shit had gone down with Rachel, and Gideon had done his damnedest to help Levi. He'd gotten him the best lawyer he could find on legal aid, but of course, there was no escaping the fact that Levi had killed a guy.

The incident had struck close to home for Zee and, at the

time, he'd debated about whether or not just to leave Royal Road altogether. It had felt too much like what he'd just escaped from, the seedy, violent world of big-time crime that his father had ruled with an iron fist. And it wasn't what Madison had wanted for him. She'd told him he was better than merely being Joshua Chase's son, heir to violence and murder. She'd told him he was a good man, that he should want more for himself.

And he'd believed her. He had to, because, fuck, her death had to mean something.

In the end though, despite what had happened with Levi, Zee had decided to stay in Royal. Gideon had taken him in, given him a job, given him a new start and he couldn't just up and leave. No, none of them knew what Zee had left behind, that Ezekiel wasn't even his real name, but he couldn't leave without explanation. Not only did he owe Madison, he owed Gideon, too.

So he'd stayed and now, here he was, eight years later, and he had the kind of life that at last he could be proud of. That Madison would have been proud of. He had a job, his own place—hell, he had his own fucking building. He kept the darkness inside him nicely controlled. He was giving back to the community and he had big plans for the future, plans that included expanding his gym, getting that teen program up and running, training and teaching kids. Hiring more staff. Getting a proper business going.

Royal Road need more shit like that. There were already lots of revitalization projects happening, projects that were injecting new life and hope into a neighborhood that had suffered a lot when the auto industry had gone bust. Things were starting to get good here and as far as Zee was concerned, they were going to stay good.

Now that Levi was coming home, things would be even better.

Except, of course, that at some point he was going to have to tell Gideon he was quitting the garage. Which he wasn't looking forward to. But shit, he couldn't stay at Black's, not when he wanted to concentrate on his plans for the gym.

"How was he?" Zee asked.

"Seemed okay. Looking forward to getting out." Gideon gave Zee a narrow glance. "You get that pretty little thing you gave a ride to last night home safely?"

"Yeah, of course."

"Good." Gideon's gaze was vaguely assessing. "What the hell was she doing hanging around your classes anyway?"

"Like I said, she was with a friend of hers."

"Bit fucking strange to come down this end of town just to hang around and watch."

And just like that, Zee's good mood began to dissipate. Christ, and he thought he was the paranoid one. "It's no big deal. I get all sorts at the classes."

"Don't normally take them home though." The other man's dark eyes narrowed, his big body going still in his chair.

Zee stared at him. "Is there a problem, Gideon?"

Zoe snorted. "And here I thought we were going to be talking about how great it was that Levi will be home soon."

Gideon glanced at her, and there was a moment's heavy silence. Then he sighed and the strange tension faded. "There's no problem." He leaned forward in his chair, his hands between his knees. "Truth is, I'm worried about Levi. I don't think he is okay."

"Like how?" The worried crease was back between Zoe's brows.

Slowly, Gideon shook his head. "He doesn't smile like he used to, doesn't laugh. He's changed. And I get the impression that he's pretty fucking angry."

"Not surprised," Zee said. "Eight years of time will do that to you." He'd seen the ex-cons his father had used for various jobs, knew the kind of anger that seemed to radiate off them. They were mean motherfuckers and they hadn't gotten that way because jail was an easy way out.

"He's gonna need help." Gideon paused and looked at both of them. "And I'm gonna have to tell Rachel."

No one knew exactly what had happened between Levi and Rachel the night she'd been attacked, but what they did know was that it had changed her. She'd always been a firecracker, but over the years she'd gotten harder, pricklier. Defensive. Not an easy person to be with in many ways and how she was going to take this news was anyone's guess.

One thing was clear to all of them though—Rachel blamed herself for Levi's jail time. And she was pissed about it.

"That's gonna be hell," Zee muttered.

"Yeah, I know. But she'll have to find out at some point and probably the earlier the better."

"True." He gave Gideon a look. "I suppose now is a shitty time to hand in my notice?"

Zoe blinked. "What the hell, Zee?"

Gideon just stared back, the beginning of a smile curling his mouth. "I've been wondering when this was coming."

Zee scowled. Jesus, don't say all his worrying about Gideon's reaction was all for nothing? "What do you mean you've 'been wondering'?"

"Well, you've gotten that gym up and running, and you told me you've been talking with the outreach center. I know your heart isn't in the garage. Shit, it never really was."

That was true. Though he liked fixing cars, liked putting pieces together and making them go, or analyzing a mechanical problem and finding a solution, it wasn't really what he wanted. Fixing cars was one thing, but fixing broken people, broken communities was better.

It was what Madison would have wanted him to do.

"You don't look very unhappy about it," Zee commented, lacing his fingers together and leaning back in his chair.

"I'm not. In fact, it's perfect timing."

"What do you mean perfect timing?"

Zoe was grinning. "I see where you're going with this."

"Uh-huh." Gideon smiled. "Poor Levi's gonna need a job. Do you think you could stay until then?"

Chapter 5

Tamara smoothed the white linen napkin over her knees and tried once more to see if she could read the expression on her father's face.

He'd descended from his top floor CEO's office to take her out to dinner right at five P.M., waving off her protestations that she had to work late. Scott had been very magnanimous despite spending the whole week keeping her under his thumb, granting her the evening off with much bonhomie and obvious sucking up, though of course this was going to come back to bite her. Scott's eyes had been cold as he'd told her that naturally she could go have dinner with her father and she knew he was viewing this as favoritism.

She'd tried to have a conversation once with her father about Scott, but he'd waved it off, telling her that she'd always come up against bosses she found difficult and she'd just have to find a way to work with it.

John Lennox always hated complaints so she'd shut up after that. Because, after all, he wasn't wrong. Showing him she could handle it was the better way to deal with it anyway.

She studied him now as they sat in one of Detroit's newest restaurants and the source of much buzz, but the expression on his slightly hawkish face was impenetrable. He'd long perfected the art of showing only what he wanted other people to see, so why she was even bothering to figure out what this dinner was about she didn't know. And it *was* about something, that was for sure.

Her father always made a big production about everything when he wanted to talk.

"So, Dad," Tamara said after the waiter had taken their order and filled up their wineglasses. "Was there something in particular you wanted to see me about?"

He picked up his wineglass and leaned back in his chair, a smile hovering around his mouth. His dark eyes were full of what could only be termed satisfaction and he looked exceptionally pleased with himself. "I just wanted you to know, Tamara, how happy your mother and I are with you at the moment."

She should have felt glad about that, because her dad didn't often hand out praise, so when he did, it meant a lot. But for some reason it wasn't pleasure that sat in her gut but apprehension.

"Well, thanks. You know I appreciate all you and Mom have done for me." She smoothed her napkin again, because they were edging into dangerous territory. "I want to make you proud."

He nodded. "Of course and you have. Very proud indeed. In fact, I hope to hear good news at the end of the month from Scott."

She ignored the apprehension that wound deeper. "That's the plan."

"Good." He took a sip of wine, studying her. "And I suppose that brings me to the point of this dinner." Another pause.

"Your future is looking very bright, Tamara, and your mother and I just want to be sure you're heading in the right direction."

Carefully she reached out for her own glass and held it, trying to still the shake of her hand. There was no reason to be nervous about this and she couldn't think why she was. "Oh? That sounds ominous." She tried a smile to help lighten her mood.

Her father smiled back. "Of course it's not ominous. I meant what I said—we're very proud of you. It's only that the next step will be an important one for you and one that's going to ensure your success." He took another sip from his glass. "So we want to make sure that the next step is the right one."

The apprehension in her gut churned. "And what's the right step?"

Her dad leaned forward, putting his glass on the table and clasping his hands together. "You and Robert are pretty serious, aren't you?"

She blinked at the question, not expecting it. "I . . . suppose we are. What's that got to do with anything?"

"Well, you're getting your career set up nicely, but that's not the only part of your life you need to consider." He gave a small self-conscious laugh. "Boy, I really wanted your mom to broach this with you."

Tamara's grip on her wineglass tightened. "Broach what?"

"Okay, well, your mom and I wondered if you and Robert have thought about tying the knot."

She stared at him. Marriage? Was he serious? "Uh, no. Robert and I haven't . . . I mean . . . we're not at that stage yet."

Her father's smile didn't change. "We think you should consider it. We like him, he comes from a great family, and he's got a great future ahead of him too. Your mom and I think you and he would make a great team."

Trying to mask her shock, Tamara took a swallow of wine. But it only sat in her stomach acidly, making her feel a bit sick. She put the glass down again, her hands returning to the napkin spread over her lap. "That's . . . uh . . . good you think that, obviously. But . . . I'm not sure I'm ready for that step yet."

"You're twenty-three, Tamara, and you've got yourself a great career path. This is the next logical move, don't you think?"

No. She didn't think that. Or at least, marriage hadn't been something she'd been considering.

And certainly not with Robert.

She looked back down at the snowy white folds of the napkin. "It might be for me. But I'm not sure Robert is ready for it."

There was a heavy pause.

She glanced back up.

Her father was looking at her with some embarrassment. "Actually," he said, "I've already discussed this with Robert and he's very happy with the idea."

The shock inside her twisted again, threaded through this time with anger. "What do you mean 'already'? Don't you think I should be the first one to speak to about this?"

Her father lifted his hands in a calming motion. "Okay, okay, settle down. Yes, I know, I should have talked to you first. But we needed to make sure Robert was on board."

"This is not a takeover meeting, Dad. This isn't business. This is marriage we're talking about."

His smile began to fade, the look in his eyes becoming harder, sharper, the way it always did when she caused a fuss about anything. "You know, don't you, what your mother and I have sacrificed to give you the future you have?"

Tamara shut her mouth, biting down on the hot flow of words that threatened to spill out. Her father hated overemotional responses and, God knew, she wouldn't make anything easier if she got angry with him. But that didn't stop the sudden spike of fury that licked up inside her.

A low blow, that reminder. Because of course she knew what they'd sacrificed for her. All the money that had been thrown around and the lies told to cover up what she'd done. To pretend that nothing had happened.

Yet even though they never talked about it, never discussed it, they still knew. Normally she didn't think about the unspoken weight of that knowledge. But now she felt it like a building falling down on top of her.

"I know," she said tightly. "I remember, Dad. Believe me, I remember."

The pressure of his gaze didn't lessen. "All we want is what's best for you, Tamara. That's all we ever wanted."

No, that's not what they want. They want you to pay. That's all they ever wanted.

Tamara ignored the thought, buried it right down deep so it would never surface again. "I understand. And I know you do."

"We love you, Tamara. Never forget that."

Of course they did. They told her that constantly ever since Will died.

She looked away again, reaching for her glass and this time taking a much larger swallow than before, hoping to drown the sick feeling inside her. "I know, Dad. I know."

There was another heavy silence.

"So," her father said eventually, his expression softening again. "What do you think? Your mom's gone a little crazy and organized something. I told her not to, but you know how she gets when she's excited."

The wine sat uneasily in her stomach, the apprehension deepening into something cold and sharp. "What's she organized?" It seemed the least problematic question to ask.

"A small party." Her father gave a rueful shake of his head. "I promised not to tell you."

Oh shit.

"Not to tell me what?"

God help her, there was actually a twinkle in her father's eye, like he thought this was great news.

"Awww." He laughed. "And now I have to tell you. Your mother planned a little surprise engagement party for you and Robert. So you're going to have to pretend I didn't tell you, okay?"

Tamara blinked. She felt like a trapeze artist who'd just missed a vital catch and was now falling and falling into the net below. Except, there was no net. And she couldn't understand how she'd missed the catch.

"But . . . Robert hasn't mentioned a word about this yet."

Her father's smile turned smug. "Oh, he will, don't worry about that. We've got it all arranged. He's going ask you at the party. So just remember to look surprised."

Tamara opened her mouth. Then closed it.

Her parents were doing what was best for her and perhaps she needed to trust that. After all, hadn't she known that perhaps this had been their aim the day they'd introduced her to Robert in the first place? They'd encouraged her to date him from the get-go, had made loud noises about how perfect he was for her, and she'd happily agreed with them. Just like she'd agreed with everything they'd told her.

But you don't want this. You never wanted this.

No, she couldn't think that. She couldn't ever think that. She had to believe this was the right thing to do. She had to trust her parent's judgment. After all, her choices were suspect and only people who hadn't taken a life got to make decisions like this.

Anyway, she had to remember: her career and Robert. Those were her moving-on strategies and this was exactly what her father had told her, another step on the path of putting the past behind her.

She pulled it together for the rest of the meal, ignoring the doubt that sat inside her. The terrible unease that wouldn't go away. Her father didn't seem to pick up on it, thank God, and luckily he didn't seem to want to make it a late night.

He dropped her back at her apartment after a couple of hours and once she got inside, she stood there staring at nothing for a long time. At the lovely whitewashed brick and the exposed wooden beams, the polished wooden floors. The furniture she'd chosen on a shopping trip with her mother: an elegant, pale gray sofa with a few splashes of color in the shape of deep blue pillows. The distressed-look coffee table and the neatly piled magazines on top. The bookshelves with her beautifully arranged knickknacks and books. The deep blue rug on the floor that her mother had spent a lot of money on because Tamara was "worth it."

A beautiful, expensive, perfect apartment. Like a movie set waiting for the actors to appear.

Waiting for her. Because she was the actor, wasn't she? Moving through her own life, saying the words, playing the part of the good, dutiful daughter. While she knew that deep inside, it wasn't really her. That none of this was really her.

She swallowed, looking around at her apartment that felt suddenly unfamiliar. As if she'd wandered accidentally into someone else's home. It was disturbing, frightening.

When was the last time she hadn't had to play the part for her parents or her boss? Or had she lost herself the day she'd picked up the gun and aimed it at her brother?

God, when was the last time she'd actually been herself?

You know the last time.

Tamara closed her eyes. Oh yes, she knew. That night a week ago in Zee's car.

She hadn't been anyone's good girl then. She hadn't had to please anyone, impress anyone. She hadn't had to hide or pretend. All she'd had to do was let herself go. And in that moment she'd been more herself than at any other time in the past eight years.

The sharp, insistent ring of her phone sounded, breaking into her thoughts.

She crossed to the couch where she'd dumped her purse and pulled her phone out of it, checking the caller ID. *Wonderful.* It was Robert.

"Okay, so John just told me he'd accidentally let the cat out of the bag," Robert said almost as soon as she'd hit the accept button.

Tamara took a breath, remembering the whole awful conversation at dinner. "No," she replied after a moment. "I don't think there was anything accidental about it at all. I think he was giving me a heads-up." Not to mention a reminder of her place in the world.

"In case you were going to say no?" His smooth voice was amused, as if that was the last thing she would say.

She gripped the phone tight, suddenly furious. "And what if I did?"

There was a silence.

"Okay." The amusement disappeared. "I'm sorry. I should have said something when you were up this way last time, but I wanted to surprise you. So you have every right to be angry with me."

So he thought she was angry because they hadn't discussed it. *Well, aren't you?*

No, it felt more than that. As if once again she was being forced into a role she didn't want and one she had no choice but to play.

"I'm not angry," she lied, trying to get herself back under control. "I'm just . . . surprised. I didn't realize how serious you were."

"Yeah, I know." He sounded so damn understanding she wanted to spit. "But things change. John and I had a talk last time he was here on business and what he said made a lot of sense. You and I getting married, I mean."

Tamara raised a hand and rubbed between her eyebrows. Of

course. This would be good for Robert's career, marrying into one of Michigan's richest families, and the New York connection would be great for her father. No wonder both of them were so keen on the match. And naturally enough it was assumed that was what she wanted as well.

Isn't it?

The unease that had been sitting inside her all evening twisted again. Her father was right. This *was* the next logical step and it *did* make sense.

And yet . . .

"But . . ." She groped around for words to articulate the doubt. "You don't love me, right? I mean, we hadn't even talked about being exclusive or anything."

Robert gave a laugh that sounded indulgent. "Well, no. I don't love you any more than you love me. But that'll come. And as for exclusivity, would you really be surprised if I told you I hadn't been?" He sounded so casual that she felt no shock at all.

"No, I guess not." She tried to ease her grip on the phone.

"I mean, did you want to be? Obviously once we're married, it'll be a different story, but until then . . ." He stopped. "Seriously, Tamara. You're in Detroit, I'm in New York. We're apart for long periods of time. I'm not staying celibate."

"I'm not arguing." Because she didn't care. And now she knew the truth it even felt . . . freeing. "As long as that goes for me, too." She wasn't quite sure why she'd said it, maybe to prove a point even if it was only to herself. That she did have some choice in this after all.

Robert was silent.

"Oh," she said. "And here was I thinking we lived in the twenty-first century. Or are you seriously suggesting you get to screw around while I get to remain pure as the driven snow?"

"Okay," he said on a long breath. "Fair point. Same goes for you as well. But once we're married, we're faithful to each other, right?"

Once we're married. The words rang weirdly in her head. "Yes, of course."

There was another pause.

"So . . . Does this mean you're going to say yes?" Robert's voice held a note of humor in it. "Or are you going to keep me in suspense until Cassandra's party?"

Ah, yes. The engagement party her mother had organized before Tamara had even known an engagement was going to be the next thing that was required of her.

What was the correct response? The Tamara of a week ago would have said, "Of course I'm going to say yes" without a second thought. But for some reason, right now, the words wouldn't come without her forcing them. "I suppose so," she said at last, and it sounded wrong, left a bad taste in her mouth.

Another five minutes and she ended the call, a mix of anger and frustration and fear sitting uncomfortably inside her. And this time it had nothing to do with the wine.

She felt suffocated, the walls of her movie-set life closing in on her. The script of the next movie, the next part she had to play already on the table before her. A role she had no choice but to take, to play.

Turning away from her perfectly arranged lounge area, she went into her bedroom and began taking off her work clothes. Kicking off her heels, peeling down her skirt. Unbuttoning the prissy Chanel blouse she had on.

And as each item of clothing dropped away, the suffocation began to ease, something else taking its place. Something stronger and more desperate. The need to not only strip away the costume she wore, but also to step away from the set. To leave behind all the props, all the pretending she had to do. Step outside the role she had to play, before she forgot she was even playing a part.

Just for one night be herself.

And she knew exactly how she wanted to do that.

Zee.

She turned back to her closet, pulling it wide open and ri-fling through all the designer clothing on the rack until she came to the red silk cocktail dress she'd bought a couple of years ago and never worn.

It was soft, stretchy, clung to her body, and left nothing to the imagination, which was why she'd never worn it. And that made it perfect. Because if she was going to go through with this, she needed ammunition.

He'd told her they'd never see each other again. She was going to prove him wrong.

Pulling on the dress, she then added a pair of red-soled black patent Louboutins and put her hair up into a loose bun. It was completely the wrong look to be going where she was headed, but she didn't care. All the more reason for him to take her in.

She called a cab and when it arrived, the driver gave her a du-bious look when she told him where she was going, but didn't protest.

A long, hot twilight had settled over the city by the time the taxi pulled up outside the familiar metal door of Black's Vintage Repair and Restoration. Tamara threw some money at the driver, then stepped out into the night heat.

All her earlier anger and frustration had drained away, left behind along with her apartment and everything else that made her who she was. Now she was only a woman in a red cocktail dress in a sketchy part of town, and she couldn't deny the sense of freedom that came along with it.

She paused a moment on the sidewalk, breathing in the thick scent of a summer night in the city. There were people around, though the stores were all closed. A bar down the street was blar-ing loud music and there were a group of teens hanging around outside. A couple of old guys sitting on boxes in front of a boarded-up building eyed her suspiciously. There was a gritty, raw feeling to the landscape, to the very air around her. Like it was full of soot and heat. Like a volcano had erupted and the ash was already settling.

"Watcha doin', girl?" One of the old men was staring at her, looking her up and down. "You lost?"

Tamara gave him a smile, anticipation rising inside her along with a hunger she didn't try to deny this time. "No, I don't think so."

Then, before she could second-guess herself, she walked up to the garage door, put a hand to it, and pushed it open. The old guy yelled something at her, but she ignored him, stepping inside, the smell of motor oil and hot machinery thick in the air.

She recognized the massive form of Gideon first. He was leaning against the workbench, a beer bottle held casually in his fingers. Another man sat back in a scuffed plastic chair and, like Gideon, was wearing his overalls with the top rolled down and tied loosely around his waist. But unlike Gideon, who wore his with a T-shirt underneath it, this man wasn't wearing anything underneath it at all.

Zee.

Tamara's breath caught. She couldn't seem to tear her gaze from the sheer perfection of his body.

He was beautiful, from the powerful width of his shoulders down to the sharply defined muscles of his chest and abs. Muscles that spoke of the hard-won strength and grace of a serious athlete. And her attention kept catching on the tattoos inked into his skin, now revealed in all their glory.

There were words across his shoulders: *The one who sins is the one who will die. Ezekiel 18:20.*

There was an image of a dragon winding around the biceps on his left arm and on his right, the flames she'd glimpsed from underneath the sleeve of his T-shirt a week ago were part of something bigger. . . .

A phoenix rose, wings outspread on a wave of flames, stretching over his biceps and shoulders, the tips of the wings reaching over his right pectoral. More flames curled across his chest, while others disappeared over his shoulder.

She'd never been one for tattoos, but this one . . . It spoke to her. There was a life to it, an energy she could almost feel flowing from it herself. As if the bird were about to lift off his skin and soar into the sky.

"What the actual fuck are you doing here?" The fine grit in his deep voice was a shock of cold water over hot skin. It made goose bumps rise all over her body.

She looked up.

He'd turned toward her, sharp silver eyes meeting hers, and she felt the impact of it like the first blow of an ax against a tree, sending shudders right through her.

No going back now.

"Hi, Zee," she managed to force out. "Bet you weren't expecting to see me again, right?"

That was the understatement of the fucking century. Tamara was the very last person he expected to walk through the garage door just as he was sitting down for an after-work beer with Gideon.

A heavy, uncomfortable silence fell and he was very aware of Gideon standing there, looking from Tamara to him, then back at Tamara again.

Because it was perfectly fucking obvious what she was here for. At least, it was obvious to him.

She stood in the garage in a slinky red dress that licked all over her curves like cherry sauce on ice cream. And Christ, what curves they were. Last time she'd been in jeans and a tee and that had given him a hint as to what lay beneath. But now here they were in all their glory.

The dress had a plunging neckline that showcased the most perfect pair of tits he'd ever seen, before skimming to a narrow waist and the luscious curve of her hips. The hem came to mid-thigh, leaving her long, beautiful legs bare. On her feet were shiny, black stiletto heels that made her legs look even longer.

With her long golden hair piled up on her head, her dark eyes outlined in black, and dark red lipstick outlining her lush mouth, he knew she hadn't come here to talk. And judging from the immediate and intense reaction from a certain part of his anatomy, his body was quite okay with that idea.

"Hey," Gideon said slowly, breaking the silence. "It's Tamara, right?"

Her gaze flicked to Gideon, a polite smile curving her mouth. "Yes, that's right. Nice to see you again, Gideon."

Jesus. So fucking polite.

Anger threaded through him, though he couldn't figure out why. Okay, so he hadn't been expecting to see her again and sure, her showing up here in her fuck-me dress and killer heels was a shock. But it was no big deal, right? It wouldn't be the first time he'd had women turn up at the garage hoping to find him.

Except all of that didn't do anything to change the restless, antsy feeling that had been bugging him all week and that seemed to rise up inside him, swamping him, the moment she'd walked through the door.

He'd thought the fights he'd had over the course of the week would have put paid to it, but they hadn't. It felt like a million ants crawling over his skin and no way to brush them all off.

Putting his beer down on the ground beside his chair, he got to his feet in a sudden, sharp movement, then swung around to look at his friend. "A little privacy here."

The other man raised an eyebrow, but after a moment, the look on Zee's face obviously doing its work, he said, "Sure. I've got some paperwork to do anyway." He straightened and gave Tamara a grin. "Catch you later, Tamara."

Zee waited until his friend had gone up the metal stairs to

the office, the door shutting heavily behind him, then swung back to the woman standing in the middle of the garage.

And just like that the tension between them pulled excruciatingly tight.

Something was different about her tonight, at least different from the way she'd been with him before. A week ago she'd seemed nervous, off balance. She'd kept looking away, her lashes veiling her gaze.

But now she stood very still, her gaze meeting his without flinching. And this time he saw the raw need glinting in the darkness of her eyes, like diamonds at the bottom of the ocean. She made no attempt to hide it or look away. She only stared back, letting him see everything.

"What do you want?" he demanded, breaking the silence and trying to lock down the hunger that rose. Like she'd turned a switch on inside him, sending a live current straight through his whole body. "I thought we weren't going to see each other again."

"I know." She was holding a red purse, no monogram anywhere on it this time around. But that didn't make her any less a lamb in a den of hungry wolves.

And you're the biggest wolf of all.

No, he wasn't. He'd left that life far behind him. He was on the straight and narrow because of Madison and that's how it was going to stay.

"So why the fuck are you here?" He tried to make his voice less rough, but it didn't seem to work. Already the seductive smell of her was filling the space, a heavy, dense scent that was now inextricably linked in his head with the hot and hard sex they'd had in the back of the Trans Am.

It made his mouth go dry and his cock get hard.

Jesus. He'd been sitting here discussing with Gideon how they were going to approach telling Rachel about Levi's release and what needed to be done to help him ease back into life in

Royal again. And he'd also been going through his own plans for the gym and the preliminary program he'd drawn up.

Basically not thinking about one hot little rich girl he hadn't been able to get out of his head for a change. And now here she was, stepping back into his life, dressed to kill or at least to seduce. With the kind of look in her eyes that made him want to back her up against the nearest hard surface and give her everything she wanted.

She shifted on her shiny black shoes that made her legs look so long. That had him thinking about them wrapped around his waist or over his shoulder or any one of a number of different positions. "I want to say that I was just in the neighborhood or something. But I guess you won't believe that." She took a step toward him, that open, bare look in her eyes. "I came for you, Zee."

He didn't move, staring back at her, feeling the hunger coil hard inside him. The hunger that wanted to tear that pretty dress of hers and get it all dirty. Put his oil-stained hands all over her smooth, creamy skin and dirty her up too. Make her scream his name the way she had back in the car a week ago.

Why did he want that? Why was that so important?

He didn't have any answers. But she'd taken everything he'd given her that night and there was a desperate part of him that wanted to do the same thing again. A part that craved release.

The dark part of himself he never showed to anyone who wasn't in the ring with him.

"Yeah, well, I'm not in the market." He didn't temper the harsh note in his voice. She had to know that he'd meant it when he'd said they weren't going to see each other again. That had been the only reason he'd caved to the urges of his stupid dick rather than listen to his own better judgment.

He wasn't going to do it again now.

Getting tangled up with hungry, desperate socialites out looking for a bit of rough was a complication he didn't need.

He was supposed to be a better man than that; at least, that was the idea.

Something flickered in her gaze. "Why not? You seemed perfectly happy about it last week."

"That was last week. And I told you it was a one-off thing. I meant it."

Still she made no move to leave. "I'm not looking for anything else. So if you're imagining I'm going to start wanting flowers and dinners and dates, you can stop. I just want what we had last week."

"Go find someone else. I'm not interested." It was for her own good—didn't she know that?

And yours, too. Don't forget that.

Yeah, he couldn't pretend this wasn't about his peace of mind as well.

Her dark eyes glinted in the harsh fluorescent lighting of the garage. She took another step toward him, then another. And this time her gaze swept down his body and stayed down. "I don't think that's true."

Oh fuck. Of course his goddamn dick would have other ideas.

"I'm in charge, pretty girl. Not my fucking cock. And if I said I'm not interested, I'm not interested."

But she didn't stop, her heels making soft tapping sounds as she made her way across the dusty concrete floor to him, the light following the sheen on the fabric of her dress, outlining each delicious curve. There was determination in her eyes and hunger, and something else. Something painful.

She was only inches away from him when she stopped and she didn't look down this time. "Okay, then," she said quietly. "Here's the truth. Ever feel like you're only an actor playing a part? That you're not really who everyone thinks you are? That's how I feel. And tonight, I just want to step off the stage.

I want to stop acting. Stop pretending. Tonight I want to be me." She paused, searching his face. "I'm sorry, I'm not articulating it very well. And I know you don't know me or any-thing. But . . . that's the best way to put it."

There was a raw honesty to the words that caught in his chest, made something inside him go tight.

You know exactly what she means.

No, shit, his situation was different. He wasn't acting. He was trying to be the man he'd promised Madison he'd be and he'd pretty much succeeded. Gideon and his friends didn't know his background or even his real name, but that didn't matter.

Damian Chase, son of Joshua, was dead. He'd died the night his father had told him Madison's death in a car crash wasn't an accident.

"I get it," he said roughly, trying not to notice how close she was standing. How the heat of her body made him want to growl down low in his chest and the pulse at her throat cried out for his hand. So he could feel how fast it was. So he could feel it get faster. "You wanna use me as your rich girl therapy? Get a bit of the dark side? Is that what this is about? 'Cause, baby, if so, there's a hundred or so guys right outside this door who'll give you that. You don't need me."

"I can't go to them." Her voice had a husky edge to it. "I don't trust them. But I do trust you."

"Why the fuck would you do that?"

"God, why wouldn't I? You give women self-defense classes. And you were so pissed off about me hanging around this neighborhood on my own that you gave me a lift home."

"Yeah, and then I fucked you in the back of my car."

That glint in her eyes flared. "Because I wanted you to."

"You were also very clear we weren't going to see each other afterward. So what the hell happened to bring you down this way again?"

Her mouth tightened. "Does it matter? Can't a woman just want sex for the sake of it?"

"Sure they can. But I don't fuck rich girls from downtown, Tamara. That's a rule and I've already broken it once. I'm not doing it again."

She stared at him for a long moment and he could see anger glittering in her eyes, mixing with the heat to create something intense, combustible.

It pulled at him like she had a string tied to his fucking dick.

"I'm getting engaged soon," she said abruptly. "I'm getting engaged and I . . . want a night. Just one goddamn night where I don't have to play a role. Where I don't have to be anyone but myself." She stopped, her breathing sounding shaky, her gaze suddenly fierce. "Where I don't have to keep it under *fucking* control all the time."

Engaged. Hell . . . There were so many reasons why saying yes would be a bad idea.

But you want to anyway. Because you want her. You want to step outside your role as much as she wants to step outside of hers.

"So you wanna use me? Celebrate your last few nights of freedom with hot and dirty screwing before you settle down?"

Her chin came up, defiance joining the anger in her eyes. "You have a problem with that?"

Of course you don't. And that's what makes it perfect. No commitments, no complications.

Yeah, and his head needed to shut the fuck up.

"You don't know me, pretty girl." He stared at her. "I could be anyone."

"You don't know me either. Which is why this works."

She wasn't wrong. So really, why was he protesting? Hadn't that restlessness been eating a hole in his gut? And hadn't the fact that he'd been thinking about her all damn week been pissing him off? Yeah, he was wary of girls like her for a number of different reasons, but in this instance she had her eyes wide open about what she was getting into. She already knew what kind of man he was.

The thread of darkness inside him twisted hard.

She wanted something and he could give it, they'd both get orgasms, it was win-win all the way.

He held her gaze. "You want me, Tamara?"

She didn't look away. "Yes."

"And what do you want me to do? I wanna hear you say it." He wanted to hear those dirty, dirty words coming out of her pretty, pretty mouth.

Her throat moved. "I want you to f-fuck me."

The stutter got him even harder than he was already. Which made him a sick fuck, but suddenly he didn't much care. "You have to make the first move this time. I'm not gonna do anything until you do." If she wanted this, if she truly wanted to step out of her good-girl role tonight, then shit, he'd help her. He'd find out just how far out she was truly prepared to step.

You want to show her as badly as she wants to be shown.

He couldn't deny it. He did. Wanted to know what her limits were and whether he could test them. Perhaps it was the vulnerability he sensed beneath the surface of her that he wanted to get at, that he wanted to uncover. Or the passion he knew burned hot and strong under that sleek, expensive dress of hers. Whatever it was, he wanted it.

Tamara reached out and put a hand on his chest, her palm like a brand on his bare skin. And he had to take a breath, because that electrical current had him in its grip all of a sudden and he couldn't move.

A lot of women touched him like this, unable to take their eyes off his body.

So he felt it like a shock when she looked up, straight into his eyes. Held his gaze like what he'd seen in her, she could see in him, too.

Unease turned over inside him, but before he could say a word or move to break the contact, she slid her hand on his chest up to his shoulder and around behind his neck, reaching up to the back of his head.

To bring his mouth down on hers.

Chapter 6

Tamara didn't know what she was expecting as she pulled Zee's head down. Perhaps the same kind of kiss she'd always had from Robert: tentative and respectful. Not demanding, not taking.

It wasn't what she got.

He was like a lion lying still and waiting for its prey to get close before pouncing. Because as soon their lips touched, his mouth opened and he simply devoured her, his tongue pushing inside without any preliminaries.

A shudder went through her whole body, the hot taste of him igniting a fire inside her she hadn't even realized was smoldering.

Her fingers curled on the back of his head, her nails digging helplessly into his scalp. Not so much to hold him there as to just hold on because it felt like her knees were going to give out.

Beneath her palm on his chest she could feel the oiled silk of his bare skin and the rock-hard muscle under it. God . . . so hot. She wanted to spread her fingers, run her hands all over that perfect body of his, feel it against her own. He smelled of engine oil and that spicy, musky scent she remembered from the car. The one that made her body ache and sent her senses into free fall.

Then, abruptly, his hand curled around her throat and he lifted his head, tarnished steel gaze holding hers.

Tamara forgot how to breathe, how to speak. She even forgot how to think.

There was only him and the heat of his hand around her throat, his palm pressing on her pulse, all demanding and possessive. Only the dark glitter in the depths of his eyes, the one that told her the sex they'd had in the car had only been a small taste of what he was capable of.

She shivered, unable to help herself, a sliver of doubt winding through her.

He was right, she didn't know him and her reasons for trusting him weren't exactly built on anything but a car ride home and gut instinct.

But it was too late to turn back now. And more, she didn't want to.

She knew what she wanted and she'd been the one to dress up like this and come down here. The one to convince him even when he'd said no.

She'd been the one to make the first move. She could have turned around and walked away at any time. But she hadn't.

So now she had to deal with the consequences.

He looked at her a long moment and she had no idea what was going on in his head. Then he flicked a glance up the metal stairs that led to what must be the office, where Gideon had gone.

"Come on." He let go of her throat, gripped her elbow instead and turned, drawing her after him as he headed toward a door at the back of the garage.

She stumbled a little, her heels not really made for oil-stained concrete floors and the metal offcuts that littered them. "Where are we going?"

His fingers on her arm were hard and sure, holding her up. "Out back." He pushed the door open and went through it, pulling her after him.

Gravel crunched under her shoes as she stepped out into a small parking area with chain-link fences on either side. The space was full of a number of different cars, probably waiting for their turn to get worked on in the garage.

Zee tugged her over to the side of the building, where the shadows lurked, then pushed her gently up against the brick wall.

Although it was deserted and they were in darkness, and there were a few cars between them and the street, she still felt exposed.

She tipped her head back and looked up at him as he put his palms on the brick on either side of her head. "H-here? Right now?"

His body was so close to hers, the heat coming from him like one of the powerful engines he worked with. "Yeah." His face was in shadow, and she couldn't see the expression on it. "You said you didn't wanna date or get chocolates and flowers. So you're not gonna get them. You want me, pretty girl, it's right here, right now."

Out on the street behind him, beyond the parked cars, a group of people walked past, laughing and shouting.

Tamara swallowed. Okay, so another thing she hadn't expected. "I just . . . People might see."

He didn't move, that perfectly muscled body looming over her, surrounding her. "They might, but it's pretty dark. And it's nothing they haven't seen before around here."

That wasn't particularly reassuring, and yet she couldn't deny a small piece of her was perversely excited by the thought.

You wanted to step outside your life? So step outside.

There was only darkness where Zee's eyes should be.

And something inside her clenched hard.

"What are you waiting for?" she whispered, suddenly shaking and not quite sure why. "Changed your mind?"

"No." He lifted a hand and placed it lightly around her throat again, making goose bumps rise all over her body, sending her pulse racing and her breathing short and fast. "I'm just thinking about what I wanna eat first." His hand moved down, his fingers trailing over her skin in a light caressing movement that made the shakes worse. "And I think..." His hand reached the neckline of her dress, brushing over the swell of one breast. "I wanna start here." And he slid his fingers inside the red silk and pulled down hard.

She couldn't stop the gasp that burst from her in a soft explosion of sound and she had to grip on to the brick wall behind her to stop from instinctively covering herself. Because she wasn't wearing a bra under the dress. There was nothing at all between the fabric and her bare skin. And now there wasn't even that.

She stared up at him and gradually the expression on his face became clear in the darkness, taut and hungry, silver glittering in his eyes.

A deep shiver caught her.

Are you really sure what you're getting yourself into?

No, actually, she wasn't.

And then Zee lifted his hand and put his thumb in his mouth. Then he lowered it again and brushed that wet thumb over her already hard, bare nipple.

Electricity arrowed through her, every nerve ending suddenly on fire. She made a choked sound and then another as he lightly began to circle, her skin now slick from the moisture on his thumb and even more sensitized.

"You wanna be dirty for me, pretty girl?" His voice was low

and dark and hungry. "You want my dirty hands all over your nice clean skin?"

His thumb moved and it felt like with every circular motion he made, he stripped a piece of her away. Pieces that weren't herself, but the costume she'd been wearing every single day of her life since Will had died.

Perhaps it was wrong to want this, to embrace it. But something was changing inside her, as if ropes that had been holding her down were slowly being cut, one by one.

"Yes," she said hoarsely, her breath catching as he began to rub his thumb back and forth over her nipple, slick skin sliding over slick skin. "I w-want that."

He leaned in, bending his head so his mouth was inches from hers. "So tell me."

She couldn't move, held by the look in his eyes and the feel of his finger on her taut flesh. "I want your d-dirty hands on me." Her voice was thick, the stutter helpless. "And I want to be dirty for you."

His head dipped, his mouth covering hers for a short, hard, blinding kiss. Then he lifted it again and took his hand from her breast, staring down at her as if debating something.

She couldn't stop shivering, that aching, restless want prowling around inside her.

Zee moved his hands to the neckline of her dress, up near her shoulders, gripping tight, then pulling apart in a hard jerk. The fabric ripped and he pulled again, tugging it down over her arms, baring her to the waist.

Her breath escaped her. All she could do was stand there naked from the waist up, the brick rough against her bare skin, feeling his gaze brush over her like the flame from a blowtorch.

Robert had never looked at her like that. Or any of the few boyfriends she'd been with in college. Never like they wanted to devour her alive. As if they couldn't wait to feast.

Zee's gaze lifted to hers, sharp-edged and blazing like a blade lifted straight out of a forge fire. And then he covered her breasts with his oil-stained hands.

The heat of his palms transfixed her, stole the remaining breath in her.

He squeezed gently, his thumbs pinching her aching nipples and sending bright arcs of sensation pulsing through her.

She groaned and he stole the sound with his mouth in another hard kiss that had her pressed up against the rough brick of the wall.

"On your knees," he demanded against her lips. "You wanted to get dirty so it's time to get fucking dirty. I want your mouth around my cock in five seconds or you're not gonna get to come."

The sound of his voice cut the remaining ropes holding her down, the last shreds of Tamara Lennox, good girl and hard worker, and she was on her knees before she could even think straight.

The ground beneath her was hard and covered in gravel, but she was barely conscious of it. All she was aware of was the fact that she was kneeling in the dirt at the back of a garage in a sketchy part of town. In front of a tattooed mechanic, a stranger, who was going to make her suck his cock. It was so wrong and yet the hottest thing she'd ever experienced.

"Five seconds, pretty girl," Zee growled. "Better open that mouth of yours." His hands were already at his overalls, shoving them down over his hips and taking the hard length of his cock out of his boxers.

Her mouth had gone dry. She didn't have a lot of experience blowing guys. But this . . . Zee . . . God. That musky, spicy hot smell of him, it did things to her. Made her hungry in a way she'd never been before.

She lifted her hands and gripped onto his muscular thighs.

His fingers curled around his cock and she couldn't take her eyes off the sight. Oil stains and smooth, hot skin. Moisture flooded into her mouth like she was starving and he was food.

"Do exactly what I tell you and you'll get yours, too." His other hand reached for her, twining in her hair and gripping on tight. "Open up, pretty girl."

And then he was sliding into her mouth and the hot, salty taste of him was on her tongue.

So good. So fucking good.

She closed her lips around him and dug her fingers into his thighs, responding to the grip in her hair as he guided her.

"Look at me," he murmured.

She obeyed, lifting her gaze to his.

Silver glimmered in his eyes, the lines of his face drawn tight. "Oh yeah." His voice was a rough whisper in the darkness. "Suck me, baby. Just like that."

And she did, taking him in as far as she could, using her tongue to stroke the underside of his cock, all down the long, hard length of him. Watching the expression on his face change, becoming tighter, fiercer. His gaze flicked to her bare breasts and back to where her mouth was stretched around him and she could see the effect that had on him. She felt it herself, too, in the ache between her legs that had her clenching her thighs together, trying to ease it.

Zee smiled, a hungry wolf's smile, his fingers pushing deeper into her hair and holding on tight. "You like this, don't you? You like having my dick in your mouth. Makes you all wet."

She nodded, increasing the suction, suddenly wanting him as desperate and out of control as she was starting to feel.

But his hips stilled, the grip in her hair almost painful. "Pull your dress up and let me see."

She would never have contemplated doing such a thing a few days ago. But she wasn't Tamara now. She was on her knees, her dress ripped, and if she looked down, she knew she'd see the marks of his hands on her breasts, oil on her clean skin.

Tamara was dead and gone.

Her hands shaking with desire, she fumbled with the hem of her dress, pulling it up around her waist, baring herself to him. And she gloried in the tight look on his face as his gaze dropped.

"Spread your thighs," he ordered roughly. "Let me see that hot little pussy of yours."

She did that too, no hesitation, adjusting her stance so she was kneeling with her legs apart.

"No." His voice was a harsh rumble. "All I'm seeing is cotton, baby. Get those panties away."

Her hands were already moving to obey, tugging aside the damp cotton, baring her sex to him.

He exhaled. "Oh yeah, that's what I'm talking about. Fucking beautiful." He flexed his hips, a long, slow thrusting into her mouth, his gaze fixed between her thighs. "Touch yourself. Let me see those fingers working that tight pussy."

She couldn't do it fast enough, shuddering as she touched her own wet flesh, sliding her fingers over her clit, the sharpness of the pleasure almost making her come on the spot.

Things began to descend into desperation at that point, her world narrowing to the slide of his cock in her mouth, the gleam in his eyes as he watched her hand move between her thighs, the intense hot pleasure of her fingers on her clit.

Everything spun out of control and she let it, embraced it as he began to thrust harder, faster, pulling on her hair and making little points of pain prickle all over her scalp. But that only added to the rush of sensations building inside her. The gravel beneath her knees, digging into her skin. The thickness of him in her mouth. The dirty pleasure of touching herself as he watched her.

It was all so good. All so intense.

The climax broke over her without warning, leaving her shaking and gasping, all her senses overwhelmed. She was barely conscious of Zee's thrusts becoming faster, wilder, his grip tightening even more painfully. And when the climax took him too, all she could do was kneel there and take it as he thrust hard into her mouth, putting his hand up to lean forward against the wall, a deep groan tearing from him.

Tamara didn't move, her whole body ringing like a bell with the aftereffects of the climax, the taste of him hot in her mouth.

And it was only in the moments afterward, as he slowly withdrew, that she began to be aware that her knees hurt and her scalp was tingling, her jaw aching.

The low, rough sound of Zee's breathing gradually penetrated her shocked brain.

She looked up and something that hadn't been satisfied one bit began to stir to life inside her.

"I'm not done," he said.

Then he pulled her to her feet.

He felt like he'd barely touched her. Barely gotten a taste. And even though the effects of the mind-blowing orgasm were still rocketing around inside him like a hit of pure, uncut cocaine, the sight of her kneeling there in the remains of her ripped dress was more than enough to get his dick excited all over again.

She looked dazed, her beautiful, pouty mouth full and red, and slightly open. And there was enough ambient light to see the glow of her pale skin and the dark marks left by his stained hands that covered her small, high breasts. His fingerprints.

He'd done that to her. He'd torn her dress and put his hands all over her, stained her, marked her. And now all he wanted was to do it all over again.

He didn't question himself because it was too late for that

shit, leaning down and sliding an arm around her waist, hauling her up into his arms. Then he turned and carried her a few steps to the vintage Chevy he was in the process of fixing, and sat her on the hood.

Her hands were holding tight to his shoulders, her dark eyes on his. "What are you doing?" Her voice sounded cracked and that only added to the fire that was still burning hot inside him.

"I told you I wasn't done. Lie down."

She stared at him a moment and then slowly leaned back on the shiny red metal, keeping herself propped up on her elbows, watching him.

Fuck, yeah, she could keep doing that.

He put his hands on her thighs and pushed them apart, the sound of her soft gasp stoking the flame higher. His fingers left more marks, staining her white skin, the sight of them a punch to the gut.

He had no idea why that was such a turn-on, why the thought of her walking away from this encounter with his fingerprints all over her made his cock so fucking hard.

A poor little rich girl pulled down in the dirt with him.

It's not the first time that's happened.

Zee growled at the thought, shoving it away as he jerked aside the crotch of her panties, revealing the hot, juicy little pussy he'd watched her fingers slide all over as she'd sucked him off.

A quiver ran through her. "Zee . . ."

He ignored the desperate sound of his name, leaning in to push his hands beneath her thighs, urging them up and over his shoulders.

Her hips shifted, a soft sound escaping her as he pressed in even closer. "Oh . . . God . . . I don't think I can. . . ."

"Yeah, you can." Christ, he was so fucking hungry and she smelled all musky and hot, like raw sex. She'd had him in her mouth. It was his turn to taste.

Burying his head between her thighs, he pushed his tongue deep inside her.

She gave a cry, her body stiffening in his hands.

But he didn't stop or pull back. She tasted hot and sweet, with a tart edge that had his heart thumping in his head and his cock hardening even more. He licked her, exploring the tender wet folds of her pussy with his tongue, listening to the ragged, desperate sounds he drew from her.

Her hips shifted restlessly beneath his mouth and her thighs clenched around his head, the sweet, raw taste of her filling his senses. He shifted his hand, sliding up one thigh and between, finding the hard bud of her clit, pinching it as he pushed his tongue deeper.

She shuddered, a choked sob escaping her.

He lifted his head, glancing up at her to see she had her head thrown back, her back arched, her bottom lip caught between her teeth. So fucking erotic. But it wasn't what he wanted.

"Look at me," he ordered, his voice gone hoarse. "Look at me, pretty girl."

She gave a soft moan, exhaling on a shaky breath, lowering her head to meet his gaze. Her eyes had gone black in the night, desire swamping them.

"Yeah, that's right." He didn't break eye contact. "I want you to watch me eating you out. And you better stay watching me 'cause if you look away, I'm not gonna let you come."

He didn't wait for her to respond, holding her gaze as he bent to her pussy again, licking deep as he pinched her clit, watching as the sharp edge of pleasure unfurled over her face like anguish. But she didn't look away. She kept her gaze glued to his with something like defiance, a challenge he couldn't help but take up.

So he kept going, using his mouth, his tongue, and his fingers, pushing her and pushing her, winding the pleasure tighter and tighter, until her hips began to shudder and shake, and she began to sob in earnest. Until at last she threw back her head again and gave a high, sharp scream, her whole body convulsing.

He clamped down hard on her thighs as she bucked against him, holding her through the most intense part of the climax. And when she at last went limp, he released her, stepping back to grab his wallet out of the pocket of his overalls and get the condom out of it.

All he could taste was her. She was in his mouth, in his nostrils, seared into his brain. He wasn't going to be able to get rid of her until he was inside her.

Jesus, he wasn't even going to be able to function until he was inside her.

He tore the packet open and rolled the condom down. Tamara was still lying on the hood of the Chevy in a wanton sprawl. Her slinky red dress was a narrow band of oil-stained fabric around her waist and she'd lost her sexy shoes. Her hair had come out of its bun and was spread all over the cherry metal of the car, her skin glowing pale. There were black marks on the inside of her thighs now from where he'd pushed them wide apart with his dirty fingers.

What the fuck have you done? Aren't you supposed to be better than this?

But he couldn't think about that now, because desire was rising inside him. And when he took his cock in his hand and rubbed the head of it all over her soft, hot pussy, she whimpered.

"You want this?" he murmured, too much in the grip of the darkness to stop. "You want my cock?"

She gave another moan, her hips lifting helplessly as he slid the head of his dick over her clit, teasing her. "Yes." The word was a whisper of sound. "But God . . . You've wrecked me, Zee. I don't know if I can."

"You did before. You can do it again."

"I don't know . . ."

He leaned forward, easing the tip of his dick inside her, then stopping. The feel of all that warm, wet flesh against his was driving him insane, but he wasn't going to give it to her yet. He wanted her to beg for it.

She groaned, her hips lifting, ready to take him.

"Tell me how much you want it, Tamara." He eased a little deeper, making her gasp. "Beg me for it."

Her eyes had closed, her teeth digging into her lower lip again. Her hands were spread on the metal of the hood as if she was holding on to it. "Please." Her voice was ragged. "Please, Zee. Give it to me. Please." Then suddenly her eyes opened and her gaze locked onto his, a dark fire burning in the depths. "I want your cock, Zee. I want you to fuck me. Do it. Now."

And like the balance of power had changed, he found himself obeying her this time, thrusting into the wet heat of her. Feeling her pussy clench around him, tight as a glove.

It nearly blew his head off.

He had to stop inside her, his hands flat on the hood on either side of her hips, just to get himself under control, because he didn't want to be the one moaning and desperate and out of control. He wanted to be the one in charge.

Yet, like she knew exactly what he was thinking, her mouth curved. And she lifted her legs up around his hips, rocking her pelvis back, urging him deeper.

His mind blanked and he knew that somewhere, somehow, he'd lost control of this. But as she moved beneath him, as the sound of her breathing got faster and faster, he rapidly found he didn't much care.

Instead he leaned forward on his hands, pushing inside her, then sliding back out. Setting up a hard, driving rhythm. Then there was nothing but the sound of flesh meeting flesh, her hoarse cries of ecstasy as he fucked her, and the whiplash of pleasure that uncoiled up his spine.

There were bright lights behind his eyes, unbearable tension drawing everything impossibly tight. Then it released and he roared as the climax burst apart in his head, a blaze of white light that annihilated him, shattering his consciousness as surely as a hammer to the back of his head.

He didn't know how long it was before he became conscious again, feeling cold metal beneath his palms and hot flesh around his dick.

When he opened his eyes, he was almost shocked to find himself behind the garage, a nearly naked woman sprawled on the hood of the car. That he wasn't in some other place, where the cities were on fire and the sky was full of flames.

She was looking at him, her eyes full of that hot darkness and he knew that he'd been lying to himself all this time. Telling himself it would be just one night, just one quick fuck and that would be it, that he'd send her back to where she came from and never think of her again.

But he didn't say anything as he pulled out of her, put his clothing back in place, then helped her with hers. She didn't speak either, sitting there silently as he pulled her dress back down over her hips, then tried to cover her breasts. When that didn't work, he picked her up in his arms and carried her back into the garage, setting her down on the work counter while he went to the lockers and got out one of his T-shirts.

She watched him silently as he came back over to her, raising her arms like a child when he gestured, letting him put the shirt on her, covering up all that pale, marked skin.

Then he said, "Get in the car. I'll take you home."

She didn't protest, nor did she speak as he drove her back to her downtown apartment.

It was as if what had happened between them had made speech impossible.

Only when he pulled up outside her apartment building and she put her hand on the door handle to get out did she speak. Even then it was only one word.

"Again?"

He should say no, he really should. But he didn't. "Yes."

She kept her head turned away. "When?"

"Day after tomorrow. I have a fight that night, but I'll come here after."

"Okay." She didn't say good-bye, didn't turn to look at him. She only opened the door and got out, slamming it shut behind her.

And this time he didn't take his eyes off her as she walked up to the building, and he kept on watching until she disappeared inside it.

Chapter 7

Tamara let the door of the theater shut behind her, the heels of her red shoes clicking on the marble stairs that led down into the foyer.

Her mother's charity event was still in full swing, the crowd raucously cheering the bachelor auction that was currently underway, and Tamara knew that slipping out wouldn't be looked on with any approval by her family. But then the evening had been tense right from the start and she needed to get out, find some quiet space.

She stopped on the bottom step and sat down, the cool of the marble seeping through the white silk of her dress. Then she leaned forward, her elbows on her knees, her fingers pressing gently against her eyelids.

Okay, so this evening wasn't ever going to be great, but it had turned out way more difficult than she'd initially expected. Her mother had kept dropping hints about how Tamara had better keep her schedule free for the end of the month because of a special "family dinner" that was being organized.

Family dinner being code for "surprise engagement party."

Her father had given her several meaningful looks across the table, warning Tamara to play along, and so she had. Acting like she didn't know a thing.

Pretending she was still the same Tamara who hadn't had hot, dirty sex with a mechanic behind his garage. In public.

And *that* had been the difficult bit.

She didn't know quite how that worked, because it had only been sex. Nothing life-changing, nothing shattering. And yet . . . she felt shattered.

After he'd dropped her back at her apartment and she'd closed the door behind her, she'd leaned back against it and slid down onto the floor, wrapping her arms around herself, her knees suddenly giving out. Unable to stop grinning.

Her blood had been like fire in her veins, her heart pumping. She felt like the entire top layer of her skin had been scraped away, leaving nerve endings raw and sensitized.

And all of it had felt . . . good. No, not good, it had felt *amazing*. Like she'd been numb for years and hadn't realized it, and only now was the feeling returning to her limbs.

Then she'd looked down at herself, at the faded black Motörhead T-shirt she wore, at the ruined silk of her dress, at the oil stains marking the silk, marking her skin. And she'd had to put a hand over her mouth to stop the hysterical laugh that threatened to come out of it.

That night she hadn't bothered to shower, wanting to keep the stains on her body, as if by washing them off she'd wash away the feeling of freedom, too, the feeling that at last, at last, she was herself. After so many goddamn years.

Of course, the next morning she had to scrub herself to get them off since she had to go to work and Scott would no doubt comment if he saw them. But she couldn't entirely get rid of them. The ghost of Zee's fingerprints lingered on her skin and that whole day she could feel them there like little spots of heat. The evidence of her own dark, secret self.

She'd loved that. It made putting on the mask of Tamara Lennox that morning so much easier, knowing that underneath it all, the marks of what she'd done with Zee were still there. A reminder of who she was inside. A woman who was free, who was passionate, who didn't have to keep it under control all the fucking time.

"Again," she'd told him, because she didn't want to give up that feeling. Wanted to hold on to it as long as she could.

Unfortunately though, the downside was that it made her aware of how much of a sham her life actually was.

As she'd sat in the theater at the charity dinner, with her parents on either side of her, she'd felt the same suffocation come over her. The feeling of being trapped in a life that she hadn't chosen for herself.

She was the good girl who worked hard, who had a great career ahead of her, who'd made her parents proud. Who was on track to marry a successful and wealthy man. And who'd had no choice about any of it. Her parents had made all her choices for her and she'd gratefully accepted all of them.

Of course you had to accept them. They saved you.

Tamara rubbed at her eyes, heedless of her makeup.

Why was this hard? A week ago she wouldn't have found any of this difficult. She'd have gone to the dinner, had a great time, been the good little socialite.

But now things were . . . different. And she wasn't sure how she felt about that. Then again, there wasn't much she could do about it, was there? She was stuck in the role her parents had created for her and she wasn't allowed to deviate from the script.

Why? What would happen if you did?

Tamara screwed her eyes shut tight. No, she couldn't think about that. Will hadn't had a choice, so why should she?

From the depths of her white sequined purse came the sound of her phone chiming and her heart seized in her chest, a burst of adrenaline firing hot and hard through her. She grabbed it, glancing down at the text on the screen, and instantly all thoughts about her family vanished.

Where are you?

Oh God. It was Zee.

Her mouth dried. She hadn't been letting herself think about his promise, about how he'd said he'd come for her tonight. But she couldn't deny that the main reason she'd slipped out of the theater tonight was to check her phone in peace. Just like she couldn't deny that she'd been desperately hoping he would contact her.

That what he'd said in the car wasn't a lie.

And sure enough it wasn't.

At the Fox Theater, she texted back. *A stupid charity thing.* And then, because she didn't want to give away too much, *Sorry, I forgot you were going to come to my place tonight.*

Her heartbeat had now accelerated, an ache gathering between her thighs.

There was no response for a second. Then her phone chimed again.

Liar.

She bit her lip, her cheeks getting hot. How stupid that he could make her blush with a one-word text.

Are you coming then? she responded, ignoring him.

Gimme ten minutes and we both will.

Tamara choked out a laugh, excitement a small, hard knot in her chest. *I'll take that as a yes.*

Wait outside. I'll pick you up.

The excitement began to spread out, expanding through her in a hot wave.

It was ridiculous, to feel this way over what was essentially a booty call, but after an evening of suffocating pretense, she wanted out. She wanted Zee's brutal brand of honesty. Hot, raw sex. No masks, no costumes. Everything straight up and way, way out of control.

This was at least one choice she'd made for herself.

"Tamara?"

She jerked her head up and turned, feeling the color rush to her cheeks as her mother, tall, slender, and beautiful in vintage Chanel, came down the stairs toward her.

Why did she find herself blushing? She hadn't done anything wrong. "Hi, Mom," she said, trying not to sound so breathless. "Sorry, just needed to get out, have a bit of space."

There was a crease between Cassandra Lennox's perfect eyebrows. "Is there anything wrong, Tamara? You seemed a bit . . . off tonight. Thought I'd check to make sure you were okay."

Tamara forced a smile. "I'm fine, Mom. Honestly. Got a bit of a headache, that's all."

Her mother descended the last few steps and, with a graceful movement, sat on the step beside her. "Are you sure that's it? There's nothing else bothering you?"

God, how she hated it when her mother got overly solicitous, soothing her and treating her as if she were a bomb about to go off.

Or a woman who shot her own brother?

The smile on Tamara's face felt like a rictus. "No, not at all. Maybe it's something I ate."

"Well, are you going to come back inside? I'm going to give my speech soon and it would be great if you were there."

Of course her mother wanted her there. She *always* wanted her there. As if she couldn't bear to let Tamara out of her sight.

Perhaps she's afraid you're going to go out and kill someone else?

The thought bubbled up from somewhere inside her, snide and sarcastic and cynical. And she nearly said it, nearly gave voice to the doubts that lingered, even all these years later. But she didn't. Instead she bit her lip hard to keep the words inside, turning away and fussing around with her purse so she didn't have to look her mother in the eye.

"Actually, I'm feeling a little sick," she said. "Would you mind if I went home early?"

"Of course I mind." Her mother smiled. "I like having you there. But I guess if you're not well . . ." There was a slight question in her voice, the merest hint of doubt.

"I'm not," Tamara said before she could question either her mother's doubts or her own. "An early night is probably what I need."

Cassandra stared at her, frowning. "You're working too hard, Tamara."

"Well, if I want this position, I have to." She kept the smile firmly plastered to her face. "It's still what you and Dad want, right? Me at Lennox?"

An expression shifted in her mother's eyes, one she couldn't read. "Of course, darling. And I suppose hard work is its own reward." She let out a long breath, her mouth tightening. "You'd better go then, get some rest. Shall I call a car for you?"

"No, it's okay. I'll get my own."

"Are you sure? Your father won't mind giving you a ride home."

Tamara stared at her mother a moment. Did she suspect something was up? Or was Tamara just being paranoid? "Mom, it's okay. I can find my own way home."

For a second it looked like her mother was going to insist, but then she lifted a shoulder. "Fine. I just worry about you, darling."

That was nothing new. Her mother was always worrying about her, always wanting what was best for her.

Maybe it's not so much best for you as what's best for them.

But she didn't like that thought, so she ignored it.

"I know you do." Tamara leaned over and gave her mother a

kiss on the cheek. "But you don't need to. Now if you don't mind, I'd better go find myself a cab and get home."

She waited until her mother had returned to the theater before stepping outside.

The entrance was bathed in white light from the theater lights above her head, making the neon-stained night seem even darker.

It was relatively late, but there were still a number of people about, bar- and restaurant-goers, or those searching for clubs and other late-night amusements.

And then she saw him, leaning against his car across the street from her.

He was in jeans tonight, worn and battered, sitting low on his hips, along with a black T-shirt that only emphasized his lean, muscled body. With his shorn head, tattoos, and the scuffed, black motorcycle boots on his feet, he radiated menace, every inch the bad boy from the wrong side of town.

A wild surge of exhilaration burst through her, carrying with it the desire that, despite what they'd already done to each other, hadn't ever been fully sated, and she couldn't get across the road to him fast enough.

His tarnished silver gaze followed her as she came toward him, the intensity of him making her blood burn and the air turn to fire in her lungs. Making her so very aware of the way her body moved and the slick slide of her dress over her skin as she walked.

She was wearing silk, a simple strapless dress with a fitted bodice and a frothy little skirt. Her mother hadn't approved of the red heels she'd worn with it, or the simple, red patent belt that spanned her waist, but Tamara hadn't cared. She'd wanted something red on her and, though she hadn't questioned the urge when she'd dressed earlier that night, she understood it now.

Red was the color of freedom.

Red was the color of passion.

Red was Zee's color.

He watched her as she approached and deliberately she let her hips sway, holding his gaze as she came closer, her heartbeat getting faster and faster as a silver flame leapt in his eyes.

When she reached the Trans Am, he pushed away from the car and the breath caught in her throat as he came around the car toward her, moving with the easy, predator's grace she remembered. The one that made her want to stand still and just watch him.

And she thought he might pull her into his arms, kiss her, devour her right there in the street. But he didn't. Instead he stopped mere inches from her, making her aware of his height, his lean strength, the heat of his body, and that spicy scent that made something pulse deep in her sex.

Without taking his gaze from hers, he reached for the car door and pulled it open, his arm almost brushing her bare shoulder, making the breath lock in her throat and shivers whisper all over her skin.

"Get in," he said.

She looked like a fucking virgin in her pretty white dress. A debutante. A prom queen.

Except for the bright splash of red at her waist where the belt was, and the high, red fuck-me shoes. That gave a hint as to the real Tamara, the passionate, hungry woman beneath the innocent white silk.

It made him so hard he could barely think.

Maybe that was his problem. Maybe he'd been thinking far too much.

Certainly that's what he'd been doing the past day and a half, going over and over in his head whether seeing her again after their encounter at the garage was a good plan or not. He knew it was a bad idea, knew getting involved with a girl like her could potentially be history repeating itself all over again. Yet a part of him—no prizes for guessing which part—kept whispering that it was just sex, that there was no danger. It was a limited-time thing and hell, she was going to be getting engaged anyway and if she wanted a bit of rough before she settled down into wedded bliss, then he had no problem with providing it.

After a while, he'd gotten sick of arguing with himself. Tonight's fight had been just what he'd needed to get out of his head and, when it was over, the adrenaline pumping hard in his veins, he'd picked up his phone and texted her.

The post-fight buzz was still there by the time he'd gotten to the theater and now all he could think about was whether he could wait till they'd gotten back to her apartment or whether they should find a handy alleyway like they had the last time around.

But no, he could hold out. He wasn't that desperate. And besides, he'd dirtied her up in his neck of the woods; it was time to dirty her up in hers.

You're curious too, don't deny it.

Zee ignored that thought, his hands tight on the steering wheel of the Trans Am. Her scent was filling the car, making it difficult to concentrate on driving let alone anything else.

She sat beside him, her fingers moving on the white purse she held in her lap, the silence between them full of tension and heat.

It lasted all the way to her apartment, but he made no attempt to break it. Talking wasn't what they were meeting for.

The tension had got to extreme levels by the time they arrived at her building, a humming, crackling anticipation that made him even more hungry and restless than he was already.

Riding the elevator up to her floor, he could barely keep his hands to himself, pushing them deep into his pockets instead.

This was a lesson in control if anything was, and fuck it, he was nothing if not controlled. One little rich girl in a sexy white dress wasn't going to get the better of him.

Like she hasn't already.

Zee nearly growled at the thought as he followed her down the hallway to her door, conscious of the harsh sound his boots made on the floor as he came into the apartment behind her.

Then he stopped as the door shut and looked around.

Christ, this place. Exposed, whitewashed brick and dark wooden floorboards. Comfortable pale gray couch and armchairs. Dark wood bookcases full of intellectual, important-looking books and delicate knickknacks. A fucking interior decorator's wet dream.

He had a sudden vision of himself in his oil-stained overalls sitting down on that pristine couch and kicking his boots up on the white coffee table, getting grease everywhere, dirtying up the place. Breaking shit . . .

He didn't know why that thought made him feel a savage kind of pleasure, but it did.

Tamara had moved through the open-plan space to where a wooden breakfast bar separated the lounge area from the kitchen. She put her purse down on it and went around and into the kitchen, going over to the fridge and taking out a bottle of wine. Then she got a couple of glasses from a high shelf and put them on the breakfast bar before pouring some wine in each one.

Wine? Jesus, who did she think he was?

He walked over to the breakfast bar and came around it to where she stood, took the bottle out of her hands, and turned her so her back was to the wooden counter. Then he put his hands down on the surface of it on either side of her hips, looking down into her dark eyes.

She was so warm, her body inches from his, and he wanted to rip that fucking dress off her, have her wearing nothing but those sexy red heels. "What?" he said. "You think I'm here for a drink and a chat?"

Her mouth curved and she leaned back, reaching out for one of the glasses and raising it, taking a sip. "Why not? Nothing wrong with a little anticipation, right?" There was a glint in her eye, something flirty and sexy and downright hot.

She was teasing him. Slowly, he smiled back, his hunter's instinct rising. "Take your fucking dress off, pretty girl. I'm done with anticipation."

Tamara raised a *wait* finger, took another sip of her wine, then said, "So you had a fight tonight? Before coming here?"

"Yeah."

"Was it a prizefight or something?"

"No. They're nothing. Just some underground matches where we beat the shit out of each other."

"Uh-huh." She tipped her head back and drained the rest of her wine, her eyes gleaming over the rim of the glass. "Why?"

"Why what?"

"Why do you do it?"

He shifted, leaning on his hands, easing his body closer, not in the mood to be discussing his fights. "What do you do?"

"I'm an intern in an investment company."

Of course she would be. Girl like her had success written all over her. "So why do you do it?"

She smiled at his conscious imitation. "It's not the same thing."

"No, but it's the same question."

"You don't want to talk about yourself?"

"Like I said, that's not what I came here for."

"I thought all guys wanted to talk about themselves."

"You've been seeing the wrong kind of guys." Gently he removed the wineglass from her hands and put it down on the breakfast bar. "Now. Take your fucking dress off before I rip it."

Something leapt in her gaze, a dark flame, and she laughed. "Show me some moves."

"What?"

Her hands came up, her palms flat on his chest. "Some of your fighting moves."

That wasn't what he'd come for either. Yet that glittering flame was still in her eyes and he wanted to see what it meant. "Why?"

"Because I'm curious." Her hands slid up over his chest, stroking. "Because I watched you at the gym that night and I thought . . ." She stopped, color rising to her cheeks. "I thought you were beautiful."

He'd been hot and sexy to women before. But none of them had ever called him beautiful. "I'm just a mechanic who beats the shit out of people at night. Nothing beautiful about that."

"You don't only do that." Her gaze had dropped to his chest, her hands stroking, petting him like a cat. "You teach people how to defend themselves too. Is that part of your fight thing?"

A thread of unease wound through him at the question, though he couldn't have said why. Perhaps it was her touch, which was gentle. And he wasn't here for gentle. "Look, you wanna get naked? So, let's get naked. Stop wasting time."

She looked up at him and he thought he saw a flash of hurt in her eyes.

Fuck. He hadn't meant to hurt her yet there had to be a line drawn somewhere. A reminder of what was happening between them.

Tamara's gaze dropped again, her hands stopping their stroking motion, and he pretended he was happy she did and not disappointed instead.

"Good point," she said after a moment. "Though I meant what I said. I want to see some of those moves. So . . ." She shoved hard against him all of a sudden and because he wasn't expecting it, he stumbled back a few steps. "You want to take my dress off, you fucking take it off yourself." She grinned, the look in her eyes all challenge. "That is, if you can."

The competitor in him, still buzzing from the fight, roared in approval at the challenge, and he found his hands curling into fists in the pockets of his jeans.

Though Christ, did she really know what she was letting herself in for, goading him like this?

"I'm not one of your pretty little rich boys, Tamara," he said flatly. "And I'm not one of your polite city guys, in a fancy suit, respecting the fuck out of you and your choices. I'm a bad man. A man you shouldn't mess with."

But she didn't look away. "Perhaps that's what I want. Perhaps messing with you is exactly what I want."

"Okay then." Well, he couldn't say he hadn't warned her. Sliding his hands out of his pockets, he deliberately relaxed his muscles, getting loose and ready. "You've got one second."

She was around the side of the breakfast bar and out into the lounge as if she had a rocket under her, moving pretty fast on those sexy shoes of hers.

But he was faster.

She'd barely reached the couch by the time he caught her, easily taking one arm and twisting it up and behind her back, while reaching around with the other and locking his fingers around her throat. Then he pulled her up against his body.

She cursed, struggled a moment, then went completely still.

She felt good, all those soft, hot curves pressed up against him. Made him want to hold her like that all day, then maybe bend her over the couch and fuck her from behind.

He lowered his head, so his mouth was near her ear. "That was too easy."

"And yet my dress is still on." Her voice was husky, an undercurrent of heat moving through it.

"I haven't finished yet." He could feel her pulse racing beneath his palm, the softness of her skin tantalizing against his fingertips. Exertion had released a soft, musky scent, sweat and the sweetness of her expensive perfume and it hit him like a pure aphrodisiac. He wanted to tilt her head, expose her neck, sink his teeth into that sensitive spot between shoulder and neck.

But it would be all over if that happened and he was now officially curious.

He wanted to see what more she could do.

Abruptly he let her go and stepped back.

She turned and looked at him, one eyebrow raised in inquiry.

"One more chance," he said. "Go."

She didn't hesitate, heading past the couch to the coffee table, obviously trying to put it between them.

He let her feel like she had the upper hand for a second, making a couple of feints around one side of the table, while she started in the opposite direction.

She'd gone pink, her blond hair coming down from the elegant bun it had been in when he'd picked her up. And she was grinning, caught in the same adrenaline high he was.

God, she was gorgeous, and he was enjoying this game she'd started way too much. It had been a long time since a woman had teased him like this—usually they were way too intimidated.

But then Tamara gave a breathless laugh and just like that, his patience with the game snapped.

He leapt over the coffee table, making her give a shriek, before taking her down onto her back, onto the fluffy deep blue rug that covered the floorboards, pinning her hands on either side of her head and keeping her down with the weight of his body on hers.

She struggled, her hips lifting like she could buck him off, her breath coming in short, hard pants. At first he thought it was part of the flirtation game, so all he did was settle down more fully onto her, using his weight to keep her still.

Then her gaze met his and he saw something wild in her eyes, and he realized it wasn't a game anymore. He knew fear, he saw it in the ring and in the women who came to him to learn how to defend themselves. In the faces of his father's enemies all those years ago. In the cold twist of his gut when his father had told him he wouldn't be seeing Madison anymore.

And now it was in Tamara's eyes too.

She was trembling.

"Hey," he said, keeping his voice sharp to cut through her fear. "What's wrong?"

She blinked a couple of times, as if she'd been somewhere else, then her gaze focused on him, the tension in her body dissipating. "Nothing."

"Yeah, there is. Did I scare you?"

Her lashes swept down all of a sudden, veiling her gaze. "No."

"Bullshit. I'm a mean son of a bitch, but this was a game and scaring you wasn't the point of it."

She was silent a moment. "It's not you," she said eventually.

"Then what?"

She let out a small breath. "I thought I'd gotten over it. Sorry."

"Gotten over what?" He couldn't think why he wanted to know, because that wasn't the point of this either. Yet he did. For some reason it mattered.

Her lashes came up, her eyes dark and wary. "Someone I knew used to . . . kind of hold me down. He never hurt me, just . . ." She stopped, her throat moving. "He was sick. Mentally unwell. It wasn't anything major."

But he could see that it was and it roused all his latent protective instincts. He suddenly wanted to know who and why and where, a surge of hot possessiveness moving through him.

Seriously? Over a chick you've banged twice?

But he ignored the thought. He didn't care whether he'd screwed her or not, something had hurt her and he wanted to fix it. "Sounds pretty major to me."

"It's not, okay?" Her expression had hardened, like a door had shut behind her eyes. "It was years ago and I'm over it. So..." Her hips shifted under his, a sensual undulation that had his cock going from semihard to hard in seconds flat.

Yet a small, insistent thread of curiosity wound through him that he found impossible to ignore.

"How many years ago?" He settled himself more firmly between her thighs, the hard ridge of his zipper pressing against the soft heat of her, and he felt her shiver.

"What? I don't know. Eight, I think." A crease appeared between her brows. "I thought you didn't want to chat?"

Yeah, that's right. You don't.

Fuck, he didn't. He really didn't. So why did he want to know what had put that fear in her eyes? They weren't here to trade their life stories, and God knew he'd sworn off vulnerable women for life. Yet, he couldn't seem to leave it alone.

He shifted, flexing his hips slightly so the ridge of his zipper hit the sweet spot between her legs. She took a sharp breath, the wariness draining from her eyes and replaced by a burgeoning heat.

Better. Yeah, that was better.

So he did it again, rocking gently against her, feeling the remaining tension seep out of her muscles. She gave a soft, shaky sigh, her thighs opening wider to give him room and that was good too. In fact that was exactly what he wanted.

He let one of her wrists go and reached down between them, pulling the white silk of her dress up around her waist so the only thing separating the rough denim of his jeans from her pussy were the white lace panties she wore. Then he flexed his hips again, harder this time. Grinding against her clit and watching as the color bloomed under her skin.

She groaned, her gaze on his as she arched her back, lifting her pelvis against his, seeking more friction, more pressure. And he gave it to her, rocking more insistently, then circling to vary the movement.

There was no fear now on her face and, though her breathing was fast and getting faster, it wasn't because she was afraid, not if that heat between her legs was anything to go by.

It made it him feel good to take away her fear, turn it into something else. Made him feel satisfied that he could make a difference to her.

But he was getting kind of sick of her clothes and the fact that her virginal dress was still on and still covering up all that beautiful skin.

So he moved, gripping her hips and rolling over onto his back, taking her with him so she was sitting astride him. She blinked, her pouty mouth opening slightly as she found her position changed. Then she smiled as if this was far more to her liking.

"This doesn't mean you're in charge, pretty girl," he said, so she understood. "I'm still gonna win this fight." Then he sat up and tugged off the belt around her waist, before putting a hand around her back and finding the tab of her dress zipper, pulling it down.

"Really?" Her eyes gleamed. "I beg to differ." And she put her hand straight down over his cock where it pressed against the denim of his jeans. Then the delicious little bitch squeezed, sending white hot streaks of fire licking up his spine.

"Jesus Christ," he growled. "You wanna play dirty? Then let's play dirty." Taking hold of the hem of her dress, he pulled it roughly up and over her head.

She gave a gasp as he did so, her face pink and flushed as he tossed the white silk away, leaving her sitting in his lap in nothing but a pair of white, lacy panties. Then he dealt with those too, simply ripping the fabric at both sides of her hips and pulling away the remaining scrap of material.

She was a delicious damn sight, sitting in his lap completely naked but for her sexy red shoes. Her legs were spread wide around his hips, revealing the neat thatch of gold curls between her thighs, and her nipples were tight and hard. The pink flush in her cheeks went all the way down her throat to her breasts and she almost fucking glowed, like someone had turned a light on inside her.

"That's not fair," she said huskily. "I want you naked."

"Too bad." He put his hands on her hips, her skin soft and smooth and hot beneath his palms. "I don't play fair." And he gripped her tight as he flexed again, stroking the hard ridge of his aching cock against that hot pussy of hers.

She shuddered, gasping as he held her down, grinding her against him. "Zee . . . God . . ."

"Fuck, you're desperate aren't you?" he murmured, his own voice starting to get hoarse. "Naked and pleading for me already. I haven't even got my cock inside you and already you've got my jeans all wet." He put his hand down between her thighs, sliding his fingers through her damp curls and tugging gently. "Shall I make you come, baby? Like this? Right now?"

She shuddered and when he twisted his hand, applying pressure to her clit with his thumb, she shuddered again. "Sure," she panted, all throaty and husky. "You can do that. And then I'll make you come in your jeans like a teenage boy."

He laughed, because fuck if that didn't sound just like the kind of challenge he particularly enjoyed. "You can try, pretty girl. You can try." Then he stroked her clit with his thumb, moving his hips, grinding the thick ridge of his dick against her tender flesh.

But she didn't just sit there and take it. Her hand came down, her fingers running over the denim, stroking the length of his cock, squeezing him, her eyes full of dark fire.

And he felt the grip of pleasure begin to wind tight because he hadn't fully understood quite how badly it was affecting him, the sight of her naked with her legs spread and his hand between them. The slick gleam of her wet flesh, the evidence of her arousal soaking his jeans. The bounce of her tits as she moved on him. The pressure of her hand on him, squeezing him. The sweet, musky scent of her making his mouth water and his cock even harder than it already was.

He tried to ignore it, tried to concentrate on driving her insane first because he'd be fucked if he was going to lose this one.

But then she one-upped him, leaning back on her hands and he could see every glorious of inch of her, giving him the most fucking fantastic view of her wet pussy. She ground down on him, panting and gasping as the climax hit her. And dear Jesus Christ, she was rubbing him in exactly the right way, and he groaned because the friction was too intense, too insistent.

And in the end he had to grab her hips and move her, growling as the orgasm snuck up on him and exploded in his head like a firework.

Making him come in his jeans like a fucking teenage boy, just as she'd promised.

Chapter 8

As Tamara's heartbeat gradually slowed, she flicked Zee a glance from underneath her lashes.

He was leaning back on his elbows, that impressive chest of his stretching tight the cotton of his T-shirt, his head tipped back, his eyes closed. God, he was a beautiful sight, the lines of his face still drawn tight with pleasure.

She'd made him do that. She'd made him lose control.

The triumph of it nearly stole her breath, made her feel so powerful.

And that was a damn sight better than the horrible, helpless feeling that had stolen up on her when he'd pinned her to the floor. Bringing back those terrible memories of Will when he'd had one of his episodes. He hadn't had them often, but often enough for her to feel terrified around him whenever her parents went out.

It should never have happened of course. She'd adored her older brother and the change that had come over him had terrified her. The mood swings, the mutterings. Speaking to people who weren't there. The sudden, random outbursts of violence.

She'd tried to tell her parents that something was wrong with him, but they hadn't wanted to know. They'd pretended everything was normal, that everything was fine. As though if they pretended hard enough, everything would be.

Exactly like you've been doing for the past eight years.

As if he'd heard the thought aloud, Zee's eyes opened, sharp silver barbs slicing straight through her. Her breath caught, afraid suddenly of what he might see. She looked away to lessen the feeling of exposure, conscious that she was sitting on his lap naked while he was fully dressed. It didn't matter what she'd made him do, she somehow felt vulnerable.

She shifted off him, unable to stop from wincing as she slid onto the floor, the flesh between her legs tender.

Then warm fingers curled around her calf and held on. "Hey."

She went still, taking a moment to compose herself before meeting his gaze. "What?"

"Are you okay?" His slashing dark brows drew down. "Sore?"

A hot wash of embarrassment moved through her. "It's nothing."

He let her go and in one fluid movement he was on his feet, bending down and scooping her up in his arms before she had a chance to protest.

"Zee." She put a hand against his chest. "What the hell are you doing?"

"Where's the bathroom?" He seemed able to carry her with no effort whatsoever. "I don't know about you, but I need to freshen up."

"It's the down the hall over there. And I can walk, you know."

He ignored her, carrying her while crossing the lounge area to the doorway that led to the hall and her bedroom and bathroom.

Okay, fine. If he was going to insist, she wasn't going to

protest. In fact, it was nice just to relax into his arms, enjoy the sensation of being carried. She hadn't been held like this since she was a child and God help her but there was something she liked about the helplessness of it. Of having strong arms around her and a warm chest to lean against.

It made her feel safe, which was a strange thing to think about a stranger like Zee. A man who by his own admission had just beaten the hell out of someone tonight. But she went with it for a while because it had been a long time since she'd felt like this and she didn't want to let go of the sensation just yet.

He carried her into her small, white-tiled bathroom, setting her down on top of the vanity unit while he went over to the bath and turned on the taps, beginning to run the water.

Tamara stared dumbly at him. "A bath? Seriously?" It was pretty much the last thing she expected from him.

"Yeah." He came back over to where she was sitting and before she could move, he gently pushed apart her thighs, glancing down between them. "You look sore too. Some warm water might help."

Oh, great. Cheeks burning, she closed her legs firmly. "Okay, thanks for that."

His gray gaze lifted, meeting hers. "You're embarrassed? After that?"

"You're still a stranger, don't forget. I don't actually know you."

He was silent a moment, studying her. "Who hurt you, Tamara?"

She had to look away. "That was not an invitation."

"You didn't like me holding you down."

"Yeah, and I told you why." Her fingers were clutching onto the edge of the vanity. With a conscious effort, she straightened them. "This is just sex, Zee. We don't have to get to know each other or anything."

Strong fingers took her chin in an irresistible grip, tipping her head back, and she found herself staring into his eyes once more. "Sure it's just sex. But when some bad shit starts to affect that sex, I wanna know what's happening. So tell me. Who hurt you?"

"You can't tell anyone, Tamara. Not a soul, understand? Not if we want this to work."

Her father's voice rang in her head, hard and sure. It had been eight years, but she remembered every word of that conversation. And she'd done what he'd asked, she'd never told a soul. So she couldn't tell Zee. Could she?

Why the hell not? Haven't you been carrying it long enough? And anyway, you don't need to tell him the whole truth. Just a bit. After all, wouldn't it be good to tell someone?

Oh God, it would. And besides, Zee was only temporary. She'd never see him again after all this was over.

"My older brother," she said at last, her voice thickening helplessly on the last word. "He would lose it occasionally, yell at me, that kind of thing. But there were a couple of times when he . . . held me against a wall and tried to choke me." It felt weird to finally say it out loud to someone else and even now, eight years later, the words sat heavy on her tongue. Like a betrayal of some sort.

Zee studied her a long moment. "You said he was sick?"

The illness her parents denied was happening, even though their son was changing right in front of them. Becoming moody and withdrawn, prone to violent rages, talking to things that weren't there. Because her parents had always denied the problem, he'd never been diagnosed, but Tamara had her suspicions.

"I think he probably had schizophrenia, though we never knew for sure."

Zee's thumb stroked absently along her jaw and she couldn't stop the shiver that went through her. "Why not?"

Again that weird feeling of betrayal twisted inside her. "Mom and Dad didn't think there was a problem. Diet and exercise. That's what they thought would make him better." God, where had that bitterness come from? Even she could hear the note of it in her voice.

Zee's gaze was uncomfortably sharp. "So what happened to him?"

She should have anticipated the question, should have prepared. But all the preparation in the world didn't stop the sliver of pure ice that drove under her skin.

Jerking her chin from his grip, she said, "Oh look, the bath is ready."

He didn't move, looking at her. "Tamara—"

"Do you see me asking you why you like beating the shit out of people? Why you live in a crappy part of town and work in a garage? Or wanting to know all about your crappy childhood?" The words tumbled out of her, the bitterness tainting all of them, and she had to force herself to shut up before any more of them came out.

Avoiding him and his gaze, she slid off the vanity and brushed past him, going over to the bath and turning the water off. "I'm sorry," she said after a moment, knowing she needed to say something. "That was uncalled for."

There was silence behind her, then he expelled a long breath. "Shit, you got nothing to apologize for. I shouldn't have asked. We're not here to tell each other our life stories."

No, they weren't. Even if she'd wanted to, her secrets were ones she couldn't tell anyone else anyway.

But as he said the words, something shifted inside of her. Almost like . . . regret.

She shook away the feeling, kicking off the only thing she was wearing—her shoes—and stepping into the bath. He was right, the water was warm and soothing, her muscles beginning to loosen as the warmth seeped into them.

She didn't look at him, but she could hear the sounds of clothing coming off, the heavy sound of boots hitting the floor.

Then there was heat at her back, the slide of bare skin along hers, the water of the bath rising massively as he got in behind her. One muscled arm curled around her waist as he brought her back against him, his thighs on either side of hers, her spine to his chest. She could feel his cock pressing against her butt, already semihard, but he made no move to do anything but hold her.

The position felt too intimate and she tensed, suddenly uncertain about where this was going.

Then he said, "For the record, it's not the beating the shit out of people I like, but the chance to let off steam in a controlled environment. I live in Royal 'cause I ran away from home when I was seventeen—my mom died when I was a kid and my dad was an asshole—and that's where I washed up. That's where I met Gideon and the others, and they're the ones that make it home for me. And in a couple of months I won't be working in a garage at all, but running my own gym."

The quiet, measured way he said it made her feel ashamed of herself and her assumptions. Assumptions she hadn't even realized she'd made until they'd all come spilling out.

She swallowed, her throat tight.

"But," he added, one long-fingered hand running down her side and along her thigh. "You're right about one thing. I did have a crappy childhood. I haven't seen my dad for ten years."

She should say something more, maybe apologize again. But she was too afraid to open her mouth in case that bitterness was still there. And she didn't want to hear it again, or examine why it might be, so instead she focused on the arm around her waist, studying the flames and the tail feathers of the phoenix inked onto his skin.

"A phoenix," she said, tracing the lines with a finger. He felt smooth and hot beneath her touch. "Rising from the ashes?"

A pause.

"Yeah."

There was no inflection in his voice, yet she heard the under-current in it anyway. The bird on his skin wasn't the only thing rising from the ashes. He was too.

"What about the quote on your back?"

"Just something I like. Nothing special."

A lie; she could hear it in his voice. Curiosity shifted inside her, unexpected and unwelcome, but she didn't push. There were boundaries here that she had to stick to and since she'd been pretty clear of hers, she had to respect his as well.

"Rachel inked me up," he said unexpectedly. "She's got a great studio in Royal. Did you see her sleeve? That's hers too."

Tamara remembered the deep red of the roses on Rachel's arm. They'd been pretty. "How did you get to meet them? Your friends I mean." Since he'd offered the information, maybe she could ask. "Though you don't have to say if you don't want to."

He was silent a moment. "I hung around the Royal outreach center 'cause there was a guy who taught fighting. Met Gideon and Zoe and Rachel there, plus another guy you didn't get to meet. Levi, he's currently doing time, but he'll be out pretty soon." Zee paused. "Gideon gave me a job, helped me find a place to stay. And the others . . . None of us got family, or at least, none we wanna have anything to do with, so we made our own."

No wonder she'd felt like she was interrupting something the night Zee had first taken her to the garage. She kind of had. They'd been having a family get-together and she definitely wasn't part of it.

Envy shifted inside her, and a grief for what she'd lost. Her own family had once felt like a family and not a prison, but that had been before Will had gotten sick, before everything had changed.

Before you destroyed it.

"So, you have to let off steam often?" she asked in a grace-less change of subject. "I mean you seem to do a lot of fights."

He shifted, the water swirling around them. "I thought we weren't going to talk about this."

"You don't have to answer."

There was a pause. "Sometimes." Then he asked, "Why investments?"

Tamara sighed. Well, she kind of owed him an answer since he'd given her one. "Would you believe it's my way of letting off steam?"

"No."

"Damn. Okay, it's my father's company and I'm following in his footsteps."

"Why? You like investing shit?"

She almost grinned at that—at least until she realized she didn't have a good explanation, not one that wouldn't involve the truth. "It's not so much that as what's expected. My parents want me to have a great career and it's a pretty great company to have a career in."

His hand firmed on her stomach. "Yeah, but that's not what I asked. I asked whether you liked it or not."

The question needled her. "Sure. Same as you like fixing engines."

"That much, huh?"

She didn't know what to say to that, so she settled for silence, her fingers moving idly to trace his tattoo. She felt him pressed against her back, hard and ready. But he didn't speak or make any demands, just kept holding her, one hand splayed possessively on her stomach while the other stroked her thigh.

There was a lingering tension in the air, but it began to dissipate and, after a while, she turned around in his arms, because her apology had been inadequate and she wanted to give him something more than that.

She wanted to give, period.

So far it had all been about her and what she wanted. She hadn't even thought about him.

Perhaps she needed to.

He met her gaze, gray eyes unreadable, and that was kind of intimidating. The fact that she didn't know him and despite their sexual encounters, she didn't even know what he liked about the sex, beyond him telling her what to do. And that made her feel ashamed too, that she hadn't even bothered to ask him.

So she forced herself to hold his gaze and say, "What would you like?"

Something flickered in his eyes, though she couldn't tell what it was. "Don't wanna keep talking?"

"Not really. Do you?"

He stared at her a second, then he reached out with one hand, his fingers sinking into her damp hair, exerting a gentle, relentless pressure, drawing her mouth down on his.

Her eyes closed, shivers racing through her as he parted her lips with his tongue, holding her in place as he kissed her, at first tentatively, lightly. Then, getting more demanding, exploring deeper into her mouth. She let him, sitting there in the bath with her eyes closed as he ate her up, devoured her, holding her completely still with a steady hand, as he nipped and bit and feasted on her.

Then at last he drew back, leaving her mouth tingling and almost bruised, the look in his eyes blazing. And slowly he exerted more pressure on the back of her head, easing her head down.

No prizes for guessing what he wanted.

Tamara shifted her position so she was lying between his thighs, her hands sliding up, reaching for the hard length of his cock. And when he pushed her head down, she opened her mouth and took him in, tasting water and salt and Zee.

She didn't think about herself or her freedom or her choices. She listened to him, let the rough, guttural sounds of his pleasure be her guide. Let his hands in her hair set the pace, his fingers knotting into the damp strands, keeping her just where he wanted her.

She closed her eyes, focusing on the warmth of the water and the hard, muscular thighs on either side of her, the thrust of his hips and the slide of his cock in her mouth. He tasted good and she licked him like he was her favorite ice cream, curling one of her hands around the base of him, gripping his hip with the other. Then she looked up, circling the head of his cock with her tongue and his silver gaze met hers. So much heat and hunger in that look. It pierced her, sharp as a sword.

"Slower," he ordered roughly, his fingers tightening in her hair, showing her what he wanted.

She shivered at the demand, slowing her movements, giving him long, languid strokes with her tongue, before closing her lips totally around him. Then she took him deep as she could, losing herself in the salty taste of him, in the musky, spicy scent of his body and the shift of the powerful muscles of his thighs.

He was pure physicality, raw and rough, and straight up. All power, all strength.

It changed something in her deep inside.

She wanted to drink him down, take some of that strength and rough physical honesty for herself. Cover herself in it until all the pain and the doubts had gone.

So she closed her eyes and lost herself completely, letting him guide her, take what he needed from her. Letting him fuck her mouth until the thrust of hips grew wild and the grip in her hair made her eyes water. Until he cursed and threw his head back, a low, gravelly roar escaping him, the sound of it echoing around the hard-tiled surfaces of the bathroom.

Afterward, the harsh sounds of his breathing filling her ears, he pulled her up for another soul-shattering kiss, his tongue in her mouth as if he wanted to taste himself on her.

She was panting by the time he released her. Then he scooped her up from the bath and dried her off himself, grabbing his wallet and pulling out a couple of condoms. She said nothing as he picked her up again and carried her into the bedroom, meeting him kiss for kiss as he put her on the bed.

Then he touched her, stroked her, took his time to caress her before protecting himself and pushing her back, sliding easily inside her. And she lost herself all over again, her legs around his waist, gripping on tight as he moved. Each stroke driving her further away from the person she'd made herself and closer to someone else. Someone new.

It was frightening and exhilarating and agonizing all at once.

She sobbed when she came, the pleasure tearing her apart, and all she could do was lie there as Zee buried his face in her neck, biting her as the pleasure took him, too.

For several minutes afterward neither of them moved or spoke. Then Zee eased from her, got off the bed, and left the room. He was gone for what seemed a long time and when he came back, he was fully dressed again.

Tamara lay on her side, her knees drawn up to her chest, and she blinked at him, noting his clothes. "You're going?"

He put a hand on the doorframe and leaned on it. "Gotta get up for work tomorrow."

A creeping disappointment she didn't want to acknowledge twisted in her gut. "You don't have to leave," she said before she could stop herself.

He looked at her a long moment. "Yeah, I do."

She could hear it in his voice, the gentle reminder of the boundaries. The ones they'd both been reminding themselves of, her especially tonight. And part of her wanted to protest. Wanted to say no, he could stay. He could crawl in beside her and help her find herself again. Hold her in his arms, cradle her against that big, warm chest of his.

But those were stupid thoughts. Stupid wants. Because soon

enough she'd have a husband to do that for her. A husband she knew better than a tattooed mechanic from Royal Road.

So all she said was, "Good night, then."

He pushed away from the doorframe. "Good night, pretty girl." And turned.

"Can I text you?" God, she hated the desperate sound of her voice.

He didn't turn back. "Yeah."

And then just like that he was gone.

Chapter 9

Gideon gave Zee a dark look as Zee stalked into the garage the next morning and headed over to the lockers to get his overalls.

"You're late," Gideon said, eyeing him. "Where the hell have you been?"

"Slept in," he replied curtly, getting his overalls out and starting to pull them on. Jesus, the last thing he felt like now was questions.

Gideon, who was standing by the Honda he'd spent the better part of two weeks rebuilding, put the wrench in his hand down and lifted an eyebrow. "You never sleep in."

"Yeah, well I did this morning." Zee slammed his locker closed with more force than was strictly necessary and moved over to the Chevy currently taking up space in the workshop.

There was a pause. "So what crawled up your butt?"

"Nothing. I'm fine." He gave the Chevy's engine a cursory look-over, then went to the workbench, trying to remember what he was supposed to be doing and what tool he needed. Except his foul temper got in the way and he couldn't concentrate.

Fuck it. What the hell was he so pissed about? He'd spent a couple of hours with a hot woman, had three incredible orgasms, and now he was slamming doors and throwing tools around for reasons he couldn't even begin to guess at himself.

"Okay. Don't give me that shit, Zee." Gideon leaned his hip against his bench and folded his arms. "You look like you could grind rocks with your fucking teeth."

Goddamn Gideon. The guy took his role as parent/big brother figure way too seriously, especially given Zee wasn't seventeen anymore. "It's nothing." Where the fuck was the wrench he wanted?

"Yeah, it is." Gideon folded his arms. "Look, if you don't want to tell me about it, that's fine, but I don't want your fucking bad temper in the workshop. You know that. We got enough problems to deal with as it is let alone fielding any mistakes you might make because you're too angry to do a proper job."

Zee let out a breath. Gideon was strict about making sure any personal difficulties stayed out of the workshop, and that was part of why Zee liked working with him. There was something peaceful, something calm about working with engines. Making sure everything fit together, that it worked and if it didn't, then you had to figure out why not. He liked that. It was easy to immerse himself in it, let the past and its demons lie.

At least, it had been easy. But today his head was full of Tamara, and not just her delicious body and carnal mouth. He couldn't seem to forget what she'd told him about her brother, the vulnerable note in her voice making his protective instincts go crazy. Making him want to fix her too, just like he fixed an engine that wouldn't work.

Obviously something had happened to her brother, because she'd been angry with him when he'd asked. Angry enough to rip him a new one with a few choice words.

He didn't give a shit what anyone thought of Royal Road or the fact that he was a mechanic; he had his reasons for being here and they were good ones and none of anyone else's business. Yet her words needled him. As if even though he didn't care about anyone else, he cared about what *she* thought, which was just insane. He'd even felt the need to justify himself, which he never did.

And then, to make matters even worse, she'd apologized, then turned in his arms and asked him what he wanted. No one did that. No one just fucking asked him.

Then she'd gone down on him like a goddess, as if his pleasure were the only important thing in the entire world, and even though he knew it was only an apology, even though he knew not to read anything more into it, he'd felt a surge of possessiveness that was a fucking bad sign if ever there was one.

He didn't get possessive over women and he didn't get curious either. He made sure he kept his emotional distance. So why the hell he should be feeling that way about Tamara Goddamn Lennox he had no idea. Somehow she was getting under his skin and he didn't like it.

She'd asked him to stay the night before and God help him, but some part of him had wanted to even though sleeping over wasn't exactly the point of their encounters.

You can't. Remember what you promised Madison?

As if he'd forget. He'd promised her he'd live a good life, be a good person, and he was pretty sure that didn't include screwing rich girls about to be engaged to be married.

Fuck, what the hell was he doing?

"Zee," Gideon said firmly, "take the afternoon off. Come back when you're feeling in a better goddamn mood."

Zee glowered at his friend, but Gideon just looked back, unimpressed.

"It's Tamara," Zee said, because there was a lot he owed the guy, the truth being the least of it. But since he couldn't tell Gideon that truth, not if he wanted to protect what he had here, he gave him something else instead. "The chick who came to the garage the other night."

Gideon didn't look especially surprised. "Oh, you mean the one you banged out back? That one?"

Oh, fucking wonderful. "You heard that?"

"It was difficult not to."

Zee cursed under his breath. Gideon hadn't said anything to him afterward, but it wasn't as if he or Tamara had been quiet that night. "Yeah, her."

"So what's the problem? She wanting more or something?"

"She's a fucking financial intern from a big-deal family, living in a downtown loft the size of the entire gym. She's not what I want."

"Uh-huh. So you're the one wanting more then?"

Zee gave the other man a belligerent look. "It's just sex. That's all it is."

"Right. And that's why you're so pissed. Because it's just sex."

Zee cursed, shoving himself away from the workbench, the inexplicable anger burning a hole in his gut. "You know you're right, I should just take the fucking afternoon off."

Gideon shook his head. "Jesus, between you and Rachel, I've nearly got the full complement of assholes today. All I need is Zoe to get pissy and I'll have the whole goddamn lot. Thank God Levi isn't arriving till next month is all I can say."

Zee flipped him the bird, then stalked over to the lockers and got out of his stupid damn overalls.

Gideon merely shrugged and went back to the Honda.

Once he was out of the garage, Zee shoved his hands in his pockets, that restless, antsy feeling mixing with his anger to become something more volatile, dangerous.

He turned toward Sugar Ink, Rachel's tattoo parlor, wondering if he shouldn't get a few more feathers for his phoenix, but then decided against it. Ever since Gideon had told Rachel about Levi getting out of jail, she'd been even pricklier than she normally was and he didn't particularly feel like trading barbs with her right now.

Instead he called into the Royal Road Outreach Center to go over the program he'd sent them and see if they wanted any changes. They were more than happy with it, which eased his mood a little. Then he fell into conversation with some of the kids and that helped too, because it was clear some of them desperately needed some kind of direction, some kind of discipline.

Just like he had when he'd washed up there, a broken, grief-stricken seventeen-year-old with a huge chip on his shoulder and an anger management problem. Back then, he'd had Gideon to pull him out and set him on the right path, but these kids weren't so lucky.

Or maybe they were, since they had him.

"*You're a good person, Damian,*" Madison had said to him that night. "*You can make a difference to this world, no matter what your father says.*"

He'd clung to those words for a long time after she'd died and they guided him still. And he hoped that in turn, he could pass them on to these kids, help them find the better life that he now had.

He got back to the gym afterward feeling calmer, then spent the rest of the afternoon working out, trying to get rid of his remaining anger with a punching bag.

By the time the evening rolled around, he was good, ready for his fight at Gino's that night. Calm and in control as usual.

The bar was packed out by the time he'd got there, with lots of newcomers come to try their luck up against the local champion. Money was already changing hands when he stepped into the circle chalked on the ground that marked the ring, the shouts of the onlookers echoing off the concrete surfaces of the bar's basement, where they always held the fights.

Fuck, he loved the raw emotion of the crowds, the pumping energy that crackled through them. Here he could channel it, focus it. Let it touch the dark anger inside him and allow him to release it, transform it into a pure, controlled violence in a place where there were rules. Where every opponent knew them and went in with their eyes open, no surprises.

Madison probably wouldn't have approved, but shit, he had to let out his dark side somewhere and this was the safest way he knew how to do it.

As the first guy stepped into the ring, Zee tried to get his head into the fight, gathering all the energy and focusing it, tuning out the sounds of the crowd, concentrating only on the man circling him, watching the expression on his face and the betraying flicker of his eyes. Waiting for the moves that everyone telegraphed sooner or later.

For some reason it took him longer than usual to find that still, quiet place inside him, the one Crazy Dave, his mentor, had taught him back when he'd been a fucked-up, angry teenager, though when his opponent finally came for him, it took Zee all of thirty seconds to end the fight once and for all.

The crowd roared, more money changing hands.

The next opponent came. Then the next. The fights beginning to blend, as they always did, into a round of circling, waiting, watching, looking for weaknesses, a chess game in earnest.

Then his last opponent went down and Zee leapt on him, his arm across the back of the guy's neck, his knee in the small of the other man's back. The man groaned and struggled, but Zee kept up the pressure. Eventually, his opponent cursed and conceded the fight, and Zee released him, rising to his feet and standing back.

That's when he saw the man in the suit.

The guy wasn't like the others, all roaring and shouting, but rather merely standing there in the middle of the crowd with his arms folded, staring at Zee. He wore a black three-piece suit like an undertaker, but unlike an undertaker he was smiling.

And even though Zee was a few feet away, the crowd between them, he felt like he'd been sucker-punched. Because he knew the man. It had been years, ten of them to be exact, but there was no mistaking those cold, dark eyes. That mirthless, menacing smile.

It was Victor Krupin, his father's henchman.

Everything in him went on high alert, his muscles tensing, his hands coming up, his body automatically readying itself for another fight.

But Krupin only smiled that still familiar smile of his, as out of place and wrong as a smile on the face of a torturer. Then he casually turned around and strolled out of the basement without any hurry at all.

Zee's heartbeat thundered in his head, the sound of the crowd becoming distorted and muffled, his blood slowly but surely turning to ice in his veins.

It had taken him a long time to stop looking over his shoulder. To stop glancing into the face of every stranger he passed, wondering if the person was one of his father's minions out looking for him. To stop leaving threads taped carefully over his doors and windows in case his apartment had been broken into. To stop carrying the handgun he kept in the top drawer of his dresser.

But it was all for nothing.

Somehow, his father had finally found him.

Tamara stared at the phone ringing noisily on her desk. She knew who it was and really didn't want to answer it, in no mood to speak to her mother today. Then again, her mother would just keep on calling until she answered so ignoring it wouldn't work either.

Cursing under her breath, she reached out, picked up the offending piece of technology, and hit the answer button. "Hi, Mom. What's up?"

"Hi, honey." Cassandra Lennox's voice was full of her usual solicitousness. "Just checking up on you this morning, seeing if you're feeling any better."

Tamara looked at the spreadsheet open on her computer. Scott wanted all the data entered into it by the end of the day and it was already three P.M. She didn't really have time to chat since she was only halfway through, but she knew her mother. Cassandra wouldn't leave it alone until she'd been reassured. "Oh, I'm feeling much better today, Mom."

She really wasn't. She felt tired and gritty-eyed, and the raw places on her body ached.

And she couldn't stop thinking about Zee. About the things he'd told her and the way he'd held her. And the secret she'd told him.

She had a sudden vision of confessing to her mother. *By the way, Mom. I told this mechanic from Royal Road about Will. About how he probably had schizophrenia even though you insisted everything was fine. No, I didn't tell him anything else, but maybe if he'd stayed, I would have. . . .*

"Okay, that's great to hear, honey." There was a pause, but Tamara knew her mother wasn't quite done, that there was another question she wanted to ask.

For some reason it made her stomach give a nervous flutter. She swallowed, her mouth suddenly dry. "I can hear the 'but.' "

Her mother gave a soft laugh. "Oh, it's nothing really. Just . . . You know your boss was at the function last night, don't you?"

Something cold wound down Tamara's spine. She'd seen Scott across the room, had known he was going to be there, but she hadn't spoken to him. "Yes, of course. And?"

There was a small silence.

"He was outside having a cigarette and he . . . saw you getting into a car with someone."

The cold began to spread out, sending tendrils of ice through her chest, and she had to take a small silent breath to calm herself. "What someone?" Thankfully the question came out sounding much less sharp than she'd anticipated.

"A man he'd never seen before." Her mother paused. "The man had tattoos, apparently. Drove one of those muscle cars."

Tamara's fingers closed hard around the plastic of the phone. From where she sat, she could see Scott in his office, talking to someone standing near his desk. He was smiling, obviously enjoying whatever conversation he was having.

The bastard. The complete and utter bastard.

What? You think this is his fault? He just caught you. You're the one who was doing something wrong.

Was it wrong though? Was being with Zee, finding out who she truly was, stepping outside her role for just a few hours, truly wrong?

Of course it is. You're going to be engaged soon. What kind of behavior is that? After all your parents have done for you.

She blinked hard, trying to focus on the silence at the other end of the phone. "Oh, you mean Zee?" she said, as if it was no big deal. "He's just a friend, Mom. He was in the area so I asked him to give me a ride home."

"A friend?" There was a world of doubt in her mother's voice. "Where did you meet him?"

Suddenly anger erupted inside her, hot as a solar flare. She tried to keep it down, to keep it under control. "Can I ask what business is it of Scott's? Or of yours? He's just a friend, that's all."

"I know, dear, I know." Her mother turned soothing. "But you have to be careful who you associate with. And Scott said—"

"Scott said what?"

There was an offended silence. "Please don't cut me off like that, Tamara. I'm not attacking you."

"I'm sorry, Mom," she said, trying for patience. "But it sure sounds like you are."

"Well, you can see how it looks, can't you? Getting into a car late at night with a strange man."

Oh hell, she needed to get it together. Protesting too much was going to make her look defensive and she didn't want that. "He's a friend, like I said. He runs some self-defense classes that I went to with someone from work, nothing more." She forced out a laugh. "I mean, did Scott think I was seeing him or something?"

Another moment of silence.

"Scott didn't know quite what to believe," Cassandra said carefully. "He was . . . concerned."

Oh, Tamara knew how concerned he was. Concerned enough to get as much dirt on her as he possibly could. "I have a boyfriend already." She tried to inject a note of amusement into her voice. "I mean, really, Robert is pretty much perfect, like you keep saying. Why would I want someone else?"

"Well, true," her mother sighed. "There is that. And I have to say, I can't see you taking up with someone who looks like a criminal. Even if he isn't."

Sure, Zee was a "criminal." Who'd held her in his arms and given her a bath. Who stayed in Royal Road because of his friends and was starting to run his own gym. Yeah, definitely a criminal.

The anger turned inside her, aiming at her mother and the assumptions she was making.

That's nothing new though, is it? She and Dad made assumptions about Will, too.

Tamara's jaw tightened as she bit down on all the words she suddenly wanted to say and couldn't. "So, is there anything else you wanted to talk about, Mom? Because if not, I've got a ton of work to do this afternoon."

There wasn't anything else and, after her mother had ended the call, Tamara put her phone back down on the desk, realizing that every single muscle in her body was clenched tight.

With an effort she tried to relax, breathing in deep the way the therapist had taught her in the torturous months after Will's death. Normally it worked, but not this time.

She leaned back in her chair, staring sightlessly at her computer screen.

Was being seen with Zee going to put her shot at the permanent position at risk? Did Scott hate her enough to use that against her? Clearly he'd had no compunction about bringing what he'd seen to her parents, so he knew they wouldn't be pleased about it. He was trying to undermine her, make her look bad. But why? What had she ever done to him but been the boss's daughter?

Ah, but what was the point in wondering about that? Whatever his reasons were, they didn't change the fact that he was out for her blood.

Which means the smart thing to do is probably not see Zee again.

The sharp edge of disappointment rested against her skin, cutting a line so thin she barely felt it. At first. And then, as she thought about the reality of not seeing Zee, the pain set in, unexpectedly sharp.

The spreadsheet on the screen blurred in her vision and she had to take a breath.

God, she was ridiculous, because it wasn't like they had anything special. It was sex and that was it. Sure, it was fantastic, mind-blowing sex, but nothing more than that. Did she really want to risk her success and alienating her entire family for the sake of a few nights with Zee?

No, of course she didn't. That would be crazy. That would leave her with no support, no nothing. Her chance for making things right with her parents, atoning for what she'd done, gone.

She couldn't risk that, she just couldn't.

Pulling herself together, she put thoughts of Zee out of her mind. She had to get this stupid spreadsheet done; otherwise she'd be here all night.

Around seven, Scott came out of his office, briefcase in hand, obviously ready to go home. He glanced at her as he locked his office door, then walked over to stand threateningly in front of her desk.

"How's it going?"

"Nearly done." She kept her gaze on her screen. "It'll be on your desk by tomorrow morning."

There was a silence.

Tamara gritted her teeth and looked up at him. "Something I can do for you?"

Scott's blue eyes were gleaming. "Boyfriend make another quick trip from New York last night?"

A trickle of ice water slid down her back. What the hell was he talking about?

He lifted a finger and gestured. "You need to invest in some scarves."

She couldn't stop herself from reaching out to touch the place on her neck he'd pointed at. The place Zee had bitten her the night before.

Oh shit. She'd slept late that morning and had rushed out the door, not even having the time to check herself in the mirror. . . .

The trickle became a torrent.

"That's none of your business," she snapped, resisting the urge to tug the collar of her blouse up.

"Isn't it? You were nearly late this morning and I'm guessing it wasn't because you'd spent the night talking with your parents at the charity dinner." His eyes were thin slivers of ice. "Oh, wait, no. That's right. Because you left early, didn't you? With some guy covered in tattoos."

Something in her chest squeezed tight. "Like I told my mother this morning after you passed on that little piece of information—and thanks, by the way—he's a friend and that's it."

"A friend?" Scott smiled, but there was nothing of amusement in it. "Since when do friends give each other bruises like that one?"

She should have been feeling afraid, because if Scott knew for certain about Zee, she could kiss his recommendations good-bye and the coveted position within Lennox along with it. Yet it wasn't fear that gripped her. It was anger.

Anger at feeling helpless. At feeling like her world was made of glass and one sharp movement would shatter it, bring it all down.

"How is that any business of yours?" she demanded. "What I do outside of work and who I do it with has got nothing to do with you."

There was a terrible silence, the delicate structure of the past eight years of her life teetering on the edge of a chasm.

Scott's gaze flickered, his mouth a hard line. "It does if you want a position here, Tamara."

Slowly, she leaned back in her seat. She wanted to pick up the paperweight on her desk and throw it at him, push her computer off her desk, break a window, scream. Do something loud and violent, smash the glass world she'd been living in since Will had died. The one where she could never make a mistake, never put a foot wrong.

But she didn't, because her parents deserved better than that and so did Will's memory.

Instead she sat there, her knuckles white on the arms of her chair, staring at him. "What do you want, Scott? Why don't you just tell me instead of threatening me?"

"I'm not threatening you." His gaze was pitiless. "Girls like you are all the same. You always get what you want. You never have to work hard, everything is handed to you on a plate. So consider this a lesson that some things aren't easy. You have to work for them. You have to play by the rules just like everyone else."

The anger rose up, swamping her, strangling her. What the hell did he know about her life? Nothing. Less than nothing.

She clutched harder onto the armrests of her chair, trying to ignore the fury gathering itself in her gut. Trying to keep it under control. "Tell me what you want from me."

"Only that you understand how precarious your position is here. And that you'll have to work very hard if you want that recommendation. Oh yes." He gave her another mirthless smile. "And I'd stay away from strange, tattooed men, if I were you. Especially if you don't want Daddy and your rich New York boyfriend to know who you've been screwing on the side."

Rage was a small, hard ball in the center of her chest, and she had to force herself to smile back, to not let him see that he'd gotten to her. "Well, sure, Scott. I appreciate the warning."

His gaze flickered as if he hadn't been expecting that, which was some satisfaction, though not much. "I'll see you tomorrow then. Have fun with the spreadsheet."

After he'd gone, Tamara shoved her chair back and got up, pacing back and forth for a few moments with her hands in fists, trying to put a lid on her anger.

How dare he? How dare he threaten her like that? Because no matter what he'd said, he was threatening her. As if she was a goddamn criminal.

Aren't you a criminal? Deep down?

Tamara stopped pacing, her heartbeat thudding in her chest.

No, she wasn't. No. Her parents had been very clear that what had happened with Will hadn't been her fault, that she'd only been protecting herself. And besides, this was different. This wasn't life or death or anything, only sex with an unsuitable man.

She hadn't done anything wrong. She hadn't.

Tamara moved back to her chair and sat down, taking a few deep breaths. Okay, so what she had to do now was be careful, let everything calm down a bit. She didn't want to give Zee up totally, not yet. Not when there was still a week or so left before this ridiculous engagement party. But maybe she needed to leave it a few days before she saw him again. And when she *did* see him again, she'd better make sure it was in his neighborhood rather than hers.

She couldn't let the hard work she'd put into building this fragile life of hers all go to waste. Her parents' over involvement in her life might drive her crazy, but they only wanted what was best for her and they'd sacrificed too much themselves for her to throw it away over some guy.

Feeling calmer, she glanced down at her phone on the desk. The screen was blank. No texts. No calls. But that was probably for the best right now.

Tamara dismissed the silent phone from her mind and concentrated on her work.

Chapter 10

"Okay, so now you've got us all here, what did you want to say?" Rachel leaned back, her elbows on the step above her, platform-booted feet on the step below where she sat. " 'Cause if this is another 'exciting surprise' like Levi coming back was, I'm outta here."

Gideon, leaning against the workbench, his arms folded, said nothing. Zoe, sitting on the bench beside him, her legs swinging like a child's, frowned. "We're not going to like this are we?"

Zee sat on a plastic chair, his elbows on his knees, his hands clasped between them. He felt calm, surprisingly so for a man about to reveal to his closest friends that he'd been lying to them for the past ten years.

But he had no choice.

After he'd seen his father's henchman at the fight, he'd spent the entire night walking the streets trying to find out where the prick had gone, the unquenchable rage he'd thought he'd dealt with years ago boiling in his veins. Yet the guy had disappeared, leaving no trace.

Eventually Zee had returned to his apartment, still burning, and had paced around and around, trying to figure out how the hell Joshua Chase had found him and what the fuck he was going to do about it.

It had taken him the whole damn weekend, working himself into exhaustion in the gym, to come to the conclusion that it actually didn't matter how Joshua had found him, the real problem was that he had. And what the fuck was he going to do about it?

If he'd still been seventeen, he would have run. But he wasn't seventeen anymore. He'd built a life here, had a future here, friends who cared about him, and he'd be fucked if he'd abandon everything just because that prick was sniffing around.

Anyway, running wouldn't help and would only put his friends in danger, because no doubt, if he left, his father would want to know where he'd gone and wouldn't have any compunction about putting the pressure on Gideon, or Rachel, or Zoe. And Zee couldn't have that. If anything happened to them, he wouldn't be able to live with himself.

Unfortunately though, that left him with only one option. Staying put. But if he was going to do that, his friends needed to know the truth about him and who he really was. And they also needed to make a choice. Zee had no idea what his father wanted, but if he stayed and his father came after him, it might prove just as dangerous for the others as if he'd left. They had a right to know that. They also had a right to decide whether they wanted him to leave.

He didn't want to, but if they thought it was better he go, then he would.

Waiting until Levi had gotten out would probably have been a better idea since then he could tell everyone at once, but if Krupin was hanging around, he couldn't afford to wait.

Fuck, nothing about this was going to be easy, was it? Then again, when had his life ever been easy?

"No," he said flatly. "You probably won't like it." He looked each of them in the eye. "I need to tell you who I really am."

"What? You're not actually Ezekiel West?" Rachel's voice was derisive. "That's not exactly the news of the century. Everyone knows that's not your real name."

Zee met Rachel's angry dark eyes. "But you don't know my real name."

"And? Please don't tell me it's Elvis Presley."

"It's not. It's Damian Chase."

She rolled her eyes. "Is that supposed to mean something? So you swapped one dick name for another, big deal."

Zee opened his mouth to explain.

"Damian Chase went missing ten years ago," Gideon said quietly before Zee could speak. "His father upended half of Detroit looking for him."

Zee looked sharply at the other man, his guts twisting.

Gideon looked back, his expression completely calm.

Realization flooded through him. "You knew?" Zee demanded. "All this time and you knew?"

Zoe's frown deepened as she looked from Gideon to Zee and back again. "Knew what?"

"That Zee is Joshua Chase's son," Gideon said, still calm. "Yes, I knew. I knew the moment you walked into the center."

Shock pulsed through him, making Zee feel like his head was ringing. "You never said a fucking word."

"No. Because I knew what you were running from. And I figured if you didn't want to tell us, you probably had reason."

"Joshua Chase?" Rachel demanded, belligerent. "Isn't he that businessman guy who's doing a lot of investing in abandoned property?"

Zee sat back in his seat and glanced at Rachel, mainly because he had no fucking idea how to deal with Gideon's little bombshell. At least her question he could answer. "Yeah. But he also owns half the Detroit criminal underworld."

"Oh my God," Zoe muttered.

But Rachel's gaze was snapping with anger. "Holy fucking shit, Zee. Why didn't you tell us?"

"Because Dad was tearing up the town looking for me and I thought the fewer people that knew the better."

"Fuck's sake—"

"Rachel." Gideon's voice was low and flat. "I know you're still pissed about Levi, but can we deal with one crisis at a time, please?"

Rachel's eyes shot daggers at him, but she shut up.

"Thank you." Gideon turned his attention once more to Zee. "Okay, so you didn't tell us who you were, that's not a big deal, understand? I don't give a shit who your father is. You've been Zee for ten years and that's who you'll stay, at least to me." He shifted against the counter. "But what I want to know is why you're suddenly coming clean with us now."

The acknowledgment should have made him feel better, but it didn't. Because trust Gideon to get to the heart of the real problem.

Zee tried to relax his tight muscles and failed. He didn't want to tell them, didn't want to be reminded again of how fragile this life he'd built for himself actually was. A normal kind of life, the one Madison had wanted for him.

But the days spent running from his past were over. It had finally caught up with him and it had tangled up the people he cared about too. Secrecy was now a luxury he couldn't afford.

"Because last night at my fight, I saw Victor Krupin, my dad's right-hand man." He paused. "And he was looking right at me."

A heavy silence fell.

"Great, so he knows you're here?" Rachel said suddenly. "Fucking wonderful." With a quick movement, she stood up. "So not only do we get Levi back, we also get a big crime boss coming down into Royal looking for you. How much better can life get?"

Gideon didn't say anything, staring at Zee.

Zoe had stopped swinging her legs, her frown ferocious.

The atmosphere in the garage became thick.

Zee didn't move. "I don't know how Dad found me and I don't know what he wants. I tried looking for Victor after the fight, but he'd disappeared. One thing is for sure though. He's fucking with me. He wants me to know that he's found me."

Rachel muttered something inaudible.

Another aching silence fell.

Then Gideon asked at last, "So what are you going to do?"

"I want to stay here. This is my home, and you guys are the only family I have left. That prick took everything from me once before and I'll be fucked if I let him take it again." Zee sucked in a breath and held the other man's gaze. "But that decision isn't mine to make. It's yours." He looked around to include Rachel and Zoe. "It's all of yours."

"What do you mean by that?" Rachel had folded her arms. Her expression was tough, but he could see she'd gone pale.

"I mean," Zee said, "that since I'm the one who brought him here, you all need to decide what you want me to do. Whether I stay." He glanced back at Zoe and Gideon. "Or I go." Sure, leaving would put his friends in danger, but he wanted to give them the choice anyway. It would be what he'd want.

"You stay," Zoe said instantly, a mutinous look on her face. "Your father can go fuck himself."

Gideon shifted on his feet. "Of course you're goddamn staying." He said it like he couldn't believe someone was even asking him that question. "No one gets chased out of this neighborhood, not while I'm here."

Rachel's mouth tightened and she looked away, down at her feet. "Fuck, Zee. I don't want you to leave either."

"Oh yeah, and Levi would agree with the rest of us," Gideon added with some finality. "We're family and you stick by your family."

A small part of Zee, a part he hadn't even realized was tense, relaxed all of a sudden. Because he'd lost a lot in his life, but at least he hadn't lost this.

"Thanks," he said, the word a little rough. "I appreciate it. But you have to know that me staying might make things dangerous."

Gideon lifted a shoulder as if he didn't give a shit. "It's always been dangerous around here, man. There's always some motherfucker who thinks he can muscle in on our territory, who thinks he can take what's ours. I got no problem showing them they're wrong."

Zee leaned back in his chair, the tight thing in his chest a little less tight. "He's powerful, Gideon. He owns half the fucking city. Believe me, I know."

"So you're just going to sit there with your thumb in your ass until he comes to get you?"

The shock was beginning to ebb and something else was taking its place. A determination. The same determination that had brought him to Royal and set him on the path to rebuilding himself.

He wasn't seventeen anymore. He wasn't going to run and hide. He was going to stand and fight, because, shit, that's what he did best after all.

"No," Zee said. "I thought I'd go get him first."

As he sat there he felt his phone vibrate in the pocket of his jeans, reminding him again that he had a text. But he ignored it, even though he knew who it was from since he'd checked it before he'd sat down. It was from Tamara, wanting to know whether he wanted to meet.

He already knew he was going to say no. He had to. The reappearance of his father had changed everything and there was no way he'd put yet another person at risk, especially a woman so similar to Madison. And it didn't matter that it was just sex, that she wasn't his girlfriend—he couldn't see her again. Because the best place for her was far away from him.

He tried to tell himself he didn't care.

And failed.

Tamara fiddled with her glass of wine, trying to concentrate on what Rose was saying. Her friend was in the middle of describing her latest date, but the bar where they'd gone for some after-work drinks was crowded and noisy, and Tamara could barely hear her.

Though, to be fair, it wasn't so much the noise of the bar that was making it difficult to concentrate as the shifting, restless energy that was churning around inside her.

The weekend had passed without a word from Zee and even though she'd tried to pretend it didn't matter, that she didn't care, it did matter and she did care.

At first she'd been fine with it, especially after Scott's little "chat." Hell, she'd even been slightly relieved that the temptation hadn't presented itself. But as Sunday came around and he still hadn't gotten in touch, she'd started to feel antsy.

She only had another week before this engagement party happened, and once it had, that would be it. She'd be Robert's fiancée, her future set. A future that did not have a sexy, tattooed mechanic and mind-blowing sex in it.

Which was fine. She could handle that, it was what she'd been working toward after all, her way of putting Will and everything that had happened afterward firmly into the past.

Yet she'd hoped for a few more nights of freedom before that. If Zee didn't contact her soon, there'd be no more time.

She'd spent the weekend catching up on work and having an awkward and stilted conversation with Robert via Skype. Then she'd had lunch with her parents, trying to pretend that everything was normal and she didn't want to check her phone every five seconds. Luckily they didn't notice her distraction and, even luckier, neither of them mentioned the tattooed man at the charity function.

But Sunday afternoon she'd given in and texted him, hoping it sounded casual and not desperate. There was no response.

Now it was Monday evening and even though she had work to do since Scott seemed bent on making her work twelve hours a day, she'd given in and gone out for one drink with Rose, hoping to distract herself.

Except all she could think about was whether Rose had gone to her self-defense class. And whether she'd seen Zee. Whether he was okay and hadn't apparently fallen off the face of the earth.

You're being ridiculous. He's just a guy you had sex with a couple of times.

It was true, all true. But all the rationalizations in the world made no difference to the restlessness that moved like ants under her skin. That had her wanting to pick up her phone and dial Zee's number, hear his voice.

She didn't know what that was all about, perhaps something to do with the fact that she'd told him about Will, given him a piece of herself, and that he'd given her a piece in return. Or maybe it was just the simple fact that he'd run her a bath and held her, and it had been too long since someone had taken care of her like that.

Whatever it was, it was driving her crazy. Which meant she either had to see him or forget him. And since forgetting him didn't seem to be working, she had to see him.

"So anyway," Rose was saying, "how'd your weekend go?"

"Work, you know. Doing a special project for Scott, which means lots of late nights."

Rose shook her head. "The guy's a jerk."

"You're not wrong." Tamara picked up her glass and took another sip, hoping the alcohol would make things better some-how. "But if I want to get this job, I kind of have to."

"Such is the life of the intern." The other woman raised a glass in a toast. "Here's to it being over quickly and permanent positions for all of us."

Tamara clinked her glass with Rose's, then took another sip. And as she did so, her phone vibrated. She looked down at the screen and everything inside her contracted.

It was Zee. A short text.

Can't see you again, pretty girl. Sorry. Z.

Tamara stared down at the letters on the screen, a lurching disappointment shifting in her gut. That's it? That's all she was going to get? Two short sentences?

What else did you expect? He's not your boyfriend. He's only a guy you had sex with, as you keep on telling yourself.

Yes, of course, that was true. So why did she feel as if something she'd longed for, was desperate for, was now slip-ping out of her reach? For a few nights he'd shown her what it meant to be herself, helped her discover the woman she was beneath the Tamara Lennox mask. Now it was over. It was time to let that go.

"No," she heard herself whisper. "No, I don't want to."

"What?" Rose was looking at her, raising an eyebrow. "Did you say something?"

Tamara blinked. Her throat felt tight, a pain digging deep somewhere inside her. It made her angry, so goddamn angry. Angry with Zee and his stupid, dismissive text. At herself and her disappointment. And she knew it was crazy to let this get to her so much, but it was and for some reason, this time, she couldn't keep it under control.

"Uh no," she said thickly. "Hey, I'll be back in a second. Just have to go make a phone call." Without waiting for a reply, Tamara grabbed her phone and slid off the barstool, making her way through the crowded bar to the entrance and slipping outside.

Finding a quieter place along the sidewalk, she pressed a button and dialed Zee's number.

It rang for a long time and she was already preparing to leave him a message when suddenly his dark, gritty voice answered. "Tamara."

The sound of it was like a caress, rough yet at the same time soft. It sent a shiver all the way through her. "So that's all I get?" she said without preamble, hating the way her voice shook. "One line and a sorry?"

He was silent a moment. "What did you want me to say?"

"A reason might be nice."

"The reasons don't matter. What matters is that I can't see you again and that I'm sorry about it."

She swallowed, trying to ease the tightness in her throat, in her chest. "Yeah, well, they matter to me. Was it something I said? Something I did?" Another thought occurred to her, making the tightness worse. "Was it because of what I told you about my brother?"

"No." The word was flat and unequivocal, a statement of fact. "You didn't do a goddamn thing. But things have changed."

"What things?"

"We had sex, pretty girl, that's all it was. I don't owe you any fucking explanations so don't go and start making this hard. It's over. Go back to your boyfriend. Have a good life."

Yes, that's exactly what she should be doing. So why did that suddenly now sound like the worst fate in the world?

Come on, pull yourself together. He's right; you know he is.

She tried to get rid of the tightness in her throat. Perhaps it was the wine. Perhaps she'd had too much. Because that was the only reason she could think of for why she was having this strange, emotional reaction to what was essentially only the end of . . . well, precisely nothing.

"Sure," she said tightly. "I will. You too."

Then she hit the end button before any of the desperation that was starting to rise up inside her could get out.

People moved around her, walking past in groups, talking and laughing. And she knew she should go back inside, have another drink, talk with Rose, and forget a man called Zee even existed.

But she didn't. She stood there for what seemed a long time, staring at the cracked pavement under her feet, feeling the walls of her movie-set life begin to close in again. The lines of her script becoming heavier, more solid.

That's all she was, wasn't it? An actor moving through a role she'd never wanted. Soon enough, she'd forget she was even supposed to be acting. Soon it wouldn't only be a role she played, it would become part of her and the other parts of herself, the ones she'd found with Zee, would be lost forever.

That's good though. That's exactly what you were hoping. Get rid of the things that hurt. All the horrible, messy urges you can't control. Because you know what happens when you let your emotions get the better of you.

The burn of terror at the back of her throat. The echo of a gunshot in a quiet room. The sound of a body falling onto the floor.

Tamara lifted her shaking hands, pressed them against her eyes.

This was good for her, this was the best thing and yet . . . She couldn't deny it. She wanted more. Even one last night. Just one to say good-bye properly. Then she could draw a line under it, put it well and truly behind her without this aching sense of . . . loss, almost.

The thought stuck in her head and even though she tried to drown it by going back into the bar and finishing her wine with Rose, it wouldn't go away.

She couldn't face going back to the office and finishing off the work she still had to do, so she went back to her apartment. But after ten minutes of staring at the beautifully whitewashed walls, she knew that was a mistake too.

She didn't want all the prissy little details of her apartment, all the color coordination and neatness. The carefully chosen white decor that was supposed to be so clean and calming. She didn't want clean. She didn't want calm. She wanted wildness and chaos and grit. Dirty, rough reality. She wanted Zee, his hands and his mouth and his cock.

Just one more time.

She'd made her decision before she was even conscious of it, finding herself in the bedroom and going through her racks of clothes. Looking at all the cocktail dresses and gowns and suits. But she didn't want those, not this time. She was going to be something else tonight.

Ditching her work clothes, she finally pulled on a pair of old jeans instead and, in an act of defiance her mother would have a fit about, she ditched the bra, too, tugging on a tight-fitting black tank without it. Then she grabbed her purse.

Okay, so Zee had said no, that things had changed, but if she came to him personally, like she had the week before, then maybe he'd change his mind about that, too. She wasn't asking for much, only one more night and that would be it. Then she could finally get Zee out of her system, put the past behind her, move forward into the future without all this stupid restlessness and longing. A final fling before she gave herself to her career and to Robert.

Of course there was always the risk Zee would say no, but it would be worth it, wouldn't it?

She called herself a cab and half an hour later she found herself standing outside Gideon's garage. This time she didn't even bother looking around at the cracked sidewalks or the broken-down buildings. Or notice the groups of people hanging around.

She just strode right up to the metal door and hammered loudly on it.

There was no response so she hammered again, refusing to believe that there might not actually be anyone inside. The thought of coming all the way here only to have Zee be out was just not happening.

A pair of old guys sitting on upturned milk crates and playing cards on a cardboard box not far off looked up from their game to stare at her, obviously drawn by the noise of her hammering.

"Shop's closed, girl," one of them said. "No one's there."

Tamara stared at the old man a second, then glanced back at the resolutely shut door of the garage. Her heart began to sink. Dammit. This was definitely not the outcome she wanted. What the hell was she going to do now? Go to Zee's gym and look there?

"Who're you lookin' for?"

She turned back to the old guy. He'd put his cards down and was grinning at her through a mouthful of broken teeth. She probably shouldn't approach him since she was obviously out of place and by herself, and Zee had made it very clear the last time how at risk she was here.

Yet he didn't look to be outwardly threatening and she wasn't getting any weird vibes from him. Besides, she hadn't come all the way here only to be scared off at the last minute.

"I'm looking for Ezekiel. Do you know where he is?"

The old man gave a wheezy laugh. "Of course you're lookin' for him. All the girls do." And he glanced at his friend, who laughed right along with him.

Tamara ignored them. "Is he at the gym?"

"Nope. He's off at the fights. Beatin' up on people."

A thrill shot down her spine, sending a prickling wash of electricity right through her.

She'd never really considered his fights, though he'd been mesmerizing to watch during the self-defense classes. Yet now that she was here, the thought of seeing him in action was . . . exciting.

Zee stripped down, moving with all that graceful power, dealing out controlled violence on his opponent. What was he like when he fought? What would he be like to watch?

Her mouth went dry as she imagined it. He would be beautiful, she just knew it.

"Where?" she asked.

The old man chuckled. "It's not boxing, girlie. You don't pay for a ticket and sit in a seat and eat a hot dog. It's not that kind of fight."

She kind of already knew it wouldn't be. "I'd still like to see it."

The old guy's friend muttered something Tamara didn't catch, making the old man nod his head and mutter something else in return. Then he turned his attention back to her. "I'll haveta take you, if wanna see it, cos you won't get in the door by yourself."

The thrill inside her gathered tighter, making her gut shift uneasily and her palms get damp. This was totally outside her experience and perhaps she should have been a lot more nervous than she was. But this was what she'd come down here for after all. Rough, dirty, hard reality.

She took a few steps over to where the two were sitting. "Okay. I . . . can make it worth your while." There was cash in her pocket if that's what they wanted.

But the old guy frowned as if she'd offended him. "Hell, I don't want your fuckin' money."

She could feel herself coloring. Great start. "I'm sorry. I didn't mean—"

"I know. Just messin' with ya." The man heaved himself up off the crate. He was holding something dark in his hand. "But you better put this on. Gotta granddaughter your age and flashin' those titties around at a fight's a big mistake. Unless you askin' for trouble, catch my drift?"

Tamara's blush deepened and she only just stopped herself from folding her arms over her chest. Instead she glanced down at what the man was holding out. A black hoodic.

Oh God, was he seriously wanting her to put that on?

Judging from the look on his face, he really did.

Gingerly Tamara took it from him. She couldn't see much in the dark of the street, but she was rather surprised when she pulled it down over her head to find that it smelled like laundry liquid.

Her surprise obviously showed on her face, because he gave another chuckle. "My wife just did the laundry. Your lucky day, huh? Come on, we're already late."

Three blocks and ten minutes later, Tamara looked dubiously up at the abandoned building in front of her and wondered if coming down here really had been a good idea after all.

The windows were all boarded up and there was graffiti spray-painted over the crumbling brick of the walls. A very dark, dank-looking alley ran off to one side, the entrance almost blocked by several overflowing Dumpsters. Trash littered the deserted sidewalk, the flickering neon from the sex shop across the street washing everything in a lurid red glow.

The old man—who'd declined to give her his name—was busy talking to the huge, muscle-bound guy who was guarding the door to the building. After a minute or two he turned and beckoned to Tamara.

For the first time, doubt curled inside her, along with a good, healthy dose of fear. But she shook off both sensations. She'd come too far now to let a little fear stop her.

The guard, or bouncer, or whoever he was, held open the door and jerked his head at her to go in.

"Past the elevators and up the stairs to the top, girlie," the old man said. "You can drop my hoodie back later."

Then with a last chuckle, he went back off down the street again, leaving Tamara on her own.

Okay, so now she was here at a shady fight, in a sketchy neighborhood, by herself. This was perhaps more rough reality than she was expecting.

Taking a breath, she went past the bouncer and into the dim hallway, making her way past a bank of decommissioned elevators and out through some more doors that she soon discovered led to the building's stairwell.

Up the stairs, the old guy had said. Kind of strange to go up, especially when she'd been expecting some dank basement.

Biting down her nervousness, she started up the stairs, sounds beginning to filter down the stairwell the higher she got. The distinctive sound of a crowd, lots of shouting and catcalling and whistling.

The nervous tension curled tighter inside her, along with a sharp, electric thrill, that had her heart pumping and her breath coming faster.

The noise grew louder, echoing down a small corridor right at the top of the stairs.

She hesitated only a moment, then slowly went down it to the door at the end, pushing it open, and was nearly flattened by the roar of the crowd as it crashed over her.

Through the doorway was the broad, flat space of the rooftop itself, and as she stepped out, she was rather surprised to see that there weren't actually the thousands of people shouting that she'd expected, but only what looked like a couple of hundred.

They were gathered in the center of the space, clustered in a big circle. Most of them were men, but there were a few women in skimpy outfits here and there too.

It made Tamara glad about the hoodie and she pulled it more firmly over her head so her features were concealed.

There was so much leather and chains and piercings and tattoos it looked like a heavy metal convention. People were drinking, beers in hands and cigarettes in mouths as they shouted and gestured to one another.

The few women were in tiny skirts or poured-on jeans and tight tops, hanging off the arms of the men. They too were shouting and gesticulating at whatever was happening in the center of the circle. Money looked like it was changing hands, bills being shoved to and from various people.

Swallowing her nervousness, she slipped through the crowded rooftop as best she was able, trying not to bump or knock into people. Not that anyone else seemed to care about that, but she really didn't want to draw attention to herself.

The crowd thickened the closer to the center she got and she finally came to a standstill, trapped behind some huge muscle-bound guy who was screaming at the top of his lungs, unable to go any farther—or at least not without shoving someone out of her way.

Twisting, she managed to see past him just at the right moment, the crowd suddenly parting in front of her, enough to see the wide-open space in the middle of the rooftop.

And the two men in the center of it.

She stilled, the breath catching in her throat.

Zee stood there, dressed only in a pair of black shorts and gloves that looked a bit like boxing gloves but weren't. He had his hands raised, his whole body motionless and yet vibrating with energy, the leashed violence and danger she'd sensed in him from the moment she'd laid eyes on him coursing through him like a current.

Light came from the city around them and from a floodlight set up down one end of the rooftop, a raw, white kind of illumination. It picked up the sheen of sweat on his hard, muscled body, making him gleam. Making the ink of his tattoos look darker and denser on his skin.

He looked like he'd been dipped in silver somehow, a battle angel fallen to earth. Magnificent. Beautiful. Terrifying.

Her chest tightened, hunger beginning to uncoil inside her.

The other man was in blue trunks and he'd begun to circle Zee, coming closer and closer, though Tamara barely looked at him. All her attention was on Zee.

The man made a few feints with one hand that Zee easily dodged, then he came in with a sweeping kick, only to have Zee dodge that one too. The two circled each other a couple of times while the crowd heaved and screamed all around her.

She found herself rooted to the spot, her heart thundering as the man in blue rushed at Zee and Zee danced back, the crowd moving with them almost to the low and dangerous parapet that bounded the edge of the roof.

Fighting on the rooftop of a building. Were they insane? Perhaps that was the appeal.

Zee was now dodging more feints and avoiding kicks, leading the guy around in a circle, and it became apparent to Tamara he was either toying with the other man or maybe tiring him out.

The crowd's excitement seemed to build the longer Zee held out attacking, people screaming at him to go for it, to rip the other guy apart, to take him down.

Zee himself didn't appear to notice. His expression was fixed, silver eyes burning and focused wholly on his opponent. As if the crowd wasn't even there.

Tamara found herself almost chanting along with the audience, her heart hammering, her hands out of her pockets now and clenched in fists at her sides. Excitement poured through her as she watched, adrenaline firing through her bloodstream. She could feel the excitement build in the crowd like a wave, as if they were all waiting for something. A moment they were anticipating. The point where the wave would break.

In the center of the crowd, Zee had come to a stop as his opponent circled and she had the impression that he was gathering himself. That the moment the crowd had been waiting for was coming, was almost there . . .

He moved, an explosion of lethally controlled violence that had him feinting a punch before dropping to the ground for a sweeping kick that took the other guy's feet out from under him.

The crowd roared their approval as Zee was instantly on top of his opponent, grappling with him, shoving him down to the ground, his hand on the back of his neck. The other guy was struggling, trying to throw Zee off, but failing. Then Zee sprang away, pulling back.

His opponent got to his feet, his hands coming up. There was blood trailing down his face from a split eyebrow and a cut lip, a bruise around his eye socket.

Tamara frowned. Why had he let the other man up when Zee was clearly winning the round?

Then Zee shifted again, another series of powerful yet contained movements that had him feinting a kick before launching a punch at the other man's face that snapped the man's head back and had him dropping to the concrete like a stone.

He didn't get up again.

The crowd gave a deafening roar as Zee looked down at his felled opponent for a long moment. Then he punched one hand into the sky while the crowd howled their approval, and Tamara found herself howling right along with them, the excitement of the victory pulsing through her like it was her own.

People began to move, some converging on where Zee stood, others gathering in groups to shout and argue as money once again changed hands. Chaos reigned and Tamara had to quickly slip away to the side of the rooftop to avoid getting trampled.

A couple of muscle-bound bouncers waded in and began shoving people away, clearing a space around Zee. The crowd pulled back muttering, more money being tossed around amid loud arguments and laughter.

Tamara inched around the side of the rooftop, trying to see where Zee was. Then she spotted him down one end. He was standing there with a towel around his neck, holding a beer bottle loosely in one hand, talking to his friend, the other mechanic she'd met, Gideon. Both of them were surveying the crowd, tense expressions on their faces.

She barely noticed, her gaze drawn inexorably to Zee's body gleaming under the floodlights, sweat outlining every perfect muscle, blood trailing from another split eyebrow down the side of his jaw and farther down the powerful column of his neck.

Everything gathered tight inside her with want. He was intimidating and dangerous, no doubt about it, and God, she liked that. So different from all the men she knew, in their suits and ties and with their country club memberships. Zee was like another species entirely. He was life in the raw, in all its gritty, physical glory. A tiger in a field of antelope.

He'd played with that guy, toyed with him, before taking him out with what looked like ridiculous ease.

He'd told her he fought to let off steam, but was it more than that? Did he like beating the shit like that out of people? What was it that drew him to this?

Why do you want to know?

Because she did. She just . . . did.

Too busy staring, Tamara didn't notice the man backing into her until it was too late. The impact almost knocked her off her feet and she stumbled, her hand going out to grab on to something.

"Shit," a male voice said. "What the fuck are you doing?"

Someone had grabbed her hand and was holding on tight. She looked up, the sudden movement making her hood fall back.

An older man with rough, brutal features and cold dark eyes

was steadying her, his grip almost painful. He smiled as her hood fell away. "Hey, honey, sorry 'bout that. Didn't see you there."

There was no mistaking the interest in his eyes. Damn.

Tamara forced herself to smile back, trying to untangle herself from his grip. "It's okay, really. I'm fine."

"Are you sure?" He didn't release her.

Double damn. "Yes. I promise. It's all good." She flicked a glance over to where Zee was, hoping he hadn't disappeared, still attempting to pull away from the man who seemed bent on holding her fast.

And met Zee's eyes, glittering like polished steel.

Chapter 11

Zee had been counting on Victor turning up to the fight tonight and he wasn't disappointed, which was just as well since the guys he and Gideon had gotten together were in the crowd just waiting for Zee's signal. A show of strength for Victor to take back to Zee's old man, a line in the sand from his son.

And Zee had nearly gone ahead and given that signal.

Then Victor had backed into a slender figure at the side of the rooftop, some chick nearly swamped in an outsize black hoodie. She'd stumbled and her hood had fallen back, exposing the bright gleam of a blond ponytail.

No mistaking that color. And when her face had turned toward him, he knew there was no mistaking the woman either.

It was Tamara Lennox standing on the rooftop and Victor fucking Krupin, more commonly known as the Pitbull, was holding on to her hand.

His blood had turned to ice at the same time as a black fury rose inside him, strong as a fucking hurricane. He wanted to go over to the other guy, smash his face in, then hurl him from the rooftop like King Kong.

Then maybe he'd fling that stupid little rich girl over his shoulder, take her somewhere quiet, and put the fear of God into her. Because what the *fuck* was she doing here? After he'd told her no? He thought he'd been very specific, been very clear that they were not going to see each other again.

She stared at him from across the rooftop, her dark eyes defiant, and no matter that his father's henchman was right next to her and that he had more important shit to do, he could feel beneath his rage the hunger for her begin to rise too.

Whatever his head was telling him about not seeing her again, his dick, the stupid fuck, had clearly not gotten the message.

Jesus. She had no idea what she was messing with. She had no idea who was holding her hand. A man who'd kill her without a shred of regret.

"What the fuck?" Gideon muttered at his side. "Is that your girl?"

"The others need to stand down," Zee said roughly. "We gotta get her outta here. *Now.*"

"I'll tell them." Gideon glanced at him. "I'll get her too. Take her back to the garage."

Zee could only nod. He couldn't go over and get her himself, not with Victor there. Doing so would single her out, make her seem special and with his father's favorite attack dog nearby, that was the last thing he wanted to do.

Luckily Gideon seemed to understand so Zee just stood there, sipping casually on his beer, pretending that the rage the fight had already unleashed wasn't about ready to blow his head off.

After he'd told his friends the truth about himself, he'd gone out himself to try to track down his father. But in Joshua's inimitable way, once he'd shown Zee he knew where he was, he'd vanished. Zee, impatient now for everything to be over, had wanted to go to his old man's house and rattle on the goddamn gates to get the guy to come out. But Gideon had had a better idea.

Make the guy come to them. Get him in Royal territory. Their territory.

So he and Gideon had engineered a fight especially to draw either Joshua or Victor out of the woodwork. And sure enough, at least one of those cocksuckers had come. But he couldn't make a move now, not with her here. She'd fucking ruined it.

Zee forced his gaze away from hers, watching Gideon move through the crowd instead. Adrenaline was a loud buzz in his veins, fury and a dread he wasn't going to admit to only adding to it.

Jesus Christ, he needed another fight to burn this shit off somehow.

Why fight when you can fuck?

He couldn't help himself; his gaze returned to where Tamara stood. The hood of her sweatshirt had fallen back completely now, her long blond ponytail a golden waterfall down her spine. The top hid her figure, except for those long slender legs, encased in worn blue denim.

Gideon had approached them and was talking to Victor, smiling as he put an arm around Tamara's waist, pulling her against him in a blatantly possessive gesture. Tamara wasn't looking at Zee and her face was white, but clearly she could think on her feet because after a moment's hesitation, she put her own arm around Gideon's waist, letting her head fall on his shoulder.

Something inside of Zee growled.

Insanity. He'd wanted this confrontation, needed it. To draw a line in the sand, to show his motherfucking father that he wasn't seventeen anymore. That he wasn't going to be pushed around or threatened. He had his territory and he was going to defend it.

But the goddamn woman had ruined it. She'd shown no sense at all by coming down here looking for him, and then, to add insult to injury, had gotten tangled up with Victor of all people.

The very last thing he should be doing was getting posses-sive because she had her arm around Gideon.

Yet all of that made no difference to the feeling inside of him. The one that wanted to rip her away from Gideon, from Victor, and show her who she really belonged to.

You? Really? You can't have anyone and you know it, espe-cially not now.

As if to punctuate how true this was, as Gideon and Tamara moved toward the entrance to the stairwell, Zee noted Victor's gaze tracking them all the way there. Then the fucker turned and that cold gaze met Zee's.

Victor smiled, gave him a salute, then casually he began shouldering his way through the crowds to the stairwell too.

The rage boiled up inside him, demanding an outlet. A rage he hadn't felt since his father had told him about Madison's car accident. About how it hadn't actually been an accident at all.

Something cracked in his hand, the neck of the beer bottle shattering in his grip, the bottle falling onto the concrete of the rooftop and smashing.

Christ, he needed to get out of here, figure out what his next move was. No, correction. First he needed to make sure Tamara Goddamn Lennox took that pretty, rich-girl ass of hers back downtown and stayed there.

It took him nearly an hour to finish up the fight, then get back to the garage, and by the time he slammed his way through the doors, he was in a towering fury.

Tamara was sitting on the white plastic chair with a beer in one hand, still enveloped by that stupid fucking sweatshirt, while Gideon sat on the metal stairs. He was also nursing a beer and the pair of them were chatting like old friends.

Zee wanted to strangle both of them.

"What the *fuck* do you think you were doing?" he de-manded, slamming the door behind him, then heading straight for Tamara's chair.

A flicker of fear chased through her dark eyes—which was good, because if she was afraid, then maybe she'd stay away from him—only to be followed by something else. Something that looked a hell of a lot like that same defiance she'd shown him up on the rooftop.

She lifted her chin as he stalked up to her, slamming his hands on the arms of the chair, caging her into it.

"Zee," Gideon said. "Calm the fuck down."

Zee ignored him, staring down at the woman in the chair. "Answer me."

She stared right back at him, her jaw tight. Then she lifted her beer and took a sip.

He growled and snatched the bottle out of her hand. "Fucking answer me, Tamara." Jesus Christ, she should not be messing with him right now. Not given the mood he was in.

"Zee." Gideon's voice was low with warning. "Don't be a prick. She didn't have any idea what was going on."

Of course she hadn't, and he *was* being a prick.

You're not pissed because she ruined your confrontation. You're pissed because Victor put a hand on her. Because she was in danger.

Zee shoved the thought away. He didn't want to care about that, he couldn't afford to.

"Fuck off, Gideon," he ground out. "This is between her and me."

Gideon muttered something under his breath. "You okay, Tamara?"

For some reason that enraged him even more. "You really think I'm gonna hurt her?" he demanded, shifting his attention to the other man.

Gideon's dark gaze was level. "Just making sure she's okay."

"Well?" He looked back down at her. "Are you? 'Cause Dad over there is worried."

Her mouth flattened into a line. "It's okay, Gideon. I'll be fine."

There was a moment's silence. Then Gideon let out a breath and got to his feet. "I'll be in the office."

Zee didn't watch him go, his attention fully on the woman sitting in the chair in front of him.

It had taken him three days to text her to tell her it was over and he'd told himself that was because he'd had other more important shit to think about. But when she'd called him back and he'd heard her soft, husky voice on the other end of the phone, he'd known that was a goddamn lie.

It had taken him that long because he hadn't wanted to do it. The end of the month wasn't up yet and he wasn't ready to say good-bye. But now this shit with his father had blown up, Christ, he hadn't had a choice. It should have been easy and definitely nothing in his chest should have clenched tight at the sound of her voice. At the undercurrent of disappointment in it, a disappointment she'd been trying to hide that he'd heard anyway. Nevertheless it had.

He'd had to force the words out. Had to make himself say them.

All for nothing, it seemed. Because here she was, having not paid the slightest bit of attention.

"What the fuck did you come down here for?" he demanded, not caring how rough he sounded. "I told you it was over. I fucking meant it."

Something he couldn't quite read glittered in her dark eyes. "I wanted one last night."

He didn't know why that made him even angrier. "If all you wanted was a fuck, then you should have found one downtown, Tamara. You didn't need to come to Royal to find it."

"I didn't want just a fuck." Her jaw had gone tight. "I wanted you."

That got him, made something twist hard inside him. Something traitorous he didn't want. "Yeah well, you shouldn't. You should be staying the hell where you belong and not coming anywhere near here."

"Why? Or better yet, why the hell are you so pissed with me?" Anger vibrated in her voice. "So I didn't take no for an answer and came to one of your fights. What's the big deal?"

His fingers curled on the white plastic of the chair. Perhaps he should tell her what she'd interrupted, so she knew exactly the level of shit that was going down. That would make her wish she'd never left her pretty, expensive apartment and her clean-cut New York boyfriend.

Once she knows who you are, she'll run. And you'll never see her again.

Which meant he should tell her. Yet the words didn't want to come out of his mouth.

The way he was leaning over her had brought her so close, her dark eyes inches from his, her full, pouty mouth right there. She smelled so good, like sex and heat and hunger. And he was so full of adrenaline and fury, and nothing was going to make it any better.

He could fight or he could fuck. He knew which one he wanted to do.

Maybe she was right. One more night to say good-bye. Then she could fuck off back to where she belonged.

Zee shoved himself away from the chair. "You wanted one more night. You sure about that?"

She blinked. Then her mouth firmed. "Yes."

"You better be. 'Cause I'm not in the mood for gentle. Understand?"

She didn't look away. "I didn't come here for gentle."

Desire wrapped around him, squeezed him. Making his heart slam against his chest and cock harden in his jeans.

"Then you'd better come with me." And he held out his hand to her.

Zee must have gotten changed somewhere because he was now in low-slung jeans and a black T-shirt. The blood had been cleaned up, a cut on his cheekbone taped, and he should have looked if not respectable then at least less threatening.

But he didn't.

There was wild lightning in his eyes and it burned bright as he held out his hand.

She shouldn't take it, not when his mood was like this. When there was so much anger in him and he refused to explain any of it.

The encounter with the man at the fight had frightened her, especially when he wouldn't let go of her hand and had looked at her with those cold, cold eyes. Then Gideon had appeared and put his arm around her and mentioned something about her being "already taken," and luckily she'd had the presence of mind at least to go along with it.

Gideon had brought her back to the garage, explaining how there were always a few weirdos at the fights and how it wasn't a good idea to turn up by herself. She'd been okay with that, though she'd felt like a bit of an idiot for not thinking it through.

It had been nice just sitting there with Gideon, chatting and having a beer. They'd talked about Zee, Gideon mentioning the work Zee'd been doing with the kids at the local outreach center, and about Zee's gym and what Zee was trying to do with it. She already knew he was a pretty decent guy and hearing about the difference he was trying to make in his neighborhood only deepened Tamara's respect for him.

Then Zee himself had come in, bringing the lightning with him.

She had no idea what he was so angry about, though she'd guessed it had something to do with her turning up at the fight. He hadn't wanted her there; that much was obvious, though again, she didn't know why. And clearly he wasn't going to tell her.

Tamara met his hot, burning gaze and briefly debated pushing the issue. But then she knew if she did that it wouldn't get her what she wanted. Which was him in all his rough, dirty glory.

So she took his hand, feeling the heat of his touch steal up her arm. Letting him draw her up and out of the chair. And when he turned and went back out of the garage, she followed him, the grip of his fingers around hers drawing her along.

Ten silent minutes later they stopped outside a building Tamara recognized. Zee's gym. He unlocked the door and held it open for her, and she stepped inside into the familiar dim hallway.

He didn't speak, taking her hand again and this time he headed not for the gym entrance but for the stairs at one side of the foyer.

She followed, going up her second set of stairs for the night. But this time they didn't keep heading up, stopping at the first floor where Zee halted outside another door, unlocking it with another key.

He turned to her as he held the door open, his eyes full of challenge. He didn't say a word, but somehow she knew what that look meant nonetheless.

Cross the threshold if you dare. The choice is yours.

Tamara didn't even hesitate. She stepped through the doorway.

The hallway beyond was plain and painted white, the light from the stairwell shutting off as Zee followed her, closing the door behind him.

Tamara stopped, unsure of where to go. Her heart was racing, her breathing coming faster and faster. She could feel his heat behind her, smell the scent of him, clean sweat and that intoxicating spice. So good. She began to turn to him, but all of a sudden his hand was on the back of her neck, and she was being propelled down the white hallway, past a few doors, down toward an open doorway at the end.

A shiver chased over her skin, her body already gathering it-self in anticipation, responding helplessly to the feeling of his hand on her neck.

Inside the room, she caught a glimpse of tall windows and the view of the street outside, a big, low bed that sat underneath them, a chest of drawers, and then that glimpse was cut off as Zee let go of her neck, then shoved her down onto her front on the bed.

She turned over, her heart racing.

But he didn't follow her, only stood there, looking down at her, all six feet and three inches of lean, hard muscle. Then, with a fluid movement, he pulled his T-shirt off over his head and threw it on the ground, his hands going to the button on his jeans and undoing it.

Tamara swallowed, unable to tear her gaze from his per-fectly defined torso. She moved forward, putting her hands out, wanting to touch, but he got to her first, one hand flashing out to grip her throat as the other one pulled down the tab of his zipper.

His fingers curled around her, holding on tight as he pulled her toward him. Then he bent his head, his mouth covering hers.

He kissed her as if she were one of his opponents and he was aiming for nothing short of her total submission. As if she were a city he wanted to conquer, shattering every defense, invading, marauding. Taking her mouth and devouring her like nothing could stop him.

He tasted of lightning, too, an electricity that grounded right through her body, from the top of her head to her toes, lighting her up with the same fire that was burning inside of him. Desper-ate and raw and primal. A force of nature.

Tamara tried to respond in kind, but he was having none of it.

He released her, leaving her panting and shivering, stepping back as he pulled down the zipper of his jeans. "Stay there and don't move," he ordered in a dark voice. "This is my show tonight."

She took a ragged breath, her body wanting to obey even if her own hunger wanted to tell him to stick it. Her fingers itched, desperate to touch, but she kept her hands to herself, watching as he got rid of his boots, then shoved his jeans down and stepped out of them.

He wasn't wearing boxers, which meant he stood there in nothing but his ink, the phoenix soaring up one arm and over his shoulder. The dragon on his other arm. The words on his back. God, it wasn't fair. She wanted to touch like she had that night in the bath, tracing her fingers all over those fascinating marks. They all had a story, a meaning, she just knew it. And she wanted to know what it was.

But not now, that much was clear.

He stood in front of her, blocking out the room, towering over her, the look in his eyes like fire, his cock hard and ready against the flat plane of his abdomen.

Then he bent and the hoodie was being yanked up and over her head. He threw the material aside and knelt on the bed, staring down at her, the heat of his gaze moving over the tank she'd put on. Her nipples had gone tight and hard, pushing against the fabric stretched across her breasts, making it obvious she wore no bra underneath it.

Zee lifted his hands and with one sharp movement, he ripped the thing in half.

She sucked in a breath as he shoved the remains of the material off her shoulders, every nerve ending she had coming alive to the touch of his hands. Her breasts ached, the pulse of desire deep in her sex. Her hands were in fists at her sides and she couldn't stand it, the need to touch him almost too much.

"Zee," she said thickly. "Please, I want—"

"Lie back."

"Zee."

His silver eyes were brilliant with desire, with anger. "Do as you're fucking told."

Tamara stared at him, feeling something inside her flare in response. Part anger, part excitement, part defiance. An answer to a challenge.

No, she wasn't going to be the good little rich girl tonight. She wasn't going to sit there and do what she was told, let him have all the control. This was her last night with him, the last night to be the woman she'd discovered she was inside.

Fuck it. She wasn't going to give in without a fight.

Tamara smiled and pushed herself back on the bed, her hands moving to the fastenings on her own jeans, undoing the buttons, reaching for the zipper.

The flame in his eyes leapt. "Stop. I was planning on doing that."

"Stop fucking around then." She jerked her zipper down and lifted her hips, pushing down her jeans and taking her panties with them, easing them down her thighs slowly, giving him a show. "For a martial arts fighter, you're pretty damn slow."

He made a growling sound and moved, his body suddenly coming over hers, his hands on either side of her head, his gaze holding hers. She could feel the heat of him against her skin like a bonfire burning hot.

She didn't look away from him and didn't stop what she was doing, sliding her jeans and panties off, wriggling to get them down her legs. The look in his eyes intensified and she felt a surge of triumph as his gaze swept down her body, almost as if he couldn't help himself.

"You shouldn't do shit like that," he murmured. "Bad girls don't get what they want."

"I don't need you to get what I want." The room was dark, but the light coming through the windows was enough to see his face, see the flush along his high cheekbones and the muscle flicking in his jaw. "I can get it all by myself." Dangerous to taunt him like this and yet it was thrilling, too. Made her feel powerful.

She slid her hand down to her stomach and then farther still, brushing the damp curls between her thighs, watching his face.

"Jesus." Zee shifted, his fingers curling around her wrist and jerking her hand away. "You're asking for trouble, baby. I'm already fucking angry. It's not a good idea to push me." He forced her hand up and over her head, pinning it to the bed.

A brief flare of panic went through her, the same as it had when he'd held her down in her apartment. Reminding her too much of Will and his inexplicable rages, his frightening flashes of violence.

But no. This wasn't Will. This was Zee. And she wasn't helpless.

Tamara gulped in a heaving breath, arching her body, her breasts almost brushing Zee's chest. He cursed again. "Fucking keep still."

She didn't, lifting her other hand to touch his chest, sliding it down over his hot skin, all oiled silk and hard muscle. Going lower and lower, reaching for his cock.

He gave another curse and grabbed her other hand, pinning that one above her head too so she lay stretched out beneath him. Ostensibly helpless and yet, she didn't feel helpless. Not in the slightest. If anything, even though he was holding her down with effortless strength, it was as if the balance of power was with her.

A bubble of excitement gathered in her chest. "Come on," she taunted him softly. "I thought you said you weren't doing gentle."

His gaze came to hers, polished steel and tarnished silver. Sharp as swords.

Then he moved again, his hands on her hips, shoving her right up against the wooden headboard of the bed, with the neon lights of the city falling down around them.

"Put your hands on the headboard," he ordered. "And hold on fucking tight."

Anticipation coiled tight inside her. She wanted to disobey him, see what he would do, push him further. There was something wild in him that thrilled her, the crackling energy like a current beneath his skin, and she wanted to let it out. Let it burn both of them.

"What would you do if I didn't?" She pushed herself up, reaching out to him again.

This time Zee didn't bother cursing. He grabbed one wrist, picked up one half of the tank top he'd ripped, and with ruthless efficiency tied her wrist to the slatted wood of the headboard. Then before she could move or protest, he did the same with her other hand.

Tamara trembled, flexing her wrists, then pulling against the ties, testing them.

"You wanted to know what I'd do." Zee's eyes gleamed. "Now are you going to shut the fuck up and let me screw you or what?"

Kneeling between her legs, he leaned over to the nightstand beside the bed, tugging open a drawer and pulling out a condom packet before ripping it open. Then he rolled the latex down over himself.

All his movements were quick, efficient. Sharp. And when he turned back to her, the look on his face blazed.

The wild thrill burned hot in her blood, her breathing coming in short, fast pants. She wanted to protest again, push him again, and yet she wanted him to touch her more. Because, God, he hadn't even done that yet and she was desperate.

"So do it," she said huskily. "Or is playing with bits of fabric all you've got?"

Zee smiled, hungry and feral, and leaned forward, never looking away from her, sliding one hand beneath her right leg and lifting it up and out. Next, he placed his hand on the bed and hooked her right knee over his arm, keeping her leg up. Then he pushed her left leg up and out, holding it to the side.

She shuddered, feeling herself spread open, held ready for him.

"No, baby," he murmured. "That's not all I got."

Then he shifted his hips, thrusting forward, pushing deep and hard into her.

Tamara gasped, her whole body trembling with the delicious, vicious stretch of him inside her. Her inner muscles clenched hard on his cock, her hips already trying to rise, to increase the friction.

Yet he didn't move, the weight of him pressing down on her adding to the sensation, maddening her. His jaw was tight, his whole body tense as if he was holding back.

"Zee." The word came out before she could stop it.

"So you're begging me now?" He lowered his head, his face inches from hers. "Not so smart anymore, are you? You got my cock in you and you're desperate already." He flexed his hips, making her groan as his gaze raked down her body, lingering at where they were joined. "You don't get to give me orders, pretty girl," he murmured, the words threaded through with darkness and raw hunger. "You're in my bed and that means you're here for me. So keep your legs spread and hold on tight. I'm gonna fuck you so hard you're gonna scream."

Then he slowly drew back, his cock sliding out, before slamming back into her again.

And again. And again.

She couldn't think, couldn't speak. With every thrust he went deeper inside her, the weight of his body shaking her, making the headboard slam against the windowsill. Her knuckles were white as she held on, trying to meet him, trying to match him.

But he was too much.

His eyes were silver fire, lightning in them as he reared over her, and she couldn't look away, utterly caught by the fierce intensity of him. Consumed by it.

Zee shifted one hand off her left thigh and pressed down on her clit with his thumb as he thrust hard and deep, keeping his other arm right where it was, up near her shoulder with her leg hooked around it. Keeping her wide and open.

She screamed at the vicious pleasure of it, trying to move with him, lift her hips and take him as much as he was taking her. But he wouldn't let her. All she could do was go with it as he stroked her, fucked her harder and faster, murmured wicked, filthy things to her, his voice all guttural and ragged.

Then all at once she ignited again, the climax blazing through her like the backdraft of an inferno, burning away every last vestige of Tamara.

Setting her free to soar like a phoenix from the ashes.

Chapter 12

He could feel her tight little pussy clench hard around him, her hoarse scream echoing in the bedroom as she stiffened beneath him, her body arching.

But he didn't stop. He physically couldn't.

Pleasure as irresistible and inexorable as a tidal wave was carrying him along and all he could do was ride it. Driving himself hard into her, the heat and musky scent of her making him feel drunk and hungry and desperate. Feeding his strange, inexplicable anger, too.

So many different sensations he couldn't work out which was which.

So he only concentrated on one: pleasure.

He moved in her, the wet heat of her body holding him tight, her desperate cries in his ears as he shifted his hand from her pussy to cover one of hers where it gripped the headboard. Then he held on too, thrusting deeper, harder. Working out all the adrenaline left over from the fight in her.

Losing himself.

The climax came and like a wave it took him under, drowned

him, shattering him completely, his own ragged cry joining hers in the echoing silence of the bedroom. And for long moments all he could do was hold on with one hand to the headboard, his forehead resting against hers, listening to her hectic breathing as the beat of his own heart began to slow.

He was buried deep inside her and he didn't want to move.

"That was incredible," she murmured at last, sounding all throaty and husky. "You're amazing, Zee."

Through the slowly subsiding roar of his climax, he felt something shift and turn inside him, though he wasn't quite sure what it was.

He'd wanted to scare her, maybe break her, frighten her enough to make her go back to where she came from and stay there.

But . . . that did not sound as if she'd been broken. Not even a bit.

Slowly, he lifted his head, looked down into her face.

She was lying back against the headboard, her hands still tied to the wood. There were marks around her wrists from where she'd pulled against the ties, and he could see some darkening bruises from his hands, too.

Jesus Christ. He'd been a fucking animal with her.

Weren't you supposed to be better than that?

He wasn't supposed to give in to the darkness. He was supposed to be in control of himself, yet tying Tamara up against the headboard and fucking her was not being in control. That was giving in to it in a big way.

And yet . . . she hadn't seemed scared by any of that. In fact, if anything she'd taunted him on.

She's stronger than Madison.

The thought came out of the blue like a roundhouse kick he hadn't seen coming, the impact shoving all the air from his lungs.

Madison had been so young—hell, they both had—but

she'd also been innocent. Brought up in one of those privileged families in Grosse Pointe, gritty reality hadn't hit her in the face until she'd come to the party where they'd met. And even then, he'd tried to protect her from it.

She'd known what he was, who he was, but he'd shielded her from the realities of his father's business, keeping their dates as normal and as far from his father as possible. Movies and fancy restaurants and picnics. Drives in his car. She'd been so soft and sweet, and when he'd first made love to her, he'd been so afraid of breaking her he'd hardly touched her at all.

She didn't know his dark side because she'd never seen it. He'd never shown her.

But he'd shown Tamara. And Tamara had liked it.

His chest tightened and for a second he couldn't breathe.

A crease appeared between Tamara's brows. "You okay?"

Fuck, he couldn't deal with this. Madison was gone and Tamara sure as shit wasn't going to be her replacement. No one would be. At least not while his goddamn father was still alive.

"Yeah." He said the word roughly, turning away to undo the ties on her wrists, releasing her.

Then he pulled out of her, moving off the bed to visit the bathroom just off the bedroom, throwing the condom in the wastebasket there.

Bending over the sink, he splashed some water into his face, trying to clear his head.

Why the fuck was he getting all wound up over Tamara? Every time he'd ask himself this and every time, he couldn't figure out a decent answer.

First he'd been angry with her, then he'd wanted to rip her clothes off. Now she'd made his chest go tight with something he didn't understand. And all because she'd let him tie her up and fuck her hard.

Jesus, he was a mess. What he needed to do was tell her what he was, then get rid of her.

In the mirror above the sink he caught a flash of movement and when he looked up, he caught her dark eyes staring at him. She was in the doorway, leaning against the doorframe, utterly and gloriously naked and seemingly not giving a shit about it. But that lovely warm smile had gone, something like anger in her gaze.

"Don't tell me," she said, her voice flat. "You want me to go."

Slowly he straightened, brushing the water away from his face with one hand, then turning around to face her.

It's easier this way. You know it is.

"You got what you wanted."

"A night, Zee. I wanted one whole night."

"And I guess you're used to getting whatever you want, whenever you want it."

She blinked. "Is that yet another rich girl dig? God, get yourself some new insults. That one's getting old."

Angry, he should be getting angry. But somehow his anger had vanished and no matter how much he reached for it, there was only emptiness inside him.

He leaned back against the basin, the porcelain cold beneath his hands. "You want another round? Then get the fuck back to bed and I'll be there in a minute."

But she didn't move. "What did I do? I know I did something. Was it the fight? I know it's not because you don't want me. Your cock's not that good a liar."

His fingers curled around the edge of the sink. He'd been so set to tell her before and now that he'd gotten rid of at least some of that sexual heat, it should have been easy to say. Yet the truth didn't seem to want to come.

Because once you tell her, all this will be over.

Well, shit. It was going to be over anyway though, wasn't it? After tonight, he was never going to see her again.

"If I tell you, it'll change things, pretty girl. I guarantee that."

She frowned. "Change things how?"

"It'll change how you see me for a start." He tried to ignore why that mattered.

She stared at him. "Why? Have you done something bad?"

He shifted against the sink, uncomfortable for reasons he didn't want to examine. Because he had done bad stuff before he'd met Madison. He'd been part of his father's empire, had tried the alcohol and the drugs and the women that had come with it—shit, he'd only been seventeen, like a kid in a candy store. He'd also been a part of roughing people up, the people Joshua thought needed a little bit of "encouragement."

You know what you are deep down. No matter how "good" a life you've made for yourself.

"Yeah," he said softly. "I did a whole lotta bad things once."

Her throat moved, her gaze searching his face as if looking for something. "Tell me."

"You heard of Joshua Chase?"

The crease between her brows deepened. "The investor?"

"Yeah, that's him. He also owns the underground here in Detroit. The drug rings, the weapons deals. He's got half the gangs in his pocket and at least two outlaw motorcycle clubs. He's a bad motherfucker." Zee paused. "And he's my father."

Tamara's eyes widened. "Holy crap."

"My name isn't Ezekiel. It's Damian Chase and I've been in Royal for the past ten years trying to build a new life for myself."

"Zee—"

"No, let me finish. Somehow the bastard found out where I am, and the fight you came to tonight was supposed to end with me confronting his fucking lieutenant and delivering a message. But I couldn't because guess what happened?"

Her face slowly paled. "Oh . . ."

"That guy who grabbed your arm? That was Victor Krupin, Dad's right-hand man."

She blinked rapidly. "But Gideon was there. He got me away. So why didn't you stay to deliver your message or whatever?"

"Because you were still around. Because ten years ago, Dad had my girlfriend's car run off the road and she died. And I'm not gonna let another woman be put in danger again just because she happened to get tangled up with me."

There was shock in her eyes. "He . . . killed her?"

"Yeah, he did."

"But . . . why? What did she do?"

Zee didn't want to talk about it, go through digging up that old shit again. But he was the one who'd brought it up and so he made himself go on. "Dad told me she was a bad influence. Because she didn't want me to join the family business. She thought I was better than that. But no one gets out once they're part of it and most especially not if you're born into it." A familiar grief locked hard in his chest. "So he had her taken out."

Tamara's mouth opened. "Oh . . . Zee . . ."

There was sympathy in her eyes, and for some reason that hurt. But he hardened himself against the unexpected pain and lifted one shoulder as if it didn't matter. "It was a long time ago."

A heavy silence fell, one he didn't particularly want to break.

Then she said, "I'm not your girlfriend, you know that, right? You don't have to protect me."

"Doesn't matter. You're not supposed to be here in Royal and you're not supposed to be with me. I can't let anything like that happen again to another woman. I won't." He held her gaze, made her see how much he meant it. "Which is why you're gonna go back to your apartment after this and you're gonna stay there. And you're never gonna see me again, understand?"

Her gaze flickered. "I know that. It was always going to be that way anyway, right?"

There was something in her voice he didn't recognize, an undercurrent he didn't understand. It made him want to justify himself. "I never promised you anything different, Tamara. Hell, you shouldn't even have come down here again in the first place."

Abruptly she looked away from him, her arms tightened across her chest, hiding her beautiful breasts. "How was I supposed to know you're the son of some crime boss? Like I told you, I just wanted to see you one more time."

Another silence fell, the atmosphere in the bathroom thick with tension.

Ah, fuck; you should never have told her.

He pushed himself away from the basin, not knowing what he was going to do, whether to go past her and get dressed or pick her up and sling her over his shoulder and take her to bed again.

Then, when he was halfway across the bathroom from her, she looked at him, brown eyes steady, direct. "You're wrong. It doesn't change the way I see you."

He stopped, staring at her. "It should. Shit, Madison died because she got involved with me—"

"Gideon told me about you before you came to the garage tonight. He told me about the gym and the programs you're setting up for the outreach center. And that you donate all your fight winnings to local charities."

The tight thing in his chest was back, twisting hard. Because if he wasn't careful, history would start repeating itself, another woman seeing something in him that wasn't there and getting hurt because of it. "No, fuck no. Don't go putting me up on a pedestal. I'm not a fucking saint."

But her dark gaze swept him up and down. "Of course you're not. Any fool can see that. But you don't want her to have died in vain and you're doing what you can to right the balance, aren't you?"

He felt like she'd punched him in the chest, clear through his rib cage, leaving a hole right the way through to his heart. How she'd understood so easily, so quickly, was beyond him.

"How the fuck would you know?" he demanded, defensive anger stirring.

"Because I know a little something about balances." She made no move, staring at him. "You wanted to know what happened with my brother? Well . . ." Her chest rose sharply. "I shot him."

Now he felt like she'd not only left a hole in his chest, but also had gotten her fingers around his heart. He couldn't think of anything to say so he said nothing.

"I told you he got violent? Well, one day he did. He was . . . going to throw me out of the plate glass window." All the color had leached out of her skin, her cheeks deathly pale. "I didn't know how to stop him. He was too big and too strong and nobody was home. So I managed to get away from him long enough to get to my Dad's study because I knew he had a gun in his drawer. I thought if Will followed me, I'd wave it at him, maybe snap him out of it." Her throat moved, a convulsive swallow. "But he didn't. I shouted at him and pointed that stupid gun at him, but he just kept on coming. . . ." She stopped. "He was shouting stuff, something about how I was the devil and he had to kill me. And I knew that he'd do it and that this time I had to stop him somehow. So I pulled the trigger."

He didn't know how it happened. One minute he was in the middle of the bathroom, the next he was in the doorway, his arms sliding around her, pulling her close. She went stiff, her hands coming up to press against his chest. "Don't. I didn't say this for pity and I don't need you to make this—"

"Shut the fuck up." He pulled her hands away from his chest and put them up above her head, pinning them there. Then he looked down into her pale face. "Did he die?"

Her eyes were huge, dark as space, and he could see the pain in them, no matter how hard she tried to hide it. She didn't try to pull away, only looked back at him. "Yes." The word was defiant. "I shot him and he died. So you see, you're not the only one with ghosts. You're not the only one who's trying to balance things out. You're not alone, Zee."

That hole in his chest hadn't gone away and that simple statement just made it larger.

You're not alone.

He'd never thought he was and yet . . . No one else knew his demons. Not Gideon. Not anyone else. Until Tamara.

"You saved yourself," he said, deciding to ignore that because he didn't know how to deal with it.

"Yes, but I *killed* him. It wasn't even his fault. He was sick."

"You had to protect yourself." He leaned down, holding her wrists crossed above her head, his free hand cupping her chin. "Sometimes that's all you can do. Sometimes it's the *only* thing you can do." There had been no one to protect Madison. He'd never even known she was in danger.

Tamara jerked her chin away. "My brother is still dead. I still shot him."

"So is Madison. And I didn't even get to protect her because I didn't know my motherfucking father was gonna kill her."

Her lashes came down, quivering on the pale skin of her cheeks. "You can't make it better, Zee. Nothing can."

"You think I don't know that? You think I don't have that very same thought, every fucking day?"

She lifted those long, thick lashes again and the darkness in her eyes was like the darkness in himself. She didn't say a word, just looked at him.

He could feel the warmth of her skin against his, bare and soft and hot. And the scent rising from it, drowned flowers and musk.

No, she wasn't like Madison. She wasn't in any way, shape, or form like Madison.

On the surface she was all blond innocence and privilege, but inside . . . Inside she was darkness just like him.

"I know one thing that can make it better," he said roughly. And he gripped her chin again and forced her head back. And he kissed her, hard and deep, pushing his tongue into her mouth and taking everything. Taking the darkness inside her into himself.

All the rigidity melted away from her and suddenly she was arching against him, making desperate sounds in her throat. Pulling against his hold, the desperation that was rising in himself rising in her, too.

Fuck his father and fuck this life he was trying to make for himself. Fuck trying to do right, be a good man. That wasn't going to make it better and it wasn't going to bring Madison back. Maybe in the morning he'd change his mind, but right now, he was ready to throw himself into that darkness and drown in it. With Tamara.

Zee lifted his mouth from hers, jerked her head to the side. Then he bit her neck, hard enough to leave a mark. She shuddered in his grip, tugging at the hold he had on her wrists, but he didn't let her go, closing his teeth around her again, then licking her, tasting her. Going lower, he licked his way over the curve of one high breast, taking her taut nipple into his mouth and sucking hard.

She gasped, her hips lifting against his, trying to grind her pussy against his cock. Electricity whipped through him as the damp heat of her pressed against him, the rough silk of her curls grazing against the sensitive head of his dick.

Maybe this would be all they would ever have, this chemistry, this pleasure. But it was enough. Right now, it was the only thing he wanted.

He pulled away from her, looking down into her face. The color was back in her cheeks, but the darkness in her eyes was never ending. "You're right," she said huskily. "It does make it better."

"Then come here." He let go of her wrists, curled an arm around her waist, and tugged her into the bathroom, positioning her so she was in front of the vanity, in front of the mirror with him at her back. He met her gaze in the mirror for one long, uncounted second.

Then he pushed her down.

Her heart thudded in her chest and she was trembling so bad it was a good thing she had the cold porcelain of the vanity to lean against because otherwise she'd be a heap on the floor.

She shouldn't have told him about Will; she knew she shouldn't. But she hadn't been able to help herself, not after hearing about his girlfriend. She hadn't wanted him to feel alone, because she knew what guilt felt like and she could see it written all over his beautiful face.

It didn't matter whose son he was or what he had done before, he'd lost someone like she had and he felt responsible. He was trying to right the balance like she was and he had to know she knew what that meant.

She hadn't expected him to cross the room to hold her, to try to make it better, and it had taken her off guard. No one had ever done that for her and it felt like he'd reached inside her chest and pulled her heart out. All her defense mechanisms had kicked in and she'd tried to push him away. Except of course, being Zee, he wasn't to be pushed.

Now here she was, bent over the vanity with him standing hot and hard behind her, his silver gaze catching hers in the mirror. And she was trembling, shaking with desperation for him no matter that it had only been a matter of minutes since the last time. But she knew now it wasn't only because of their physical chemistry. There was something more here, something deeper.

They'd shared secrets and that forged a bond, no matter how much they didn't want it or tried to deny it.

It was there in his eyes as he stared at her, into her. As his hand trailed down her spine in a long, stroking movement. Bracing herself for hard and rough, the gentle touch made her shiver uncontrollably. Reminding her that for all that he was rough and dirty, there had been moments of gentleness. Moments when he'd taken care of her, been concerned for her comfort. He'd noticed her fear when he'd held her down the first time, and then afterward he'd run her a bath to soothe her tender skin. And then, just now, he'd crossed the room to hold her, an instinctive move to offer comfort.

She stared at him in the mirror, a sudden thought catching at her.

Was anyone gentle with him? Did anyone comfort him? Hold him? Did anyone look after him at all? He was a hard man all over, physically and emotionally, and given his past, it was no wonder. But everyone needed someone to hold them sometimes. Everyone needed to feel that there was someone there for them.

Zee's fingers trailed down her spine again and over the curve of her butt, sending another shiver through her, and she kept her gaze on those fascinating eyes of his, metallic, glittering.

Was anyone there for him? He had those friends of his at the garage, but she got the feeling that the relationships there were complicated, difficult. That they might be his friends, but they all had their own problems.

You could be there for him. It could be you.

But she couldn't. She had her own problems, her own debts to pay. Her own atonement to make. And if she wanted to be there for Zee, it could only be for tonight.

It would have to be enough.

His hand stroked the back of her thighs, still gentle, the tips of his fingers brushing her sex, making her shake. God, she'd have to do this now before he distracted her.

"Zee," she said softly. "Stop."

His hand on the back of her thigh halted. "What?"

She straightened and turned around, staring up into his face. Then she put her hands back on the vanity and pushed herself up on top of it. He frowned. "What the hell are you doing?"

Spreading her knees, she held out her arms. "Come here."

"Pretty girl, you're not in charge here. You don't get to give me orders."

So he was going to play hard to get, was he?

She leaned back on her hands, allowing her knees to fall open, letting him get a good view. "Why? Scared I might make you do something you don't want?"

His gaze dropped between her thighs. Stayed there. "Don't play with me, baby. You might not like what happens if you do."

"I'm not playing. But we've done this your way all night so far. I want to do it mine for a change." She paused, shifting her hips in a deliberately sensual movement. "Unless you're not secure enough in your manhood to let me have a little control."

Slowly he looked back up at her. "Jesus, Tamara."

"Well?" She raised an eyebrow. "I'm not going to ask again."

The intensity in his face eased, his mouth curving in an almost smile. Then he shook his head. "Fuck. Well, when you put it like that." Stepping forward, he came to stand between her thighs, sliding his hands up her legs, his fingers gripping her.

She looked up at him, held his gaze. Then she closed her legs around his hips, pressing her sex right up against the hot length of his cock. The flame in his gaze burned higher and his fingers slid farther up her thighs, pushing beneath her butt to gather her in his hands, squeezing her.

Bastard. He was hoping to distract her, no doubt.

Tamara put her hands on his chest and pressed them there,

the heat of his body slowly seeping through her. His skin was hot and smooth, the flames and feathers of his phoenix reaching across his right pec. She touched it, tracing the lines, stroking gently. It was beautifully drawn, a work of art. "This is gorgeous," she murmured.

He squeezed her again, his hips shifting, his cock pressing a little harder. Oh yeah, definitely he was trying to distract her. "I like it."

She ran her finger along the flaming wing that ran from his shoulder and down. "You said Rachel did it, right?"

"Yeah." He pushed his hands farther beneath her, his fingers heading for her sex.

Sneaky.

Tamara shifted on the vanity, angling herself against him. "She's an amazing artist." She ran her fingers along his collarbones, tracking the lines of them, the dips and hollows, the only fragile architecture in his strong frame.

He shivered. "What are you doing?"

"Admiring you." She let a finger rest in the vulnerable hollow of his throat, feeling the beat of his pulse. "What about the words on your back? What do they mean?"

"Stop." His hands on her butt squeezed hard in warning. "I'm not a fucking art gallery."

She looked up at him, keeping her fingers moving on his skin. The expression on his face had gone tight. "You don't like me touching you?"

"That's not exactly what I had in mind." He flexed his hips again, his cock pushing insistently against her. "Let me in, baby. Stop screwing around."

"I'm not screwing around." She spread her hands, slid them up over his broad shoulders and down his arms, caressing. "I think you're beautiful and I want to touch you."

"You wanna touch me, then how about you wrap that mouth of yours around my dick."

She could feel his muscles shifting and moving under her hand, the tension beginning to radiate off him. He didn't like her doing this, that much was obvious, and probably, if she kept it up, she'd lose him. He'd either walk away or turn it back on her, and this moment would be lost.

Well, that wasn't going to happen.

He was going to accept this from her whether he liked it or not.

Tamara ran a hand up behind his neck, curving her fingers around his nape. Then she urged his head down, his mouth meeting hers, and she kept it there, unmoving.

He stilled and she got the impression he was waiting to see what she'd do.

Gently, she traced his lips with her tongue, before deepening the kiss gradually, keeping it sweet and gentle, an exploration rather than a demand, rubbing her thumb against the back of his neck in a caress. Showing him that this wasn't just about mutual hunger and satisfying her desires.

That this was about him.

Another shudder went through him. "Tamara," he murmured roughly against her mouth, and she could feel him tense even further. "What the fuck?"

She exerted more pressure on the back of his neck, keeping him there. "Let me do this, Zee," she whispered. "Let me do this *for* you. Touch you. Kiss you. Please, let me give you this."

He pulled back and just for a second she saw the pain burn bright in his eyes. And grief and longing, and something in her own chest tightened in response.

"Why?" His hands were hard on her. "You don't need to give me anything."

"I know I don't. But I want to. You ran me a bath last time and you . . . held me." She swallowed. "Why can't I hold you?"

"Because I don't want you to." The words were bitten off, abrupt.

She didn't know how she knew, but she could tell he was lying. "Just for tonight." She raised her other hand, slid it over the short, black velvet of his hair. "Just this once. Please. For me."

He didn't speak, the look in his eyes unreadable. But he didn't pull away and eventually, when she pulled his mouth down again, he let her. And when she kissed him again, his mouth opened, letting her in.

Such a sweet kiss. Deepening into something hotter, more intense.

She ran her hands over his shoulders and down his back, tightening her thighs around his waist, desire clenching hard inside her as she held him, all that powerful strength between her hands.

Then she drew away, kissing down the strong column of his neck, licking the hollow of his throat. When his hands tangled in her hair, she thought he was going to pull her back. But he didn't, he just wound his fingers in deep and let her kiss him farther down the wide expanse of his chest, let her graze her tongue over his flat nipples, then feeling them harden. Hearing the harsh hiss of his breath.

Her hands slid down his sides, tracing the contours of his six-pack before sliding around his lean hips and down over the tight muscles of his butt. Stroking, caressing.

He was so beautiful, so strong. And though he might be rough, he was hugely protective too. A man who cared. A man who let things matter to him.

Tamara closed her eyes, his skin salty and spicy beneath her tongue, and she was suddenly desperate for more of him. To get closer to him.

Zee's fingers tightened in her hair and beneath her palm she could feel the beat of his heart, getting faster. "Tamara." His voice was harsh. "Pretty girl . . . I gotta be inside you. Please . . ."

Please. She'd never heard that from him before.

She lifted her mouth from his skin and looked up, reaching

to touch the hard, firm line of his jaw, his skin a little rough from his stubble.

There was something brilliant in his eyes and, this time, it wasn't anger. Only desire. Only hunger.

He reached for a drawer in the vanity near her thigh and opened it, pulling out a condom packet and holding it up. She took it from him and opened it, taking out the condom. Then she leaned back, making space between their bodies so she could roll it down over his cock, nice and slow. He shuddered as she did so, the breath hissing between his teeth. But he didn't move or touch her, letting her take the lead.

So she did, gripping the base of his shaft in her hand and guiding him, feeling the head of his cock pushing into her, the stretch of her sex around his a delicious burn.

She let out a soft ragged breath, because he was big and he felt so damn good. Then she flexed her hips and took him deeper, watching silver flare in his eyes and hearing the sharp intake of his breath.

She took him as deep as she could, then she locked her legs around his waist, holding him there. And then she began to move, deep and slow, never taking her gaze off his.

He kept one hand tangled in her hair, the other moving to the small of her back, bracing her as he followed her lead, the shift of his hips slow and deep as the swell of the sea.

"Christ," he whispered, his silver eyes searching hers. "What have you done to me?"

"Same thing you did to me." She slid her hands up his chest and around his neck, holding on to him. "You ruined me, Zee."

And because it was easier and because she'd said too much already, she pulled his mouth down for another kiss.

Letting the heat and the desire work its magic until they were both lost.

*   *   *

Much later, complaining he was ravenous, Zee urged her out of bed and took her to a nearby diner that, in his opinion, did the best Coney dogs in Detroit.

It was late, the night was sticky with heat and loud with the drunks on the sidewalks and spilling out of the bars, and she would have much rather been in bed with him. But she was hungry too, and besides, she couldn't deny that there was something special about walking the streets of Royal at his side, his fingers laced through hers. As if they were truly a couple and not just two people indulging their chemistry. As if, somehow, she belonged with him.

It was a dangerous thought, so she ignored it, concentrating instead on how different the streets seemed now she was with him. That first night, after his class, she'd stood out on the sidewalk and the place had seemed a jungle, while she'd been a prey animal among the lions.

Now, although it was still dangerous, there was something familiar about the streets, something recognizable. Two girls standing near a streetlight and taking selfies on their phones. A couple of young guys sitting on the sidewalk and drinking beer while they chatted. A family who'd had a late night on their way home, screaming, overtired kids in tow.

The same kind of people you'd see anywhere, in any neighborhood.

Zee gestured across the street to the large brick building they were passing. A pink neon sign that said SUGAR INK glowed in the windows. "Rachel's studio," he said.

It looked like a cool place, Tamara had to admit. "Does she do all your tats?"

"Yeah."

"Including the line from Ezekiel?"

His mouth curved, an almost smile. The first she'd seen that seemed to be genuine amusement. "You really wanna know what that means, don't you?"

"I'm curious." She tightened her fingers around his. "Come on, it's our last night. Might as well tell me."

"'The one who sins is the one who will die,'" he quoted softly. "It's for my dad."

She waited for him to elaborate, but he didn't and she decided not to push. They'd already talked too much about the painful stuff anyway. "Rachel seems nice," she said, changing the subject. "I mean, prickly, but nice."

His smile deepened and her heart turned over inside her chest in a way that should have worried her if she'd been paying attention to it. Because, damn, his smile was amazing. "You mean, she's a prickly bitch."

"Hey, I didn't say that."

He lifted a shoulder. "She is. Some stuff went down with Levi that . . . well, she's never been the same since."

Tamara glanced up at him, his beautiful face painted with neon as they walked. "What's Levi like? He's the one in jail, right?"

"Yeah. He's a good guy. At least he was." The smile faded from Zee's face. "Gideon says prison's changed him. Things are gonna be tough when he gets out."

She didn't know what to say to that, so she just squeezed his hand in wordless comfort.

He turned his head, glancing down at her, and for a moment she was lost in the silver gleam of his eyes. "You don't need to care about me, Tamara," he said softly. "That's not what this night is about."

Yeah, she knew. But it was too late. She did care.

"You had to protect yourself. . . . Sometimes that's all you can do."

He'd said that to her to make her feel better, to comfort her, and that meant whether he liked it or not, he cared too. A dangerous thing to think. Then again, here she was, out in one of

Detroit's dangerous neighborhoods, with a man who was danger incarnate. How much worse could it possibly get?

"I know," she said, and smiled. "Think of it as an acceptable sex side effect."

His eyes glimmered in the light and the grim set of his mouth relaxed. Then he lifted her hand and kissed the back of it. "Come on, I'm hungry. And for once it's not for you."

The diner was kind of low-rent, with scratched Formica tables, red booth seats, and cheap red neon signs. But Tamara didn't care. For once, in her borrowed T-shirt and hoodie, she blended in fine with the clubbers and drunks all after a late-night protein hit.

She slid into one of the booths, ignoring the stained table, grinning as Zee was pounced on by the very pretty waitress. He ordered them both Coney dogs and a Coke each, seemingly oblivious to the waitress's attempts at flirting.

"I think she likes you," Tamara murmured as the waitress left with their order.

He lifted a shoulder. "A lot of women like me."

"If you do say so yourself."

"Hey, it's a fact." He leaned back against the booth seat, fixing her with those silver eyes of his. "But it's not me they're looking at. It's this." He bent one arm, his biceps flexing in a way that had her mouth going dry. "The muscles and tats. The fight shit. That's all they want." His voice was causal, as if it didn't bother him. But she remembered how he'd been in the bathroom, when she'd touched him gently. How it had made him uncomfortable. She didn't think that was because he didn't want it.

"You are a fighter, it's true," she said carefully. "But that's not all you are."

He tipped his head back against the seat, staring at her from beneath surprisingly thick dark lashes. "And you know all about me, pretty girl?"

"You're also really protective." She leaned her elbows on the scratched Formica. "A warrior. Kind of like a knight or something."

His mouth curved. "A knight?"

"Sure." She grinned back at him. "My knight in shining armor. With a really big . . . sword."

Zee laughed and Tamara promptly forgot everything she'd been going to say. Lost her whole train of thought entirely. Because the laugh lit him up from the inside, the smile turning his mouth like sun coming up on a cold winter's day. Making everything around her seem brighter.

He was a beautiful man anyway. But when he laughed, he was to die for.

Her heart flipped, turning over and over, and she understood all of a sudden what was worse.

She could fall for him.

Chapter 13

Zee couldn't have said what had woken him. Perhaps it was the light that filled the room, which must mean it was morning. Or maybe it was the warmth of the woman in his arms, her blond hair lying like silk across his chest.

More likely though, it was the man standing at the foot of his bed holding a silver baseball bat in one hand and slapping it lightly across the palm of the other.

Every single cell in his body froze.

Holy fucking Christ.

The man was older, heavier, and there was gray in his black hair, deep lines around his light blue eyes and his mouth. But there was no mistaking the cold gleam in those eyes, or the edge in that smile.

Joshua Chase. His father.

There were a couple of guys in suits standing behind him, their expressions stony. The usual thugs.

Dread coiled tight in Zee's gut, but he ignored that, fixating on the fierce, black rage that came along with it instead.

So. After all that, his father had come to him. And not only had the prick broken into Zee's goddamn apartment, but he'd also found Zee with his arms wrapped around Tamara.

It's all a little too familiar. . . .

The dread coiled tighter. Jesus, he'd need to act fast if he wanted to get Tamara out of this without her attracting his father's attention. And the only way to do that was to pretend she meant nothing whatsoever to him.

Disentangled himself from her and not bothering to be gentle about it, Zee sat up. "Dad," he said flatly to the man at the end of the bed. "Wondered when you'd fucking turn up. Didn't bother to knock I see. Well, you can give us some goddamn privacy, okay?"

Beside him, Tamara had started to stir, shifting and turning over, her eyes opening. Then, as she spotted the fact they weren't alone, she gasped, grasping at the sheet and pulling it up over her.

"Hey boy." Joshua Chase's voice was a low rumble. "Been a while, hasn't it? Nice little piece you got there. Hope I'm not interrupting anything important."

Zee didn't bother looking at Tamara, keeping his gaze on his father instead. "No. Just some bitch I hooked up with last night."

"In that case, she might wanna get out of here." Joshua swung the baseball bat in a casual arc. "There's some father-son shit you and I need to sort out."

Tamara said nothing, but Zee could feel the tension in the warm body beside his.

The dread twisted inside him. "You heard the man," he said, keeping his voice utterly cold. "Time's up. Get your clothes and get outta here."

At first she didn't move and he wondered if she hadn't realized what was happening. But then, no, Tamara was smart. She'd know. Which meant she was probably hesitating because she was naked and didn't want three strange men looking at her while she got dressed.

Zee let out a breath and met his father's gaze. "I'm not fucking talking to you bare-assed. Go wait in the lounge and I'll be out in a minute."

Joshua stared at him a long moment. Then, abruptly, he laughed. "Ah, you always were a rebellious little shit. I like it. That attitude'll take you a long way." He glanced at the men behind him. "Whaddya say, boys? Shall we give him some privacy? Or do you feel like a free show from the pretty piece of pussy beside him."

"I feel like a free show," the prick closest to the door said.

"Yeah, me too," prick number two added, grinning.

His father shrugged. "You heard 'em. Come on, share with your old man."

Rage began to curl up inside Zee, but he said nothing, keeping it locked down and cold. He couldn't afford to show anything in front of this man, not a goddamn thing. Which meant if he was going to save Tamara, he had to throw her to the wolves.

Fuck. *Fuck.*

But she was already moving, sliding out of bed without hesitation and grabbing her clothes. She ignored the men standing there as she pulled up her jeans and there was a sulky look on her face, as if men with baseball bats coming into her bedroom was nothing out of the ordinary.

She was brave, his pretty girl. He had to give her that.

Since she had no bra and he'd torn her tank top the night before, she grabbed his T-shirt, pulling it on over her head and then flicking her hair out from under the collar. She didn't seem to care that complete strangers watched her dress, their eyes following her every movement.

It made him so angry she had to deal with that. Angry and possessive. It made him want to take them down. Smash their faces in, deal out some pain. A couple of minutes and he'd have them begging for mercy. Of course that was if they weren't packing any handguns, which obviously they would be.

Christ, he'd love to get his fingers around their throats. Especially his father's.

Joshua smiled benignly at him as Tamara moved toward the doorway, her chin lifted, and Zee held the other man's gaze, making sure not to look after her as she left.

That's it. You won't see her again. You won't get to be her knight in shining armor. . . .

He crushed the flash of pain that went through him at the thought. Crushed all the fucking feelings. He couldn't afford them, not now.

"So," he said casually, throwing back the sheet and reaching for the jeans that lay on the floor. "What the fuck do you want?"

Joshua swung his bat again. "I'm impressed with you, boy. Got away from me real good. And I gotta admit, it was smart to stay in Detroit. I had people looking out for you from New York all the way to fucking Florida."

Impressed? Jesus. When he'd been ten that had been all he'd wanted. To impress his dad, make him proud. But that was years ago, before he'd realized how big a bastard his father actually was. How much greed and power had overtaken him, turned him into the monster he was now.

A monster Zee would have become himself if not for Madison.

"Yeah, well, they didn't look hard enough, did they?" Zee pulled his jeans up and fastened them. "Get to the point. I gotta get to work."

"Nice. Holding a down a job and everything. You've made good." His father nodded approvingly. "Like I said, I'm impressed. Been watching you for a while now, did you know that? Finally tracked you down a few years back."

It took effort, but Zee managed to keep the shock from his face. Shit, how had that happened? What had he done wrong? Had someone seen him?

His father gave a soft laugh. "You look surprised, boy.

Think you were safe here? Think you were hidden? This is my town, remember. Nothing stays hidden from me here for long. Especially when word gets back of some fighter taking on all comers and beating the shit out of them."

Ah. Fuck. He should have known that in the end, it would be the fights that brought him down. It had always been a calculated risk, but he'd done it anyway because he'd needed the outlet they gave him.

Zee pushed his hands into his pockets, clenching them tight into fists, trying to calm himself. Trying to find the space he went to when he fought. Clear and cold and calm. "Why wait then? Why are you here cluttering up my fucking bedroom now?"

"'Cause I had other more important things to do. And it looked like you weren't going anywhere in a hurry." Joshua took a scan around the room, pursing his lips. "Yep, nowhere in a hurry is where you're going all right. A mechanic in a shop, teaching kids in a gym. It's downright adorable."

Rage licked down Zee's spine, black and intense. He clenched his fists tighter. "Like I said, get to the point, cocksucker."

"Such a thing to call your old man. You need to learn a bit of respect, *Damian*." He glanced behind him, to prick number one. "Time for his first lesson."

Typical. His father always resorted to violence to make his point, something Zee had learned from him after all. Well, let him. Pain didn't frighten Zee, this was what he knew. The threat and the response, pure physical aggression. The prick could certainly try to deal out a lesson. Good thing Zee had aced that particular class.

"Oh," his father said casually, as the guy moved toward him. "By the way, you're gonna stand there and take it like a man. 'Cause if you don't, that outreach center you love so much might have a fire on its hands."

Zee went still, a spear of cold slicing through him.

*Did you really think you could take him on? He has too
many resources. Too much power. And you have none.*

His father's prick of a henchman was in front of Zee now,
grinning as his fist pulled back.

"Be a good boy and take your punishment," Joshua said.
"I'm sure you wouldn't want to be responsible for anyone else
getting hurt."

Zee felt the rage, bright and fierce. He wanted to take the
guy in front of him out; one hard punch to the jaw should do it.
Then he'd move fast, grab that bat out of his father's hands . . .

The fist that came at his face hit him hard. Lights exploded
in his head, pain radiating out in jagged spikes like a cracked
pane of glass. There was blood in his mouth, a hard pressure
against his knees. And he realized with a sudden shock that he
was on the floor.

"Sorry about that." Joshua's voice sounded muffled. "But
I'm a big believer in the school of hard knocks and Jay here is
expert in dealing them out. He used to be a boxer, did you
know?"

Zee spat out the blood in his mouth. There was a black haze
over his vision, fury roaring in his head. He wanted nothing
more than to get to his feet, then get his hands around his father's throat, the way he had years ago before his father's body-
guards had managed to pull him off.

Then something cold rested against the back of his head.
The muzzle of a gun.

The rage froze inside his chest.

His father's smile faded, leaving nothing but the cold blue
glitter in his eyes. "Get up, boy."

Slowly, Zee straightened and pushed himself to his feet, resisting the urge to touch his throbbing jaw.

"Here's the deal," Joshua went on. "You've had a lovely va-
cation down here in Royal, but now it's over. Now it's time to
come home. Understand me?"

You always knew it would come to this. You always knew you couldn't run forever.

"Come home?" His voice sounded thick. "To you?"

"Of course to me. No one leaves, Damian. No one ever leaves. Except in a box."

Fury and a strangely familiar helplessness gathered in his chest. "If you want someone to be your bitch, you've got hundreds of pricks to choose from. You don't need me, you fucker."

"True. All true." His father wandered over to him, that bat swinging in another slow arc. "But here's the thing." Joshua stopped right in front of him and it gave Zee a perverse kind of pleasure to see that the prick was shorter than he was. "You're my blood, boy. And my blood does not skulk in an alleyway like a dog. 'Cause that's what this neighborhood of yours is. It's an alleyway. It's trash. And you're wasted here."

A terrible echo of Madison's voice sounded in his head. *"You're wasted here, Damian. You should be out doing something better for yourself."*

"No," Zee said, to his father. To her. "I'm not going fucking anywhere with you."

"Hmmm. I was afraid you'd say that."

The cold muzzle of the gun pressed harder against the back of Zee's head, but he didn't flinch. "Kill me and I still won't be going anywhere with you."

His father smiled. "Why would I kill you? That would be all kinds of wrong. No, I have something better than that. Let's call it . . . incentive."

Just like that, the dread was back, worming deeper inside him, chilling him right down to the bone.

Tamara.

No, it couldn't be her. They knew nothing about her, nothing at all. As far as they were concerned, she was just a chick he'd slept with, whom he'd just tossed out of his bed without a second glance.

Which meant . . .

His stomach gave a sickening lurch.

His father's smile widened. "I'm sure you don't want anything to happen to the lovely folks at the garage. Nice bunch. Especially the little one with the golden eyes. She's pretty."

"Touch them and I'll kill you," he said, the fury bleeding helplessly into his voice.

"Ah, well, that'll be up to you." His father slapped the bat against his palm again. "Come back home and I'll forget all about this corner of Detroit. It'll be my gift to you."

You always knew there would be no escape.

"And if I don't?" A stupid question, but he had to ask. He needed to hear it.

"If you don't?" Joshua shrugged, but there was a feral light in his eyes. "Then I'll torch this shithole down to the ground and your friends along with it."

Tamara stumbled over a broken crack in the pavement. She barely noticed, walking as quickly as she could without actually breaking into a run. A run would definitely draw attention and she couldn't afford that, not now.

The breath burned in her chest, fear a cold weight pressing down on her, and she had to keep resisting the urge to look behind her to see if she was being followed.

The moment she'd opened her eyes, she'd known the man standing at the foot of Zee's bed wasn't going to be good news. When the sleep had cleared from her eyes, she'd even seen the resemblance. The hair was grayer and there were many more lines, but she'd traced the shape of that face with her fingers the night before. She knew. It was his father, the apparent godfather of Detroit.

Zee hadn't even looked at her, telling her to get out and get dressed, his voice cold. As if they hadn't gotten hot dogs together, then spent the night in each other's arms. But that didn't worry her because she'd guessed he was trying to kill any link between them to protect her.

She'd played along, ignoring the cold clutch of fear inside her at the sound of that bat slapping against Joshua Chase's palm. At the lascivious looks in the eyes of the two goons standing behind him. She'd even tried to be a bit sulky, as if she was offended her night was ending like this.

But getting out without any further incident didn't make her feel any better, or dislodge the fear sitting like a stone in her chest. Because Zee was still in that room.

She had no idea what his father wanted from him, but whatever it was, it was bad. She couldn't leave him there to deal with it on his own. She had to get help. First thing to do would be to call the police, but she had the sense that if she called the police to tell them a man with a baseball had threatened her in Royal Road, they'd probably tell her to get in line.

No, she needed help and she needed help fast, and since there was only one other place she knew of in Royal to go to, that's where she went.

Gideon's.

It felt like it took forever to get there and this time she didn't bother knocking, just pushed open the door and went right in.

Gideon was standing at the workbench, where he had a motorcycle up on a stand, fitting some piece of metal onto it. He turned as she came in, the smile that started to curve his mouth fading away as he caught the expression on her face.

"Tamara?" He dropped the piece of metal back on the counter. "Are you okay?"

"No . . . no, I'm not." She came right up to him. "They've got Zee. You've got to help him. I don't know what to do. I woke up and there was a guy with a baseball bat and he had others with him and—"

"Stop." Gideon's voice vibrated with command, and she found herself shutting up almost instantly.

His dark eyes had gone hard, but the hand that took her elbow and guided her to the plastic chair was gentle. "Now. Sit down and explain what happened properly."

Her legs gave way and she collapsed into the chair, feeling like she'd run around half of Detroit. Fear burned inside her, but she fought it, taking a couple of deep breaths. "Okay, so you know about Zee's father?"

"Yeah, I know."

"Well, I stayed with Zee last night. And when we woke up this morning, his father was standing in the bedroom."

Gideon's expression became blank, the black glimmer of his eyes the only sign of his fury. "When was this?"

"Now. I came from Zee's straight here." She took another breath. "Zee told me to get out so I don't know what's happening or what his father wants or anything. But . . . he's by himself in there, Gideon. We have to help him."

Gideon cursed, low and vicious. His gaze went to the office up the stairs, then he looked over at the entrance to the garage. "You gotta get out of here, Tamara. Because if they've got him, we're gonna be next on the list. And if you wanna help Zee, the best thing you can do is be far away from here."

"But—"

Loud voices drifted in from beyond the metal front doors, the sounds of car doors slamming.

Before she could say anything more, Gideon grabbed her elbow and hauled her out of the plastic chair, hurrying her to the back door of the garage.

"Wait, Gideon," Tamara said breathlessly. "I can't leave."

He pushed the door open. "Yes, you fucking can. Go home, Tamara. Believe me, Zee wouldn't want you messed up in this."

She knew he was right, that there was nothing she could do

to help Zee now. But pain had lodged in her chest, along with frustration and anger. Goddammit, she hated feeling so helpless like this.

"I want to know he's okay," she said fiercely, grabbing his arm and holding on tight. "I *have* to, Gideon. Please."

Gideon stared at her a moment. Then he gave a sharp nod. "Yeah, okay, I promise I'll let you know." His voice deepened, that commanding note rumbling through it once more. "Now get the hell out of here."

He gave her a little shove, pushing her out the door and locking it behind her.

Tamara stood there for a moment, suddenly cold and shaky.

There was no Zee now to take her in his arms and push her up against a wall. Do dirty things to her. He was having to confront the man who'd killed his girlfriend and he was having to do it alone.

She wrapped her arms around herself, taking yet another deep breath. Unfortunately though that meant inhaling the scent of him since she was still wearing his tee.

That's it. You'll never see him again.

Her eyes prickled, but she blinked hard. No tears. Gideon was right, she had to get out of here, get back to safety. Zee didn't need to be afraid for her as well as all the other shit he was no doubt having to deal with right now.

Forcing herself to move, Tamara quickly walked out of the garage's parking lot and headed down the sidewalk, digging her phone out from her jeans as she did so and calling herself a cab.

It took fifteen minutes for the cab to arrive and then, once they were on the road, the morning traffic was horrendous. It reminded her suddenly that it was, of course, a workday and that she hadn't even bothered to check the time.

Oh shit. This was going to be bad, she just knew it. And sure enough, when she checked her phone, she saw it was after nine.

Almost as soon as that fact settled over her, cold as a dusting of light snow, her phone rang. Of course it was Scott, no doubt checking to see where she was and why she wasn't at her desk.

She hit the deny button and shoved her phone back in her pocket, fear still sitting like lead in her gut. Scott was the last person on earth she wanted to talk to right now and he could damn well wait until she was ready, work or not.

Once she'd gotten back to her apartment, she stripped off her clothes and got into the shower, trying to wash away the terrible cold feeling inside her. But unfortunately she didn't feel any better as she got out again and dressed, going back into the kitchen on autopilot and putting coffee on.

Then she paced back and forth, unable to settle. Eventually she couldn't put it off any longer and gave Scott a call, piling on the bullshit about having a cold and being too sick to come in. He sounded disbelieving and she couldn't say she blamed him. She was full of shit and sounded it. Yet she couldn't bring herself to care.

She didn't know what Zee's father was going to do to him, but she couldn't shake the feeling that Zee was in danger. That his friends were in danger.

Keep it locked down, Tamara. Keep it under control.

She went over to the couch and sat down, her arms wrapped tightly around her.

That's what her parents had always said. Keep calm. Keep it under control. So that's what she'd always done, fearful that somehow the thing that had made her pick up that gun and shoot her brother would escape again. That desperate fear, that intense anger.

She could feel it inside her now, burning a hole in her gut like acid, needing an outlet. Wanting to go help him, save him, protect him any way she could.

But what could she do? She'd only get in the way. Besides, it wasn't her world. It wasn't her problem and she definitely hadn't fallen for him. He was only some guy she'd slept with a few times and told a few secrets to, and no doubt he could protect himself very well. He was the warrior. He didn't need her.

It wasn't as if he was special.

Tamara stared sightlessly at the windows opposite her.

She should chalk him up to experience, put him behind her once and for all. He was only supposed to be temporary in the first place, a chance to step outside herself if only for a moment. His life and his past weren't anything to do with her.

That's what he'd wanted anyway.

With an effort, Tamara forced away the feelings of helplessness, of anger, of frustration. The need and the longing and the sharp, painful thing that had taken root in her heart.

She kept it locked down and under control.

Then she called Scott back, told him she was feeling much better now.

Then she went to work as if nothing had happened.

Zee wiped away the last of the blood, then examined himself in the mirror. It was only a cut to go with all the rest. Only another bruise. Nothing major, no big deal. He wouldn't even need stitches.

Somehow that made it even worse.

He dumped the bloody towel into the laundry hamper, then turned and walked out of the bedroom.

In the middle of the bed was the present his father had left him. The metal baseball bat, sleekly gleaming in the middle of the white quilt.

A part of him wanted to pick up that bat and take to the walls with it, smash great holes in the drywall, shatter the windows, break the bed. Let out the thick, black anger that seemed to be woven through the fabric of his very soul. And why not? Why the *fuck* shouldn't he?

His father had given him two days to end his life in Royal

and smashing shit up here would definitely be one way of saying good-bye. It was almost expected since he was, after all, Joshua's son and causing a bit of property damage would probably end up being the least of his crimes.

No doubt his father had worse planned for him.

Zee took in a slow breath, his hands curling into fists.

What he really wanted to do was take that bat to his father's smug face. Smash him into oblivion and his fucking empire with him. But of course he couldn't. Not without putting at risk everyone he cared about. Everything that mattered to him.

Still, he'd managed to get one concession from his father—if Zee went back to him, Joshua would stay out of Royal for good. Joshua didn't give a shit about much, but he'd always prided himself on being a man of his word and Zee had made him give it. Which meant that at least Royal was protected and that was something.

What about the promise you made to Madison?

The anger inside him twisted. That was a promise he should never have made. He'd been naïve, stupid. Blinded by his grief for her and his desperate hope that she was right. That he was a better man. That he could make a difference.

She was wrong and so was he. He couldn't escape his destiny any more than she'd been able to escape the car that had run her off the road. This was the way it was always going to end and the sooner he accepted it the better.

So you're just going to be the old man's bitch for the next twenty years?

The fury cooled, hardened. No. Fuck no. He'd made the decision to stand and fight, and he would. Except now he'd have to do it in a way that would protect his friends, and that meant embracing his dark side fully. Going all the way.

He'd kill the fucker first opportunity he got. A suicide mission any way he looked at it, but so what? Royal would be safe and so would his friends. And most especially so would Tamara.

Seemed a fair trade.

A ragged bit of black fabric beside the bed caught his eye. Forcing himself to move, he went over and picked it up. It was a piece of soft cotton, expensive shit. One half of the tank top he'd torn off Tamara the previous night.

It felt as if someone had put their hands around his heart and squeezed hard.

He lifted the cotton and inhaled, smelling flowers and musk. All the soft, beautiful things he couldn't have anymore. Could never have anymore. Her touch on his skin, gentle, as if he mattered. As if he was worth something.

You're my knight in shining armor. . . .

His chest ached. No, he couldn't think about what she'd said to him last night in the diner. He'd never been anyone's knight, still less hers. At least now he wouldn't have to worry about her. Waking up to find Joshua standing at the foot of the bed should have scared her into the middle of next week and with any luck, she'd never come down Royal way ever again.

The hands around his heart squeezed tighter and for a second he couldn't breathe.

She'd felt good in his arms that morning. In the moments between waking and realizing they weren't alone, the warmth of her there had felt . . . right. Christ, if only he'd had another couple of hours with her. Just the morning. The chance to say a proper good-bye . . .

Zee curled the fabric into a ball in his fist.

Fuck that. No point in thinking about it. They didn't get a proper good-bye and that's the way it should be. Better for her, better for him. Tamara was safe now and that's the only thing that mattered.

He moved over to the wastebasket in the corner of the room and tossed the soft bit of fabric into it.

Dismissing Tamara utterly from his mind, Zee finished dressing, then he let himself out of his apartment and began heading in the direction of Gideon's. Because the guy needed to know what was happening, the decision Zee had made. Gideon would probably be a prick about it, but that was too fucking bad. The deal was done already. Pity he wouldn't be able to tell his friend his real plan, but that would involve Gideon trying to argue him out of it, no doubt. Zee couldn't let that happen.

There was a black car parked discreetly down one end of the street, not far from the garage. No prizes for guessing who that was. One of Joshua's men sent to keep an eye on Zee and those who mattered to him. Checking up to make sure Zee did what he was told, like the good son he now had to pretend to be.

Resisting the urge to flip the guy off, Zee pushed open the garage door and stepped inside, ignoring the familiar smells of engine oil and grease, forcing down the knowledge that this would be one of the last times he'd come here and the pain that came along with it.

Gideon was sprawled in the plastic chair, a beer in one hand despite the fact that it was relatively early in the morning. He looked like he was relaxing after a hard day's work, except for the black flame of rage in his eyes.

Ice slid down Zee's back. Fuck, looked like his goddamn father had paid Gideon a visit too.

Zee didn't bother with a hello. "You okay? Zoe? Rachel?"

"Yeah." Gideon didn't ask him what he was talking about. Which meant that fucking Joshua had definitely been here. "We had an early heads-up. Tamara came here and told me what had gone down at your place so I sent Zoe to find Rachel and take her to my place."

Something shifted inside Zee's chest. Shock. "Tamara came here?" And then the shock became colder. "Where is she now?"

"I pushed her out the back before your dad's boys showed up. She sent me a text to tell me she got a cab and was on her way home."

Thank Christ for that. He didn't want to acknowledge the relief that flooded through him so he pretended it didn't exist.

"Glad to hear it. But I gotta talk to you, Gideon."

The look in the other man's eyes was hard, unyielding. "I can guess already what you're gonna say. You're gonna tell me that you're leaving Royal to join his fucking empire."

Well, he'd known Gideon wasn't going to be happy about it. But knowing that didn't make seeing the anger and hostility in his friend's eyes any easier to deal with.

Zee folded his arms and kept his voice utterly cold. "It's the only way, man. If I don't go back to him, he'll torch the place. Do you really want that to happen?"

Gideon picked up his beer and took a long, slow sip. "You fucking idiot. You really think I'd let it? I have connections, Zee. I have people I can call to help. We're not in this alone."

Of course Gideon was going to argue. The prick had a thing about not being pushed around by anyone.

"You can't win this fight," Zee said flatly. "He's got half the fucking city in his pocket and most of the gangs, too. There's no way to take him down, not if you don't want a full-on war on your hands. And this neighborhood can't deal with that, you know it can't."

It was the truth. There would be no good outcome to an outright fight, or at least none that didn't involve possible loss of life and that was not acceptable. This was the only way. The best way.

Gideon's jaw was tight. "It's not your decision to make."

"I don't care who's fucking decision it is. You really want all we've worked for here in Royal to be destroyed? You want Zoe threatened? Rachel?"

The look in Gideon's eyes became blacker, harder. Sharp as obsidian. "No one fucking threatens my family, Zee. No one."

The guy had no idea. He really thought a few connections

were going to make a difference compared to what Joshua was capable of? Jesus.

"I made a deal, Gideon," he said, holding the other man's gaze, unflinching. "I go back to Dad and he stays out of Royal. For good."

"No," Gideon said. "Fuck no. I did not take you on at the center, give you a job and a place to stay just so you could walk out on us. I don't care what that prick promised you."

"Like you said, it's not your decision to make. I gotta do what I gotta do for the good of everyone, and if that means leaving Royal to make sure my fucker of a father stays out of this neighborhood, then that's what I'll do."

The other man's lip curled. "Oh sure, make it all about keeping Royal free and us safe. I never thought you of all people would be such a fucking pussy, Zee."

Just for a moment, the black anger escaped Zee's grip and he found himself taking a step toward the other man before he could stop himself. "What the fuck would you know about it?" he demanded. "You ever had a death on your conscience?"

"I got a lot worse than a death on my conscience." Gideon's face was hard, his black eyes fathomless. "And I know when it's time to stand and fight."

"He killed my girlfriend, Gideon. My dad had her car run off the fucking road. Wanna know why? Because I wanted out. Because I wanted a normal goddamn life. Get married, have kids, all that shit. Dad took exception to that, thought Madison was a bad influence. So he got rid of her. Now you tell me, wouldn't that make you think twice if people you cared about were threatened?"

Gideon's expression didn't change one iota. "No." His voice was hard with certainty. "Because I'd fucking fight for them."

There was no getting through to him, as Zee should have known. The guy had a huge blind spot when it came to defending his patch, and telling Gideon his actual mission would probably only end up making it worse.

No, the only way to make sure everyone stayed out of harm's way was to do what he'd always done and keep it to himself. That way the only person who got hurt was him.

"Call me a pussy all you want," Zee said. "But going back to him will keep you all alive and everything we've worked toward here safe."

Gideon carefully put his beer bottle down on the floor. There was something menacing about the way he did it, something dangerous. "You seriously think I would let him hurt us?"

"I'm not arguing about this, Gideon. I'm telling you. This is what's gonna happen."

His friend stared at him long and hard. Zee had to steel himself to hold the other man's gaze. "You don't trust me," Gideon said at last. "Even now, even after ten years, you don't trust me."

He's right. You know he is.

The realization was harsh and, unfortunately, true. Zee *didn't* trust him. Mostly because he didn't trust anyone and never had. Not since the moment his father had told him why Madison had to die.

"No," Zee answered in the same flat tone that Gideon had used. "Not where my father is concerned. Shit, I don't even trust myself."

Gideon's eyes were black as tar. "It wasn't your fault that your girlfriend died. You know that, right?"

"Of course it was my fucking fault. If I hadn't wanted to get out, she'd still be alive."

But Gideon slowly shook his head. "You didn't run her car off the road. Your dad did. Killing her was his choice. And that's the thing. It's always a choice, man. I thought you knew that."

Of course it was a choice. Except sometimes there were

right choices and sometimes there were wrong ones. And he'd made a shitload of wrong choices in his life. It was time to make the right one for a change.

Zee gave a short laugh, the sound hollow. "Yeah, and I've made mine."

"Bullshit. You're not making a choice, you're just reacting. A real choice would be to stand and fight with us, with your fucking family."

His anger stirred, fighting against the leash Zee kept on it. Because what if he did? What if he told his father to stick it?

Everyone would fucking die.

"You'd really want me to do that?" he demanded. "Risk some collateral damage?"

"Sometimes you have to make a stand when something's important."

"And if that collateral damage was Zoe?"

Ice shifted in Gideon's eyes. "Not gonna happen."

"I thought that about Madison. And she died. So that's not a risk I'm gonna take, Gideon. Not now, not ever. I thought you of all people would understand."

The other man's gaze was impenetrable. "So that's it? You're just gonna leave us? What am I gonna tell Levi when he comes back and asks where you are? And what about Tamara? You're gonna turn your back on her, too?"

Another twist of the barbed wire that felt like it was threaded around his heart. Fuck, what was this shit? Now was not the time to be getting soft. He had to be cold. Hard as ice. "What about her? She was just some chick I fucked. No big deal."

"Uh-huh. Right. So you're gonna deny her just like you denied us? Nice move, asshole. She was terrified for you. You should at least let her know you're okay."

"You don't know shit about Tamara so how about you just stay the fuck out of it?"

"But you just told me she was some chick you fucked so why the hell do you care?"

Christ, why the hell was he *still* arguing? Hadn't he decided there was no point?

Zee swung around, turning back toward the garage door. He didn't have time for this crap. Gideon was going to find out soon enough about the choice Zee had made.

"You're a fucking coward, Zee," Gideon growled from behind him. "You're isolating yourself when you should be standing strong with us."

Zee didn't turn. He pulled open the door instead.

"You're better than this, you fucker. You're better than him and you know it!"

Zee slammed the door behind him as he left.

Yeah, that's what they all said, but they were wrong.

Because the truth was he wasn't better. He never had been. But at least this way he'd take his father with him. Surely Madison would have to be proud of that.

Chapter 14

Tamara leaned against the white stone parapet that ran around the terrace of her parent's massive Grosse Pointe house. The whole place had been modeled on a fifteenth-century French chateau, with terraces and rolling lawns that faced the lake, an avenue of oaks bordering the driveway, and two stories of the most expensive decor money could buy.

Tamara hated it. And she hated it even more since her mother had told her to go out on the terrace to get some air for fifteen minutes—a pretext to get her out of the house so they could prepare for the "surprise."

The night air was thick and hot, carrying the scent of roses from the gardens not far off, and she couldn't help shivering, which was odd because it wasn't cold.

Perhaps it was just nerves. There were a lot of people in her mother's formal drawing room and she knew what they were all waiting for even though they thought she didn't.

As she'd gone out onto the terrace, her father had caught her eye and given her a meaningful look. Then Robert—having made the trip from New York especially for the weekend—had caught her just as she was walking out the doors and slid an arm around her, leaning in as if for a kiss. For some reason she'd found herself wanting to pull away from him, the heat of his body making her uncomfortable. Strange when, although she'd never been all that attracted to him, she'd never actually found it uncomfortable being near him.

Not so strange. It's not him you want.

Tamara turned around and leaned against the cool stone of the parapet.

No, it wasn't Robert she wanted. She never had. And she'd been okay with that once, had thought that it didn't matter. But of course it did.

You can't think about him. You can't think about Zee.

But that didn't stop thoughts of him creeping into her head, following her around like ghosts. Anything could set it off. The throaty roar of a car in the street outside. The heavy step of someone's boots on the ground. Or even just the perfectly pressed suits and polite conversation of the men she worked with, each and every one of them the opposite of the man she couldn't stop thinking about.

She'd thought throwing herself into her work would help, but it hadn't. She'd gotten a text from Gideon the afternoon she'd left Royal telling her that Zee was okay, but he hadn't said anything else. And she'd had to stop herself from texting back more questions, because they'd had their one night, her final fling. That was supposed to be the end, that's what they'd agreed.

Yet those questions went around and around in her head, haunting her. Gideon had said he was okay, but what did that mean? And what was his father going to do? Did it mean he was going to have to go back to him? Leave the life he'd created for himself and be sucked into the world that had killed his girlfriend?

She hadn't been able to leave it alone. Hadn't been able to stop thinking about it, and that wasn't supposed to happen.

She'd told herself the night of his fight that she'd let herself have him one more time, then she'd go on with her life, with her career, and with Robert. Moving on and putting her terrible past behind her, the way her parents had encouraged her. Giving them the future they'd wanted for Will, the future she'd taken from them when she'd pulled that trigger.

Zee was *not* part of that future. He wasn't part of the life she and her parents had planned, and he definitely didn't have anything to do with putting her past behind her. In fact, being with him had only brought it all screaming back.

She couldn't see him again. No matter what he'd begun to mean to her, she couldn't.

Yet despite that, she'd taken to Googling Joshua Chase at work, trying to find out anything she could about him. There wasn't much other than articles about him being one of Detroit's biggest property investors, particularly interested in buying up the city's abandoned buildings. There was nothing that suggested he was anything other than totally legit apart from a few rumors that he wasn't quite as "clean" as he made out. But those rumors were a couple of years old and there hadn't been anything that suggested sketchy behavior since.

It was definitely a cover-up, Tamara was certain. She remembered the sound of the bat slapping against his palm, the utterly cold look in his blue eyes. The face of a man who'd done terrible things and who didn't give a shit about it. A man who was prepared to do anything to get his own way.

Even kill an innocent woman whose only crime had been to love his son and want better for him.

In many ways, she should have stopped there. Left well enough alone. But thoughts of Zee had her going deeper into Joshua Chase's business dealings. She had access to a lot of financial databases through Lennox and she used that access shamelessly, delving into the many companies that all seemed to relate back to Chase in some way, that he'd either invested money in or were owned by him.

He had his fingers in all sorts of different pies, enough for her to realize just how powerful the guy was, how much money and influence he had. It was scary. No wonder Zee had wanted to get out. In fact, it was a damn miracle he'd managed to stay out for as long as he had.

Then she found something. A connection that had made her get up from her computer and go for a walk just to turn over all the implications in her head.

That Joshua Chase had political ambitions was obvious from all the news sources she'd read about him, and they were quite serious political ambitions. Given that, it was amazing no one had made any connection between him and the criminal underground, but no one had so far. Which meant he was very good at cleaning up after himself—handy since he was currently running for mayor. He already had a campaign fund and, judging from the number of donations it had received, there were a lot of people who were quite happy to support those ambitions.

Especially the biggest pledge. Her father.

It didn't surprise her that her father would donate to his campaign fund—he'd always been a man who looked for opportunities where he could get them, and perhaps he was hoping for a little mutual political back-scratching should Chase become mayor.

Tamara didn't know how she could use this or even whether she should, especially when she'd been telling herself that she was supposed to be putting Zee behind her once and for all, but the information stuck in her brain and refused to budge.

Maybe it could help; maybe at some time, in some way, she could use it to help Zee.

Later that day she'd texted Zee that she had something that

might be useful and to let her know if he wanted it. But all she'd gotten back was a terse message telling her to never text or call his number again.

It had hurt, no denying it, even though she'd told herself not to take it to heart. He was probably trying to protect her by pushing her away; at least that was the explanation she clung to rather than that he genuinely didn't care.

She hadn't heard anything since and, no matter what she told herself, it continued to hurt.

You're supposed to be moving on, remember?

Music from inside drifted over the terrace, the sound of laughter slipping through the windows.

Of course she was. And soon her mother was going to come to get her, leading her inside to her "surprise." Robert and an engagement ring, and a bright, successful future. There would be a massive society wedding here at her parents' place, and eventually she and Robert would shift to New York, since Lennox had a branch office there. She'd work her way to the top and then maybe she'd take some time off to have children. Or maybe she wouldn't. Maybe she'd hire a nanny and work while she had her kids.

Whatever, it would be a busy, fulfilling life that would make her parents proud, give them what they should have had if Will hadn't died.

Her phone chimed. She looked down where she'd put it on the parapet beside her. The screen had lit up, telling her she had a text.

She blinked, then went utterly still.

Meet me at the top of the driveway. Z.

Tamara sucked in a shaky breath, unable to stop herself from glancing at the doors that led to the terrace. They were firmly closed and it didn't look like anyone was coming to get her soon.

She reached for her phone and picked it up, her hands shaking. She shouldn't text him. She should be putting him behind her and moving on. Right?

Yeah, and look how well you've been doing that the past week.

Crap. Who was she kidding?

Tamara typed out a reply before she could second-guess herself. *Why?*

His response was quick. *I need to talk to you. Not long.*

Didn't you tell me not to text or call you again?

Please, Tamara.

It was the please that got her. She swallowed, her throat gone tight, her heartbeat wild. *I'm at my parents' place.*

I know. Come to the top of the drive.

Oh hell. Was she really going to say no? This would be the last time she'd ever see him again and, after all, they hadn't even had a proper good-bye thanks to his damn father. There was that information she had too. She could pass that on to him in person. And if her mother came out and she wasn't there, she could always say she'd gone for a walk in the gardens, get some fresh air and crap. It wasn't as if she was leaving for good or anything.

Taking one last glance toward the doors, Tamara went down the terrace stairs and down onto the perfectly manicured lawn in front of the house. Then she headed toward the driveway and the big stand of oaks that lined it.

Shadows moved around her as she walked, gravel crunching beneath the deep blue Jimmy Choo stiletto sandals Robert had brought her back from New York and insisted she wear. They were perfect with the strapless blue silk cocktail dress she'd bought with her mother the day before so clearly he'd had help.

She was conscious now of how the sandals hurt her feet and how tight the dress was, a costume that didn't seem to fit very well.

It's never fitted and you know it. You've just been ignoring it all these years.

No, it never had. The only time she'd felt truly at ease, truly herself, had been when she wasn't wearing anything at all. When she'd been naked in Zee's arms.

The warm night breeze blew over her bare shoulders, making her shiver. Making her want things she shouldn't. Things like getting into his car and telling him to take her away from her parents, from Robert, from the obligation of trying to be something and someone she wasn't and never would be. From the need to atone for what she'd done.

But she'd killed her own brother and there was no escape from that.

The shadows by the oaks were deep and she should have been scared. But she felt no fear as she moved toward the massive wrought-iron gates that both warned people off and trumpeted the importance of the owners.

There was a small gate to the side that she pressed in a code for, unlocking it and stepping outside onto the sidewalk. The street beyond was wide and leafy, with only a handful of houses on either side, and no traffic whatsoever.

Well, almost no traffic.

Opposite the gates and a little way down the street, a low-slung black car was parked under a tree, a still figure leaning against it. A figure that suddenly straightened as she came out and yet made no move toward her.

Tamara's heartbeat accelerated, a great rush of adrenaline flooding through her veins.

Zee.

She crossed the street, her heels tapping on the asphalt, trying to get a handle on herself, trying not to lose it completely and fling herself into his arms. Because now he was here, now he was close, she wanted to touch him, feel his hands on her skin, have his arms around her. Wanted to look into his intense silver gaze, the one that saw the woman she was deep inside.

The figure by the car didn't move, waiting there tall and broad and still. So very still.

She came closer and her heart squeezed tight in her chest, turning over and over and over. Because even though it had only been a week, it felt like it had been years since she'd seen him. Since she'd last seen that darkly intense face of his and those astonishing, brilliant gray eyes. Since she'd touched that lean, powerful body and heard his husky, gritty voice, been enveloped by the sheer electricity of his presence.

How could she have forgotten this? How could she have thought she could put him behind her so easily? There was no ignoring Zee, there never had been.

She came to a stop all of a sudden, not wanting to get too close to him. Because she just didn't trust herself not to be able to reach out and touch him. Hold on to him and never let go.

Zee swept her a look from her head to her feet, and even in the darkness, the glint of hunger in his eyes was unmistakable. "Tamara."

The sound of her name sent a wave of heat through her and she had to fold her arms over her chest to keep herself from reaching out to him. "Hey, Zee." She swallowed, her throat thick. "Long time no see."

He had his hands in the pockets of his jeans, every line of his body radiating tension. And he was staring intently at her as if trying to imprint her on his memory.

The thickness in her throat intensified. "I suppose I don't need to ask you why you're here. This is good-bye, isn't it?"

He should never have come. It was immediately obvious to him the moment he'd watched her walk out of the gate and cross the road. The streetlights had illuminated her lovely face and he'd seen the glow in her eyes as she'd approached, looking at him like she was excited to see him. Like she was glad.

She was so fucking sexy in the blue dress she was wearing and blue heeled sandals that made her legs look even longer and more delicate than they were. And he could feel his dick get hard, wanting to be inside her with those amazing legs wrapped around his waist. But that in itself wouldn't have actually been disturbing.

It was the way his heart felt like it was getting larger the closer she got, pushing against the walls of his chest, squashing his lungs so he couldn't breathe. Making everything inside him go tight with longing.

And when she'd looked at him with those knowing dark eyes, the ones that had seen right inside him, down to his soul and hadn't flinched away, what he'd felt was pain.

Because it was true. He was here to say good-bye.

He'd thought he'd forgotten about her. Forced her entirely from his head. Made her exactly what he'd told Gideon she was—a chick he'd hooked up with for a couple of nights and let go just as easily. A lie he'd believed right up until the point he'd shifted into the downtown apartment his father had instructed him to move into, keeping up the pretense of the obedient son, and unpacked his meager belongings, and discovered a small ball of expensive black fabric at the bottom of one box.

Fabric he'd thought he'd thrown in the trash. Tamara's tank top.

He'd taken that scrap of fabric out of the box and spread it out over his hands, inhaling the fading scent of her before he'd had a chance to stop himself. Then, angry about the fact he hadn't thrown it out like he thought he had, he'd tossed it directly into the wastebasket.

Yet no matter how many times he threw it away, somehow he ended up fishing it back out again and putting it back in his pocket. Where it was now, the cotton pressing against his palm, all warm and soft. Like a fucking security blanket.

He didn't know what was wrong with him. And that was why he was here, risking her safety, which was a damn stupid thing to do when his father was having him tailed everywhere he went. But he'd needed to do something to get her out of his head and if that meant going to see her one last time, then he had to. He couldn't afford any distractions from what he had to do, not now.

So of course he was here to say good-bye. But he didn't want to say it quite yet so he ignored the question. "You're looking beautiful tonight, pretty girl. What's the occasion?"

She had her arms folded over her chest, the sequined bodice of her dress sparkling under the streetlights. "It's a surprise party. For me."

"Oh? Is it your birthday or something?"

Slowly she shook her head. "I'm getting engaged tonight."

It felt like she'd just kicked him straight in the nuts and for a second all he could do was look at her.

You dickhead. She told you all about it, remember? The night she came to the garage in that tight little dress you pulled off her in the parking lot out back.

Fuck, that's right. She'd said "soon." And soon was apparently now, tonight.

Yet for all that, he found himself struggling to get a breath. "Engaged?" he echoed like a goddamn parrot.

She turned her head, looking away, shifting on her long legs, the sequins on her dress glittering like tiny stars. For a moment she looked exactly like fucking Cinderella, beautiful and innocent, and completely untouchable, especially by the likes of him.

Except, he knew she wasn't untouchable. And he knew she wasn't Cinderella. No matter how beautiful and perfect she was on the outside, she had her darkness inside. A darkness she showed to nobody but him.

A hungry, possessive part of him growled in satisfaction at the thought. A part that wanted to leap on her now, drag her down onto the grass beside the car and let that darkness out to play with his. To glory in it one more time.

Except he wasn't here for that, was he?

"I told you, remember? My dad gave me a heads-up a couple of weeks ago that my mom was throwing me a surprise party where my boyfriend was going to propose," she said quietly. "And I'm going to say yes."

"Why the fuck would you do that?" The question came out harsh, his tone probably revealing way too much, but he didn't take it back. "I thought you didn't love him."

"I don't. But it's the right thing to do."

Familiar anger was coiling inside him, an anger that seemed completely out of proportion to what was happening. Because Tamara wasn't his girlfriend. They'd had sex a few times, had shared a few secrets, but nothing major. So why the hell he should be getting so pissed about her wanting to get married was ridiculous. He didn't understand it.

"What do you mean 'the right thing to do'?" he demanded, unable to help himself.

She stared at him, the look on her face unreadable. "I mean, it's the next logical step for me. I have a great job and a secure career path. Robert comes from a good family and my mom and dad like him. There's no reason not to."

Yet the words sounded . . . off. As if she was repeating something someone had told her.

Zee clenched his fists in the pockets of his jeans, trying to ignore the urge to reach out and touch her. Because he'd told himself before he'd gotten here that he wouldn't. A good-bye, that's all this was. Yet now she'd gone and changed things with this fucking "engaged" bullshit.

Struggling to rein in his anger, he forced out, "Okay, then. If that's what you want."

Tamara looked down at the ground, hugging herself as if she was cold. "It's . . . it's not what I want." Her voice sounded thin and uncertain, a needle sliding beneath his skin. "I don't want to marry him, Zee. I don't."

He'd taken a step toward her before he could stop himself. "Then don't. Just fucking don't."

"I have to." Her head came up, her eyes black in the darkness. "I have to move on. And this is the only way I can do it. I mean, how else can I ever make it up to my parents?"

Oh Jesus.

He didn't need to ask her what she was talking about. He knew. It slid the needle deeper, a sharp spear of pain reaching all the way down to his soul.

"This is about your brother, right?"

Her face had gone curiously blank. "Yes."

"You don't owe them a thing, Tamara," he said fiercely, forcefully. "Not a single, goddamn thing. His death wasn't your fault. It was theirs. They didn't get him the treatment he needed. They didn't listen to you when you told them you needed help. They put you into that situation. It's all on them."

"Maybe. But that doesn't change the fact that I pulled the trigger. I killed him. I have to pay my debt somehow and this is it. This is what I have to do. They covered it up—did you know that? Mom and Dad made it look like suicide. They didn't want the mental illness stigma and they didn't want me to go to jail." Her arms dropped to her sides, her fingers curling into fists like his were. "They erased what I did entirely." There was a note in her voice that he knew, a note that was as familiar to him as his own name. Rage. "So you tell me, how else am I supposed to make what I did better? How else am I supposed to pay my *fucking* debt?"

Zee took another step toward her, coming closer. The night air carried the sweet smell of her scent and the streetlight made her skin look so pale and smooth and perfect. It wasn't that which drew him this time, but the helpless rage in her voice and the gleam of it in her eyes. The note of pain that somehow drove that needle deeper into his heart.

"You don't have to pay any damn debt." Fuck, he wanted to take her in his arms, hold her. Take away the hurt. "Like I said, it's not your fault."

But she only stared at him. "That's rich coming from you. I suppose you being here now to say good-bye isn't part of the debt you have to pay either?"

He stilled. "What are you talking about?"

"Well, why else are you here? I presume you didn't come to see me just to tell me Will's death wasn't my fault."

She saw so much. Too much. "Yeah, okay. I did come to say good-bye since we didn't get to say it properly last time. But that's got nothing to do with any debt."

Her mouth had gone tight, her knuckles white where they gripped her upper arms. She didn't speak, only stared at him.

The tension between them now had changed and he didn't understand it. She was looking at him like she wanted something from him, something he couldn't figure out.

You know. You just don't want to see it.

His heart had gone tight, the needle of pain driving deeper and deeper.

"Tamara," he said thickly. "Don't—"

"I don't want to say good-bye, Zee." There was desperation in her voice now, a raw, naked emotion that made him feel like she was stripping him bare. "I don't want to get engaged to Robert and I don't want to say good-bye to you." Her eyes were black in the night. "What I want is to get in your car and just . . . go."

"Go?" he demanded roughly. "Go with me where?"

Her throat moved. "Anywhere. I don't care. I just . . . want to be with you."

Now she hadn't just kicked him in the nuts, she'd flat out

KO'd him completely. It made him angry for reasons he didn't understand. As if it wasn't him she wanted, but only a reason to escape. "What? You think running away is the answer? That you can just walk away from shit you don't like?"

"No, that's not what—"

"Because you can't, Tamara. Believe me, I know all about it. No matter how fast you run, the past will always catch up."

"Well, maybe it's time your dad's past caught up with him." She took a step toward him and this time there was no mistaking the burning look on her face. Hope. "Do you know he's trying to run for mayor? And that my dad made a massive pledge to his campaign? All I need to do is convince Dad that Chase is shady and he'll withdraw the funds. I'm sure he'll also spread it around among the business community, too, which'll totally kill any chance Chase has of any kind of political office."

Zee found himself standing utterly motionless, staring at her. No, it couldn't be that simple. He hadn't known about his father's political aims, in fact he'd deliberately tried not to think of his father at all while he'd been flying under the radar. But if what she'd said was true . . .

Are you willing to take that chance though? What if she's wrong?

If she was wrong, fuck, everyone would pay. And it would be his fault.

Christ, she was so near, the distance between them was so small. All he'd have to do is take one more step and he could pull her into his arms. Yet it may as well have been the Grand Canyon for all the good that did him.

He'd believed in a woman before and made the wrong call, and he'd lost everything. He wasn't going to do that again. There was only one path before him now and he had to walk it to the end. It was the only way any of them could ever be free.

Tell yourself it's about Madison. Tell yourself it's got nothing to do with the fact that you can't ever give Tamara what she needs.

Zee ignored the thought, went to the calm, quiet space in his head that he went to before a fight. Where he was cold and focused and his goddamn emotions didn't screw with him. "No," he said, his voice coming out sounding flat.

She blinked. "No what?"

"No to everything. I'm not fucking risking it, and neither are you."

"Zee—"

"I said no. There's only one way to keep you safe and that's for you to walk away. So that's what you're gonna do, understand me?" Something in his head raged and shouted, but he tuned it out. Hardened his heart against the needle that tried to pierce it. "Go back to your safe little life, pretty girl. Marry your boyfriend. Give him kids, whatever. Just don't, whatever you do, come anywhere near me ever again."

She flinched as if he'd slapped her, that burning emotion in her face slowly dying. Making him feel as if he'd just dropped weed killer all over a beautiful flower. "Okay," she said in a brittle voice. "I get it. But don't pretend you're doing this for me, Zee, let's be honest. The only person you're protecting is yourself."

The coiling anger tightened. "Like you'd know the first fucking thing about it."

All the hope had died out of her face, her expression shuttered. She looked small and cold and alone, and no matter how hard he tried not to feel it, his chest ached like someone had smashed him straight in the center of it. "Of course I know," she said quietly. "You think you don't deserve it, do you? You think you don't deserve anything better, anything more."

He couldn't speak all of a sudden, every part of him wanting to deny it. Tell her she was wrong, that it wasn't about him and what he did and didn't deserve, but the people he was trying to save.

"No," he forced out. "It's got nothing to do with that."

The look in her eyes was bleak. "Really? But maybe you're right. Maybe I don't deserve to have anything either."

"What the fuck do you mean by that?" The cold calm around him felt almost as brittle as the sound of her voice. As if it was going to shatter at any moment. "You deserve everything."

"But apparently not the chance of something real with you."

"Jesus Christ. How many times do I have to say it? I can't—"

"I know, believe me, I get it." She gave a little shiver and looked away. "I did want to run away. I did want to escape. And you're right about that, too, we can't escape the past. We don't deserve to. We don't get to have anything more than the debts we have to pay." She sounded like she was talking to herself. "Maybe we never stop paying. I guess that's justice after all."

"Tamara—"

"It's okay, Zee." She glanced back at him and there was something in her eyes that cracked his cold calm like a beer bottle dropped on a concrete floor. "I killed my own brother. I don't deserve a thing."

Every cell in his body screamed at him to go to her, touch her. Tell her she was wrong, that she deserved everything good this world could give her. But how could he?

She's right. Everyone has a debt to pay and nothing ends until we pay it.

Going after his father, ending him, that was his debt. He'd tried to make amends for Madison's death with the paltry life he'd built for himself, giving back the way she'd told him he could, making a difference to people, improving things. But in the end, it wasn't enough. Life demanded more.

So he said nothing as Tamara looked at him for one long, endless moment.

Then abruptly she turned away and walked past him, moving back toward the gates of her parents' driveway, her steps crunching in the gravel. Walking back to her life sentence.

Zee bit down hard on the urge to call her back and go after her. Throw her into the back of the Trans Am and take her away with him where no one would ever find them.

But no. He had his sentence too.

So he didn't move. Just watched as she disappeared into the darkness.

She swore to herself she wouldn't cry and she didn't up until the moment Robert gave her the box and she opened it. There was a single diamond solitaire sitting inside, sparkling in the light from the chandelier in the drawing room. A tension set stone, the two halves of the ring clutching on tight to the jewel, squeezing it, holding it firmly in place.

She couldn't hold back the tears then, her chest so sore it felt like someone had stabbed her repeatedly with a blunt knife. She couldn't speak either, so all she did was nod her head, watching as Robert took the ring out of the box and put it on her finger.

Everyone was cheering and smiling, thinking her tears were from the surprise of it, the sheer happiness of the moment.

No one knew that they were tears of pain.

Because as Tamara looked at the ring glittering on her finger, she knew one thing.

She was the diamond locked into her setting and nothing was going to set her free.

It was what she deserved after all.

Chapter 15

Zee leaned forward and reached into the glove compartment of the Trans Am, his fingers curling around the handgun he kept in there and drawing it out. Checking the safety was on, he stuck it down the back of his jeans, then he got out of the car and did another quick check around.

He'd come straight from Tamara's to the meeting Joshua had demanded. His father had wanted him to come look at the abandoned warehouse he'd just bought out east of the city center, fuck knows why. Maybe it was going to be the site of some new drug operation or something.

Whatever, Zee could not have cared less. That motherfucker wouldn't have it long enough to do anything with it because as soon as Zee got in there, he was going to put him in the ground.

The warehouse parking lot was surrounded by a chain-link fence, the concrete cracked and broken, weeds everywhere. The warehouse itself was a huge brick monolith, the windows as cracked as the ground he stood on and the ones that weren't cracked were boarded up.

Fucking place reminded him of Royal.

Starting toward a pair of big double doors, Zee kept an eye out for any trouble. But the area remained deserted. Clearly his father hadn't brought his usual entourage with him, which was a good thing. Zee had spent the past week trying to be the good, obedient son to allay his father's suspicions, make it look like he'd do anything Joshua wanted him to for the sake of his friends.

Looked like he'd succeeded.

As Zee pulled open the door and stepped inside, he checked his gun again for reassurance.

He only had one shot at this and fucking up was not an option.

In the back of his head the desolate expression on Tamara's face kept replaying, the sound of her voice saying she didn't deserve anything. But he tried not to think of that. Had spent the whole goddamn drive from Grosse Pointe trying not to think about it.

He couldn't afford to, not now.

She'd be okay anyway. She was safe where she was and shit, even though she might have to marry some dick for the sake of her own demons that was better than being dead. Wasn't it?

Yet the pain in his chest wouldn't go away, the nagging ache of that needle stuck deep in his heart.

Jesus Christ, he had to get it together. Getting emotional would only screw things up and he couldn't afford to do that if he was going to go through with this.

It was a suicide mission, of that he was clear. He'd die in all probability, be gunned down by whoever else was protecting his father and if not now, if he managed to take them out too, then sooner or later they'd get to him and take revenge. He was under no illusions about that.

That's justice, though, isn't it? Justice for Madison. You don't deserve more, just like Tamara said. . . .

Zee shoved the voice away, shoved everything away, keeping his focus centered on the moment and his surroundings.

The warehouse was a massive, empty, echoing space lit by harsh white fluorescents. Chains hung from the ceiling here and there, but apart from that, there was nothing else but the bare, pitted concrete floor and the brick walls.

And his father standing in the center of it, his hands in the pockets of his black business pants.

Not far off stood Krupin, his Russian henchman, because of course it would be too much to hope for that Joshua would be by himself. Then again, if Zee played this right, Krupin wouldn't be a problem. He'd be Zee's executioner, no doubt about that, but with any luck he wouldn't be able to stop Zee getting off the first shot. The guy had always been slow on the draw after all.

"Whaddya think?" Joshua didn't look at Zee as he approached, staring around at the walls of his newest acquisition instead. "Got big plans for this place. Gonna turn it into apartments, yet keep the industrial feel. People lap that shit up by the bucketful." Finally he turned and looked at Zee, his blue eyes glinting. "How did it go?"

Zee folded his arms. "How did what go?"

"Your visit with that rich bitch you've been fucking."

It took everything he had to keep his face completely still, to not let the shock that coursed through him show.

Why are you surprised? Wasn't this exactly what you were expecting?

Behind his father, Krupin was staring at him, an evil smile twisting the guy's mouth.

Fuck. Okay, so somehow, someway, even though he'd thought he'd managed to throw off whoever was tailing him, he'd been seen with Tamara.

His heart slammed against his chest and it was only through sheer force of will that he managed not to go for the gun sitting warmly at his back.

But no, it was okay. If everything went according to plan, his father wouldn't leave this warehouse alive and then it wouldn't matter.

"Oh, her?" He managed to keep his tone casual. "Bitch keeps calling me. I had to go talk to her to tell her to back off."

His father eyed him. "Pity. Because I've been thinking a lot about how we might use that to our advantage. Her daddy's got a lot of influence that might be beneficial to us, know what I'm saying?"

Holy shit. The prick was seriously considering using Tamara?

Zee struggled to keep everything locked down. "Huh. I thought that shit wasn't what you wanted?"

Joshua lifted a shoulder. "It wasn't. But times change, boy. Thinking the underground influence might not be all I want. I mean, come on. This city could use some street smarts and who's the guy to give it if not me?" He smiled. "I got ambitions. More than pimping whores and running drugs. I want power. Real power. Power the fucking Lennoxes might just hand me on a plate if I'm lucky."

Something trickled down Zee's spine, but he couldn't figure out what it was. Shock or anger or pain, he didn't know. He tried not to think about it as he stared into his father's face, watching greed gleam in Joshua's pale blue eyes.

This was the man who fathered him. He was cut from the very same cloth. And perhaps in the end, this was the way it should always have been. Poetic justice. He would kill the prick and then he too would die just as his mother had, and that would be the end of the Chase family. The end of the death and destruction that always came in their wake.

The one who sins is the one who will die.

He almost laughed. He'd been thinking of his father when he'd had that inked into his skin, but shit, it could be applied to himself, too.

"I think I saw some junkies fucking around with the one of the windows out back," he said flatly, looking past his father to Krupin. "Whatever, you might wanna go deal with them."

Krupin snorted. "Deal with it yourself, *boy.*"

"Hey," Joshua said, turning around unexpectedly. "Keep some respect in your tone when you're talking to my son. Now go do what he fucking says. I could use some father-son time."

"But, sir—"

"*Now.*"

The man shot Zee a look that promised retribution, then stalked past him, heading for the door without another word.

But Zee didn't bother looking at him, more shock cascading through him. He hadn't expected his father to back him up like that, not at all. Was this a test of loyalty for him? Because Joshua did love a good test, that was certain. Or was it that his father was so blind he simply couldn't see how much Zee hated him? Maybe he didn't even remember what he'd done, because not once, not in the whole week Zee had been around, had the man ever mentioned Madison to him.

Joshua hadn't moved, standing facing Zee with his hands in his pockets. Smiling.

"There," he said, sounding pleased with himself. "Now we can have a chat."

"Sure we can," Zee replied smoothly. And pulled out his gun, unlocking the safety. "Chat away."

The smile on Joshua's face didn't budge. He looked at the gun pointed at him, then back to his son. "You waited a whole week. Congratulations. I've been expecting this for days."

"You've had it coming for *years*, you fucker." The gun felt heavy and sure in Zee's grip, like the certainty that this was the right thing to do. Shit, it was the only thing to do, the only thing that made sense.

Joshua's smile turned wolfish. "Oh probably. But you know you're gonna go down with me if you pull that trigger, right?"

"Yeah. I know." He cocked the gun, the sound echoing around the warehouse.

Still, Joshua didn't move and didn't stop smiling. "This is all because of that little bitch I had taken out years ago, right? The whiny rich girl? Please don't tell me you're still mad about it."

Christ, it would be so good to pull that trigger right now. Wipe that stupid smile off the sonofabitch's face. "You should have had me killed along with her," Zee said coldly. "Letting me go was a mistake."

"You got that right. You were such a whiny bitch yourself back then. Seems like nothing has changed." Joshua swept him a contemptuous look. "I was doing you a favor getting her out of your life. You weren't meant to play house in the suburbs or Robin Hood in Royal. You're better than that shit. You're like me, you're in it for more, for the adrenaline rush. 'Cause that's what the money is and that's what the power does."

"You're wrong. I'm nothing like you." The metal felt cool against his finger. All he had to do was pull it and all this would end.

"Sure you are. Why the hell else have you got a gun pointed at me? You think killing me will give you the higher ground?" The expression on Joshua's face was almost feral. "It won't. All it'll mean is that we're just the same." He laughed. "So go on, boy. Do it."

Yeah. So do it.

His palms were completely dry and he felt no fear. Killing his father would mean absolutely nothing to him. Which made it kind of strange to discover, right at the end, that the old man was right. He was like him after all.

So pull the trigger already.

He was going to. In fact, he should have done it seconds ago. "Maybe I am," he said harshly. "We all get what we deserve old man, especially you."

Does Tamara?

Zee blinked. Where the fuck had that thought come from? She had nothing to do with this.

"I killed my own brother. I don't deserve a thing."

The ache in his chest was back, a heavy dragging sensation. And suddenly all he could see was her face and the hope that had burned there as she'd looked at him. As she'd told him what she wanted was to get in his car and go with him, wherever that was. A hope he'd killed stone dead, leaving her with nothing but bleakness in her eyes.

It was for her protection. For her safety. And you couldn't run from the past anyway.

"Maybe we don't get to have anything more than the debts we have to pay."

Well, he sure as hell didn't.

But does that mean she has to?

Tamara, who was passionate and loyal. Who'd seen in him something more. A man whom she'd thought worthy of her deepest secrets. Who'd listened when he'd told her his and hadn't flinched away. Who accepted him for who he was in a way no one else ever had.

Was it really that she'd been trying to escape her past? Or was it that she'd dared to want something more, to reach beyond the prison sentence she'd given herself? And he'd thrown it back in her face because he was in the same hell she was in, paying for a death he'd caused, and hadn't been able to see a way out of it.

Except maybe . . . Maybe he was starting to see now. Not for himself and his guilt, but because he cared about her. Because if he killed this man here and now, who would be there for her? Who knew her like he did? No one. And if he wasn't there, then she would be stuck in her prison cell for something that wasn't even her fault.

That mattered to him. That hurt worse than anything else he could imagine.

"You gonna shoot me, boy?" Joshua made a show of looking at his watch. "'Cause I ain't got time for this bullshit."

Fuck, he should just shoot this prick and be done with it. Because no matter how much that might hurt him, Tamara being at risk was far more painful than anything else.

Yeah, because you're a selfish dick. It's not her pain you're thinking of, it's your own.

The realization was cold as a mountain stream sliding over his skin. Of course this wasn't about her. This was about his own fear. Of making the wrong choice. Of being responsible for someone else's death. Of never being able to wipe away the stain of the death he'd caused.

But killing his father wouldn't make it right, just like his own death wouldn't. Tamara would still be stuck in a life she didn't want, paying for something she'd already punished herself enough for. And he would end up having caused her yet more pain.

He couldn't stand the thought of that.

Joshua stared at him, a sneer twisting his mouth. "Fuck, I knew you didn't have the guts."

Zee lowered his gun, his heart thumping in his chest, adrenaline firing through his blood. "I'm not gonna kill you, Dad. But I'm not gonna stay either."

His father frowned. "Hey, we had a deal—"

"No, you had made the fucking deal." Zee put the gun back in the waistband of his jeans. "And I've decided I'm not gonna be part of it anymore."

For the first time, anger slid over Joshua Chase's features. "What the fuck? You know what I'll do if you don't toe the party line, boy. I'll fuck up all your friends and I'll—"

"You wanna know what I was talking to Tamara about?" Zee interrupted flatly. "She was telling me that if I didn't come back from meeting with you alive, she was gonna get her father to pull his pledge. And she'd reveal your sketchy business deal-

ings to the whole business community, spread around the rumors you're as shady as hell." It wasn't exactly true and he had
no idea if she'd be able to do that or not, but if she thought she
could get her father to do it, then he had to trust her. Christ, he
had to start trusting someone sometime, didn't he?

His father's expression abruptly wiped clean. "She can't do
that."

"Yeah? Guess you'll find out if you kill me." He turned
around. How weird to feel like something heavy had fallen
from him, a weight he'd been carrying for years that he hadn't
realized was there until now.

"Don't you fucking turn your back on me, boy," Joshua
growled from behind him. "I can make you wish you'd never
been born."

Zee paused, but he didn't turn. "Touch her, touch any of my
friends, or touch Royal and I'll give Tamara the go-ahead to get
her dad to pull the pledge. And you can say good-bye to being
mayor."

There was silence behind him for a long time.

"So that's what you're gonna go back to?" Joshua finally
said. "Your sad life in that shithole you call a neighborhood?
You're right. I should have killed you when I had a chance. Done
us both a fucking favor."

"Yeah," Zee said. "You should have. But you didn't. And
hey, whaddya know? I'm not like you after all."

He walked out of the warehouse, his father still hurling
curses at his back.

But no shots came after him. And it wasn't until he'd gotten
to his car and pulled open the door that he realized that if he
was still alive it was because his bluff had worked. And maybe,
if he was lucky, it would keep on working.

What if it doesn't? What if he finds another way to hurt her?

Zee got into the Trans Am and slammed the door, started
the car.

If that happened, then Zee would just have to find another way to protect her. Because, shit, he wasn't going to let her punish herself for the rest of her life. She'd wanted something more than that and apparently that something was him. He couldn't understand why that was when all he'd done was push her away, but shit, if that's what she wanted, then that's what she'd get.

She deserved to have it.

Zee pulled away from the warehouse, tires screeching, and he didn't look behind him to see if anyone was following him. Something told him they wouldn't be.

Tamara sat on the couch in the drawing room, her mother sitting on one side of her, Robert on the other. He was holding her hand in a proprietary kind of way as he chatted to one of her parents' friends, the smug sound of his voice washing over her like warm oil.

There was nothing gritty in his tone. Nothing harsh. He sounded well educated and well spoken, exactly like the rich New York stockbroker he was. And she shouldn't hate that, she really shouldn't.

She'd allowed herself one moment to cry, but that was it. The mask shouldn't drop again. She was in costume, the role was hers for good now, and she had to play it to the end. No point thinking about anything else.

This was for Will. For her parents. She had to stay focused on that.

She kept a smile plastered to her face, feeling more than ever like the diamond in her engagement ring, forced to sit between her mother and Robert, kept there. Held there. Forever pinned in her setting.

Maybe it wasn't strictly true, because of course she could choose to walk away if she wanted to. But she wasn't going to.

Will had never been given the chance to walk away. Will had never been given any chances at all. So what right had she, as his killer, to do so? Zee had been right; running away definitely wasn't the answer.

Yet all the rationalizations in the world didn't stop her throat from feeling tight and sore, or keep the walls of the drawing room from closing in around her.

Or make the memory of Zee's cold, hard expression as he'd told her to stay away from him any less painful.

She'd thought for a moment, as she had stood in the darkness by his car and told him about Robert, about the party, that maybe he'd changed his mind about saying good-bye. Because he'd been so angry, the aura of leashed violence around him almost vibrating in the air. And she'd seen something in his eyes, something possessive and hot, and all the words had come spilling out. Secret hopes she hadn't even realized herself until right at that moment. That together they'd take down his father with the information she'd gotten, that they'd both be free. She'd get in his car and they'd drive away, she didn't care where.

Because all that seemed important in that moment was being with him.

Except he didn't feel that way. She could understand it. He was still paying his debt to his girlfriend and that was more important to him.

You wanted to matter more than that.

Tamara's vision blurred, the colors of the Persian rug on the floor all blending together, reds and blues and golds. She blinked. Hard.

No, she had to get it together. Zee was gone for good, wherever he'd gone, and she had to get him out of her head once and for all.

This was her life now and she had to accept it.

Voices drifted in from the hallway. Loud voices.

The conversation in the room began to fall silent as people's heads turned in the direction of the doors.

Tamara could hear her father talking angrily to someone and someone saying something back in a low, harsh, gritty voice.

She froze, every muscle tensing.

No, it couldn't be him. It couldn't. He was gone; he'd let her walk away.

Then suddenly the doors crashed open, bouncing on their hinges, and everyone in the entire room stared and fell silent in shock as a man strode through the doorway.

Tall, dark, tattooed. In a faded black T-shirt and worn jeans, scuffed motorcycle boots on his feet. Violence rode the air around him, menace pouring off him in a wave, and those closest to the door scrambled back as if even getting anywhere near him was dangerous.

His intense, beautiful face was drawn tight with determination, eyes the color of polished steel glinting. He paused, sweeping the room with a glance so sharp it cut like a scythe. Then it settled on her and she trembled, something squeezing so hard in her chest she thought she might break.

Because he was here, in front of her entire family and everyone she knew. He'd come for her.

He didn't pause, coming straight toward her, and they may have been the only people in the entire room for all the notice he took of the crowd of her parents' friends all gathered around.

Behind him she could hear her father shouting something about calling the police and trespassing, and a couple of male guests had started to approach, obviously with the intention of escorting him from the house. But it looked like they hadn't quite gotten up the gumption yet because they kept eyeing him warily, as if he were a bomb that might go off.

Beside her, Robert had risen to his feet, his expression full of righteous anger. He said something, but Tamara couldn't hear him. There was a roaring in her ears, her blood rushing hard through her veins.

Zee stopped right in front of her, towering over her, not even looking at Robert. "You said you wanted to come with me." The gravel in his voice was like cold air after a sauna, waking her up, kicking her out of her lethargy. "So come with me."

More people were shouting and one of the men made a motion toward Zee, but Zee just snapped his head around and stared the man down like he was controlling a vicious dog.

Robert started speaking and suddenly that soothing-oil voice of his was the last thing in the world she wanted to hear.

"Shut the fuck up, Robert," she snapped, and a wave of shock rolled around the room.

"Tamara!" her mother exclaimed.

"You too, Mom," Tamara cut her off. Then she looked at Zee, her heart beating wildly in her chest, his silver gaze meeting hers.

Shaking off Robert's hand, she rose to her feet.

Zee was close enough that when she stood there were only bare inches between them. She could feel the rough, raw heat of him, so out of place in her parents' carefully decorated living room, like a scrawl of graffiti across an Old Master.

God, he was dangerous, all leashed violence and lightning. Making everyone else in the room seem insubstantial and blurry. As if he was the only one in focus.

"Why?" She had to force the word out, yet she made herself do it. Because suddenly it was all becoming very clear what she wanted. But she was done with putting it all out there for him and having it thrown back in her face. She wanted to hear it from him first. "Give me one good reason."

This was worse than the ring. Because at least in the ring he knew what he was doing and he felt like he belonged. And his opponent was here for the same thing he was.

Everyone knew where they stood and what to expect.

But here in this fucking fancy room full of fucking fancy people all staring at him, he was out of his depth. He didn't know the rules. Part of him wanted to put up his fists and start swinging, impose his own rules on people, return to what he knew, what he was comfortable with.

Yet that wasn't what he was here for.

What he was here for was standing in front of him right now, with her golden hair all up in that sleek ponytail. In her blue dress with the sequins glittering, that left her shoulders bare and all that perfect, smooth skin on show. Whose dark eyes, deep and soft as the night outside the windows, met his. They were full of shock and wariness, and yet despite all he'd done, there were glimmers of the hope he'd seen in them before. It was that hope that caught him full in the chest, a kick to the heart.

It struck him, forcibly, that he wasn't only here for her sake. He was here for his, too.

Fucking hell.

He'd never asked for anything from anyone, because he'd always made sure he never wanted anything.

But he did now. He could feel it inside him, that hungry, desperate ache, that terrible yearning. It was growing, getting larger and larger all the time, and Jesus, if he didn't get what he wanted, he didn't know what he would do.

The only thing he did know was that here in this beautiful, perfect room full of people, where he didn't belong, he was going to have to ask her. Fuck, he'd beg if he had to, humiliate himself in front of everyone. If only she'd give him what he wanted.

So Zee dropped to his knees in front of her, keeping his gaze on hers, hoping like hell that the glimmer he'd seen in her eyes when he'd walked into the room was what he thought it was.

Everyone in the entire room fell silent, staring.

"I'm not good with words," he said, hating how his voice sounded like sandpaper scraping across vulnerable skin. "I can't put it so it's all pretty and poetic. And I can't give you what you got here. A fancy house and career and a fucking diamond ring. I haven't got anything at all. The only thing I got is me. So here I am." He took a breath, staring into the darkness of her eyes, the room around them utterly silent. It was a wonder no one could hear his heart since it was beating so fucking loud. "I want you to come with me, because you deserve more than a prison sentence, pretty girl. And so do I."

Tamara didn't speak, the look on her face absolutely unreadable, and it came to him that he'd never been so scared in all his fucking life.

Then her throat moved as she swallowed, and she turned to the smug prick standing beside her, the one who'd been holding her hand so possessively. The one Zee had wanted to punch with every breath in him.

"Here," Tamara said, and with a quick movement she pulled off the diamond ring on her finger and dropped it into his hand. "I'm sorry, Robert. I'm not marrying you."

Zee found his hands were in fists, his heart pulling wildly against the leash he'd put around it, slamming against the walls of his chest as if it could claw its way out. "Tamara." He forced himself to say it. "Remember. I'm just a mechanic in a shitty part of Detroit. A guy who likes letting off steam with his fists. I'm nothing much at all. So be sure about what you're gonna do. About what you're gonna leave behind. Be real sure."

But there was nothing guarded in her face now, nothing wary. "I know what you are, Zee." The words were heavy with certainty, with truth. "I know *who* you are. You're exactly what I want. Exactly. So yeah, I'm sure. I've never been surer in my entire life."

He could feel it now, something strong and hot surging in his veins. A hope he'd never allowed himself. A hope he'd never allowed himself to even think about. He got to his feet in a sudden rush, trying to still the weird shake that went right through him. "You don't want me to do anything?" he asked, because he had to. Because the only people who'd taken him for who he was had been his friends. Even Madison had wanted him to be something else, something more. "You don't want me to be anything?"

"No," Tamara whispered, her hands raised as if wanting to touch him but not daring to quite yet. "I just want you."

Somebody said something then, but Zee ignored it. In fact, he pretty much ignored everything but the woman standing in front of him, staring at him as if he was the only thing in the entire world worth looking at. Which he was certain he didn't deserve, but fuck that. He'd never had anything like this before. Never felt anything like this before.

It wasn't the right place or the right time, not with all these people standing there staring at them, but he suddenly didn't give a shit. He couldn't hold back anymore.

Reaching for her, Zee put one hand behind her head, pushing his fingers into the warm silk of her hair, while he slid the other hand behind her, settling it into the small of her back and drawing her in. Tipping her head back so her mouth was right there.

Then he covered it with his own. A deep, possessive kiss that told everyone in the fucking room exactly whose she was.

She didn't protest. She only opened her mouth and kissed him back.

And this time it wasn't darkness he tasted in her kiss but pure, unwavering light.

She'd never been able to resist him and she didn't now. And the fact that Zee was kissing her in her parents' living room, in front of all their family and friends, didn't matter a bit.

Because there was nothing in the world more important than his mouth on hers, than his hands in her hair and his body right up against her. Freeing her. Nothing more necessary or vital.

When he finally pulled away, he didn't let her go, twining his fingers through hers. And she knew, without a shadow of a doubt, that if she went with out of the room with him there would be no turning back. No matter what happened afterward, her life here was ended one way or another.

What about Will? What about what you owe? What about moving forward?

She stared at Zee's face, at the burning look in his eyes.

She could stay here, spend the rest of her life trying to make up for what she'd done. Kidding herself that a career and a husband was the way to move forward, the way to give back to her parents what she'd taken from them. But the truth was nothing would make up for that. Nothing would pay a debt that large, still less a lifetime spent in unhappiness.

Will deserved a better memorial than that. Didn't he?

Stupid question. Of course he did.

Tamara followed Zee without a backward glance as he led her out through the doorway, ignoring the calls of her name and the rising hubbub of voices that drifted in her wake.

They had ceased to matter. Everything had ceased to matter but him.

He led her down the grand hallway to the front doors, pushing them open and stepping out into the night. There was a pillared entranceway with magnificent stairs that went down into the gravel driveway, and Tamara went down them without hesitation.

Her feet crunched in the gravel, her stilettos wobbling. And it was only there that she stopped.

Zee was still holding on to her hand and he turned, and looked at her.

She smiled, letting go of him to take off her shoes one by one, throwing them carelessly onto the driveway. Then she walked barefoot over the gravel to him.

"You'll hurt your feet," he said.

"I don't care. It's worth it. Besides, they're not my shoes anyway." She looked up at him. "Are you going to tell me what happened?"

His eyes glinted in the darkness as he reached for her hand, his fingers twining around hers again. "I went to see my dad," he said. "He wanted me back. Threatened to torch Royal if I didn't agree to go back to him. So I did. But basically I've been waiting for the right moment to put a bullet in his head."

Tamara went cold. "Did you—"

He shook his head once, sharply. "Killing him would have been a suicide mission. Don't get me wrong, I was actually okay with that. That's why I let you go earlier, because that's what I was planning on doing. Go and put him in the ground and let whatever happened after that happen."

It felt like her heart was shriveling up inside her chest. "Oh God, Zee." She took another step to him, wrapping her arms around his waist. "Were you completely insane?"

His hands settled on her hips. "I had to protect you. I had to protect my friends. And I thought that was the best way. I was gonna shoot him, I even held the gun to his fucking head. But I couldn't pull that trigger because . . ." He paused, looking down at her. "I was too busy thinking of you. Thinking about what you said you deserved."

Her arms tightened around him, remembering. "I felt pretty shitty."

"Your brother's death wasn't your fault, Tamara. And you don't have to pay any fucking debt. You deserve to be happy. You deserve to have what you want. And I couldn't pull that goddamn trigger because I knew if I did, you wouldn't get what you wanted."

Despite herself, her eyes filled with tears and she had to blink hard to clear them. "So what happened?" she asked huskily. "Did he let you go?"

"No. I walked away. I told him your father would pull his pledge if I didn't get out of there alive." A glimmer of a smile curved his mouth. "That was clever by the way. You're smart, pretty girl."

God, even just that hint of a smile made her insides turn inside out. What would it be like if he laughed? "Thanks," she murmured, leaning against him. "I hoped it would come in useful."

"Very useful. I told him I'd do it if he so much as touched a hair on your head or hurt my friends. And since I'm here, I guess that threat worked." His silver gaze on hers was like pure, concentrated lightning. "You said you wanted something real, Tamara. You meant it, right?"

Tamara swallowed, her throat thick. Leaving behind the life she'd had, hadn't been hard, not in any way. But that didn't mean the rest of it was going to be plain sailing. Still, the most important thing in the world was right here, between her hands, and as long as he remained there, she could handle anything.

"I meant it." She put all her conviction into the words, all her belief, all her trust.

"Fuck," he said on a long breath. "I still don't know why."

She looked up at him. "Then you're an idiot. You must know that I've been falling in love with you for weeks now, don't you?"

Love. What did he know about love? Nothing. Dimly he remembered it being something to do with kisses on his head and hugs from his mom before she died, but after that? Nothing. Maybe he'd had it with Madison, but then they'd only been kids. They hadn't really understood what it was. Christ, even now, he couldn't say he even knew what it felt like.

Except, maybe that was wrong. Maybe he did know what it felt like now.

It felt like Tamara's arms around his waist and the softness of her body against him. The way he felt like the sun had just come up as he watched her smile. And the fierce, bright burning in his chest as she told him she'd been falling in love with him.

Was that it? Was that love?

The sensation deepened, intensified, and it wasn't just because he wanted to push her down beneath him and bury himself inside of her. It went deeper and was far hungrier than that.

"I don't know anything about love, baby," he said huskily. "Madison was a long time ago and shit, we were just kids."

She lifted her hands from around his waist, cupped his face between them, and the pressure inside him felt suddenly overwhelming. "You understand what this means, don't you?" Her voice was soft. "That if I deserve this, then you deserve it too?"

His throat had gone tight. "Tamara—"

"We can't live our lives with debts, Zee. Hell, it doesn't work financially and it sure doesn't work emotionally."

He met her steady gaze and felt a wall he hadn't realized was inside him start to crumble, a whole lot of pent-up need spilling out. Hopes and dreams and yearnings he hadn't dared let himself have, not a man like him with a death on his hands.

"I don't know that I deserve anything," he said hoarsely. "I didn't protect her."

"You didn't know you had to. Just like I didn't know I had to protect myself." Her thumbs stroked his cheekbones, a gentle movement. "I think we have to let it go, Zee. I think we have to let Madison and Will both rest in peace. And I think . . ." Her voice thickened. "I really believe, that we need to forgive ourselves. That they would have wanted us to be happy, not torturing ourselves with guilt."

She was so strong, his Tamara. And smart. And he knew in

his heart she was right. Because hadn't Madison wanted that for him? She'd never have told him to reach for more if she hadn't.

"I wanna believe you, baby," he said finally. "But ten years of guilt doesn't just go away like that."

Tamara only smiled. "I know. But we have time. And in the meantime, I can teach you all about love."

Gently he pulled her hands away from his face, holding them in his as he bent to kiss her mouth. "You'll have to be patient. I was never good at school."

"That's okay." She was leaning into him and it felt so good. He wanted to keep her there forever. "I'm an excellent teacher."

The night was warm and there was soft-looking grass off to the side of the driveway. But even he knew that getting started with their lessons here was a pretty dumb idea. So he swept her up into his arms and started walking fast down the driveway toward the gates.

Tamara laughed, her arms tightening around his neck. "Where are we going?"

"Where do you think? Back to Royal, pretty girl."

Epilogue

Tamara placed the last few personal items from her desk into the cardboard box she'd brought with her. Scott was watching her from his office, his blue eyes narrowed with suspicion, but she ignored him.

Funny, she thought she'd feel more regret about this. But she didn't. Only a kind of satisfaction at tying up the final loose end. The last bit of her old life to get rid of.

She surveyed her empty desk, then grinned at Rose, who'd been watching her pack up, a hint of mournfulness in her brown eyes.

"It won't be the same without you," Rose said, pouting.

"Hey, I haven't gone far." Tamara tucked away the last thing into the box, her favorite coffee mug. "I'm just down in Royal. And you're still doing Zee's classes. We can meet up, go for a drink at Gino's."

Rose scrunched her face up. "Yeah, I know. But still. This place sucks."

Wasn't that the truth? This job had once been everything to

her, the only way she had to atone for her sins. But in the past couple of days, she'd found a different way, a peace of sorts.

She'd offered her financial advice to the outreach center Zee was working with and they'd been ecstatic at the offer. Sure, the pay was minimal, the benefits package nonexistent. But she got to make a difference in a way she'd never expected to, a way that was far more real than merely getting a position in her father's company.

Plus, there was one extra benefit she got in Royal that she didn't get at Lennox Investments.

As if on cue, silence began to ripple through the area as that particular benefit made his way toward her, drawing the stares of just about everyone in the entire office.

Zee wore jeans and boots again, his T-shirt white this time, making the ink on his skin stand out and the glow of his silver eyes more intense.

Among the suits and ties, he stood out like a demon amidst a horde of angels.

An incredibly hot, sexy demon.

Ignoring the stares and the silence he left in his wake, he came to a halt in front of her desk, hands jammed into the pockets of his jeans. "Ready to go?"

The rough sound of his voice still made a shiver go down her back. God, she'd never get tired of hearing his voice.

"Bitch," Rose muttered good-naturedly. "Can't believe you get to tap that."

There were some days Tamara couldn't believe it either. She smiled at the man on the other side of her desk. "Yeah, that's all of it."

"You sure you wanna do this?" Zee's gaze was direct, sharp. "You're giving up a lot for me, pretty girl. Don't think I don't know that."

Well, it wasn't really up to her, especially considering her father had made it clear, in no uncertain terms, that a position at Lennox was out of the question.

She wasn't surprised. Her parents had been extremely unhappy after she'd gone off with Zee and it was going to take time for them to come round. But she thought they might eventually—after all, they'd lost one child. Would they really want to lose another?

Then again, if they didn't, she was prepared to let them go. Because if they didn't want to build bridges with her, that was their choice and their decision, not hers.

Besides, she had all she needed right here.

"What am I giving up? A shit job? Money?" She shrugged. "Because I'm okay with that. Especially if that means I get you."

He smiled and it felt like the light in the office got momentarily brighter. "I'm not complaining." He reached for the cardboard box and picked it up. "Come on, I gotta surprise for you in the car."

"Oh, I hope it's what I think it is."

Zee laughed, clearly reading her mind. "Time for that later. This is something else."

Tamara grinned back, then, giving Rose a hug good-bye and Scott the finger as she passed by his office, she followed Zee out of the building.

But he didn't give her the surprise immediately, not until he'd pulled into a familiar alleyway.

She raised an eyebrow at him. "Here?"

"Sure, why not?" He was smiling. "I wanted to take you out to dinner, do it all special. But you know me, I can't wait." Twisting his seat, he started digging something out of the front pocket of his jeans.

"What couldn't wait?"

Zee opened his hand and sitting in the center of it was a small black box.

Tamara blinked, abruptly feeling as if all the air in the car had vanished out the windows. "What's that?" Her voice sounded all weird.

"Open it." There was something she didn't often see in his eyes. Uncertainty.

Slowly, she took the box from him and opened it up. Sitting inside it was a small, glittering red ruby caught in the delicate gold claws of a ring.

Red for passion.

Red for Zee.

Tamara looked at him, unable to speak.

"Like I told you before," Zee said, holding her gaze. "I'm not good with words, baby. And love isn't something I know a lot about. But you've been teaching me these past few days and I'm starting to get an idea." He paused, and his smile faded, the familiar intensity coming back into his eyes. "You told me you loved me and I never said it back, mainly 'cause I didn't know what it meant. But I do now. Tamara Lennox . . . Christ . . . I love you. And this ring, it doesn't have to be an engagement ring or anything, not if you don't want it to be, but—"

"Yes," she said simply, because anything else seemed inadequate. "Whatever it means, Zee. Yes."

He stopped speaking, just looking at her. Then he reached out and cupped her jaw in a touch that would have stolen her heart if he hadn't stolen it already, bending in to kiss her, deep and slow.

After a moment he lifted his head, took the ring out of the box, and slid it onto her finger, where it sparkled in the light, already feeling like part of her.

And neither of them spoke for a long time.

"You got me something too," he murmured eventually. "Rachel did it for me."

"I did? What?"

He was smiling again, a naughty, wicked smile that made her heart beat faster. Then he turned without a word and presented her with his back, drawing up his T-shirt.

Words were inked on there on the smooth, tanned skin. New words.

I will give you a new heart and put a new spirit in you; I will remove your heart of stone and give you a heart of flesh. Ezekiel 36:26

Tamara's vision blurred. "Oh . . . Zee . . ."

Then he turned around and she saw the heart inked on the left side of his chest, with her name in a cursive, flowing script beneath it. All in red ink.

Because red was for love, too.

If you enjoyed *Dirty for Me*, be sure not
to miss the next book in Jackie Ashenden's
scorching Motor City Royals series

WRONG FOR ME

Read on for a special sneak peek.

A Kensington trade paperback and e-book
on sale December 2016!

Chapter 1

Rachel Hamilton came to a stop outside the battered metal roller door that was the entrance to Black's Vintage Repair and Restoration, the motorcycle repair shop owned by her friend Gideon Black. She took a breath.

The acid eating a hole in her gut wasn't from fear.

It didn't have anything to do with the fact that Levi was back.

It was only because she hadn't felt like breakfast that morning and hadn't eaten anything. Perfectly understandable and explainable. Nothing whatsoever to do with how sick she'd felt, how her stomach kept turning over and over like a gymnast doing a complicated floor routine whenever she thought about Levi getting out of jail.

Nope. Nothing whatsoever to do with that.

Her palms were damp, but that was because it was hot. Same with her dry mouth. She should have had some water or something.

But you didn't because you would have thrown it up.

Rachel closed her eyes.

No fear. None. That's what had gotten her through life so far and that's what would get her through this. She just had to pull her armor on, pretend she gave no fucks whatsoever. It was the only way to protect herself. It was the only way to deal with the man who'd been inside for eight years.

The man she'd put there herself.

Her former best friend.

Oh Jesus. She was shaking.

Okay, so perhaps she shouldn't think about that. Think about how many fucks she gave instead. Which was none at all.

But naturally all the pep talks in the entire universe weren't going to help and when she opened her eyes, the nausea was still sitting right there and she was still shaking like a leaf.

Get. Yourself. The. Hell. Together.

Mentally she put herself in her usual snarky, sarcastic armor, the one specially designed to keep the world at bay, digging her nails into the palms of her hands. They were nice and long these days so they hurt biting into her skin. But that was good and she welcomed the pain. It helped her focus, helped her center herself.

Taking another breath, she pushed open the small metal door inset into the big roller one and stepped into Gideon's garage.

For a second she paused, trying to normalize her breathing, letting the familiarity of the garage settle her. It had always been a safe place for her, somewhere to go when she needed company, a good friend, a sympathetic ear. Gideon had gathered together a small group of kids from the Royal Road Outreach Center years ago, kids who were alone in the world, and even now, ten years later, they remained close friends. Gideon, Zoe, Zee, and Levi. They were still there for one another, still looked out for each other.

Except you didn't. You weren't there when Levi needed you most.

Rachel swallowed, ignoring the thought. She couldn't afford

to be thinking that kind of shit, not now. Not when she was barely holding it together as it was.

The smell of engine grease and oil filled her lungs. It was a comforting smell. There was a big metal shelf and a classic Cadillac up on a hoist blocking her vision, but she could hear the sound of voices. Gideon's, deep and rough, and Zoe's lighter tones. And then someone else's . . .

She stilled, the sound going through her, painful as a sliver of glass pushed beneath her skin.

A masculine voice. One that used to be deep and rich, full of laughter and bright with optimism. A warm, encouraging, friendly voice. One that used to make her heart feel lighter whenever she heard it. But now . . . now it sounded dark, with a roughness that hadn't been there before. Like someone unused to speaking aloud.

Levi.

A shiver ran the entire length of her body.

He was here, only a few feet away. After eight years.

Come on. You have to do this. Stop being such a fucking coward.

She forced herself to move forward, past the metal shelf, heading down toward the end of the garage where a long workshop counter was positioned against the wall beneath a massive row of grimy windows, some with different colored panes of glass.

The summer sun was shining through those windows, illuminating Zoe, small and slender, her black hair pulled back in a ponytail, sitting on the counter with her legs dangling. Beside her was Gideon in his blue overalls, all shaggy black hair and heavily muscled shoulders, leaning back with his arms folded.

Another man stood with his back to her. He was as tall as Gideon, which was pretty goddamn tall at nearly six four, and built just as massively. The cotton of his black T-shirt stretched over shoulders that would have done a gladiator proud, while his jeans hung low on his lean hips. The combination of sun through the dirty windows and harsh fluorescent lighting of the garage drew out shades of tawny and deep gold in his shaggy dark hair.

Her heart twisted painfully hard.

She remembered those shoulders, that lean waist, that dark hair turning gold in some lights. Except he'd been . . . not quite as built back then. He'd been thinner, more greyhound than Rottweiler, and his hair had been cut short.

He's changed.

Well, of course he had. No one went to prison for eight years and came out the same person.

Perhaps if you'd even gone to see him once in all that time . . .

She blinked hard, digging her nails deeper, using the pain to focus once more.

And maybe she'd made a sound of some kind, an inadvertent gasp or the soles of her platform motorcycle boots scraping on the rough concrete floor, because suddenly, the man standing there with his back to her swung around.

She stopped dead, as if that sliver of glass had finally reached her heart.

Levi looked the same. Exactly the same. Still shockingly handsome with the strong line of his jaw, now rough with deep gold stubble, and high, sculpted cheekbones. Straight nose and long, deeply sensual mouth. Silver blue eyes that . . .

Her breath caught, glass cutting straight through her heart and out the other side.

No. She was wrong. He didn't look the same. Not at all. There were lines around his mouth and eyes, lines that hadn't been there before, and that wasn't due to age. That was something more. There was a ring piercing one straight, dark eyebrow, and beneath that it looked like his eye had turned completely black, his pupil huge, a thin ring of silver-blue circling it.

She couldn't stop looking, couldn't stop staring, the shock of seeing him hitting her like a wrecking ball. And then there were more shocks, more blows, as the differences in him began to filter through her consciousness.

The piercing. That one dark eye. The width of his shoulders and the way his T-shirt molded over a chest and stomach ridged with hard muscle. And his arms . . . Jesus, his tattoos. Around each powerful arm was a series of black bands, each one decreasing in width until the bands around his wrists were merely black lines. They were simple, beautiful, highlighting the strength of biceps, forearms, and wrists, and the deep, dark gold of his skin.

When the hell had he gotten those? Levi had never wanted tattoos, no matter how much she'd told him they'd suit him. She'd even teased him about being afraid of the pain, though she knew that wasn't the reason. Levi hadn't wanted the tattoos because he hadn't wanted anything to get in the way of his dreams of escape.

Escape from their shitty Royal Road neighborhood. Escape from Detroit.

He'd planned to get money enough to leave, get a good job in a high-flying company. Have an apartment that didn't have dealers lurking on the stairs and drunks on the sidewalk out front. Build a life that was about more than mere subsistence and struggle. A life that didn't include tattoos.

Looked like he didn't give a shit about that now.

You can't get a high-flying job with tattoos on your arms. You can't get one with a record, either.

The acid in her gut roiled and she had no idea what to say.

Levi didn't break the heavy, impossible silence and he didn't smile. He just stared at her as if she were an insect he'd found crushed under the heel of his boot.

Say something, you idiot.

But her voice seemed to have deserted her entirely. All she

could do was stare back at him, this man who'd once been her best friend. Whose dreams used to help her believe that there was more to life than existing on her grandma's Social Security checks and hiding from the child protection agencies that wanted to take her away and put her in a foster home. More to hope for than a crummy job in the local diner or behind the counter at the 7-Eleven.

But that friend had once been Levi Rush.

She didn't know who this man was, with his pierced eyebrow, tattoos, and aura of leashed violence and menace. A man like all the other thugs that seemed to infest Royal Road.

And then as suddenly as he'd swung around to stare at her, the quality of his strangely asymmetrical stare changed. Became focused, intensifying on her the way a sniper locks onto a target.

It was unnerving. Frightening. And Levi had *never* frightened her before.

He looked even less like her friend than ever before. More like a general about to conquer a city. With her being the city.

Her protective mechanisms, ones she'd built up over a lifetime of being on her own, kicked in with a vengeance and she'd lifted her chin almost before she'd had a chance to think about whether being prickly really was the best way to handle this.

Eight years ago she would have launched herself into his arms for a hug.

But it wasn't eight years ago. It was now. And she'd made so many mistakes already, what was one more?

"Hey, Levi," she said, her voice sounding pathetic and scratchy in the echoing space of the garage. "Long time no see."

Levi had waited a long time for this moment. Eight years to be exact. And it was happening just as he'd predicted.

He'd thought she'd stand there with her chin lifted, that guarded, fuck-you expression on her lovely face. Staring at him like he was a stranger, holding him at a distance the way she did with people she didn't know and didn't trust.

And sure enough, she was.

But even though he'd braced himself, the sight of her again after all these years emptied his lungs and killed his voice anyway.

He should have known. She'd always had that effect on him, even right back when she'd been fifteen and still in school, and he'd been eighteen and feeling like a dirty pervert for wanting her so badly. Even when she'd been his best friend, the person he was closest to and being near her had been such goddamn torture.

But now he wasn't her friend any longer and he'd spent almost a decade in jail.

Maybe that was why he felt like he'd been hit over the head with an iron bar. He was just deprived of female company.

But no, it wasn't that. Because on the drive back from St. Louis to Detroit with Gideon there had been plenty of women all over the goddamn place. And then there had been the warm hug Zoe had given him, yet none of that had inspired this kind of feeling in him. Only Rachel did. Only Rachel *ever* had.

She stood there now, not far away from him, with her long hair loose down her back and dyed a brilliant, electric blue. She wore a tiny, tight-fitting tank top that plastered over her full breasts like plastic wrap, a little black denim miniskirt that barely grazed the tops of her thighs, fishnet tights, and black platform boots that made her long legs look even longer.

Jesus, she was so beautiful. Snow White, he'd once thought, back when he'd been that dumb fucking teenager and in love with her. Back when her hair had been black and her dark eyes had looked at him with warmth and trust and friendship.

No warmth in those dark eyes now though. Or sweetness in that full, sulky mouth of hers. Her lovely face was hard, her expression as tightly closed as the door to the cell that had been his home for so long.

Anger, the simmering rage that had become so much a part of the fabric of his life that he almost didn't notice it anymore, tightened inside him.

He ignored it. There was plenty of time for that. Plenty of time for everything now.

Levi almost smiled. Because that expression on her face wasn't going to last long if he had anything to do with it. And he was most certainly going to have something to do with it.

After eight years inside he had some justice to claim.

And he was going to claim it from her.

Levi straightened and folded his arms. Stared at her. He could feel his dick begin to get hard, reacting to all the honey-colored skin revealed by her fishnet tights and the luscious curve of her breasts beneath her tank top. But he'd had a long time to learn how to control his bodily responses and so he controlled them now. Effortlessly.

Something in her gaze flickered briefly, but he knew what it was. He'd become very adept at looking for fear in people and he could see it in her right now.

She was afraid of him and it didn't cause him any regret at all. Because she should be.

Rachel shifted on her feet, betraying her nervousness, which was hugely satisfying. "So, not even a hello?" Her husky, sexy voice was edged with a familiar sarcasm, yet even so, he heard the fear running underneath it like a cold current in a hot spring.

Satisfaction turned over inside him, settling right down in his gut like a sleepy animal.

Nervous and afraid. Just the way he wanted her.

Slowly, he began to walk toward her.

Rachel's eyes widened, but she held her ground.

He didn't stop.

And when it became clear that he wasn't going to, her eyes widened even further, a momentary flare of fear lighting up the darkness in them. She took a couple of steps back.

He didn't stop, moving inexorably forward.

She cursed and began to back up faster, stumbling a little as his longer stride brought him closer, until she was walking backward quickly, her breathing getting faster. "Levi, what the fuck are you—" Her words were cut off as she backed straight into the door to the garage.

And he kept coming, closer and closer, right up to her, putting out his hands at the last minute and placing them with great care on either side of her head, caging her against the door with his body.

She shrank back against the metal, obviously trying to pull away from him, but there was nowhere for her to go.

And this time, he did smile.

Because finally she was exactly where he'd pictured her for so many lonely fucking years. So many *angry* fucking years.

At his mercy.

"Hello, Rachel," he said softly, clearly.

She stared back at him for a second, the fear large and black in those wide, dark eyes. Then the actual fact of her nearness began to penetrate his consciousness.

They weren't touching, but he could feel her heat, smell the scent of her skin—sweet, like she was something good to eat and yet not too sweet. Vanilla maybe or some kind of flower smell; he wasn't sure which. He didn't remember her smelling like that before, but underneath that there was a slight hint of feminine musk that was all Rachel, so achingly familiar.

Someone behind him was shouting at him, but he ignored it, as desire, want, need rose up inside him, hungry and raw, desperate to claim her. Because she was so close, so fucking close, and it had been so fucking *long,* and he'd promised himself . . .

But right at that moment the fear vanished from her eyes

like a light turning off and anger flared instead. "What the hell is wrong with you?" Her hands came up and she shoved at his chest. "Get the fuck away from me!"

She was surprisingly strong, but he'd had eight years of re-sisting people who'd tried to push him in various ways and if he didn't want to be pushed, he wouldn't be. Then again, he'd made his point, so he let her shove him back a couple of steps, putting some distance between them.

He heard his name being called again—probably Gideon getting pissed with him—but again he ignored it, his focus en-tirely on the woman in front of him.

Her cheeks had an angry flush to them, her chest rising and falling fast in time with her breathing. Anger glittered in her eyes and filled the space between them, tight, hot and dense as a neutron star.

Then she stepped forward and this time it was her turn to get right up close, to get in his face the way he'd gotten into hers. "What kind of hello is that, Levi?"

As if she was the one who was justified in getting angry. As if she had the right to demand things from him.

His own anger, already simmering away, boiled over.

He reached for her again, sliding his arm around her waist and hauling her against him, eight years of rage dying to be let loose. He had so much he wanted to say to her, and yet, when it came down to it, only one thing mattered.

She had to pay. She had to pay for what she'd done to him.

Their gazes clashed, both of them furious. Her hands were flat against the plane of his chest, pushing at him hard, her body rigid. Yet despite all that, she felt so good against him. Warm and soft, everything a woman should be. . . .

"Hey!" Gideon shouted from behind him. "What the fuck is going on? Let her go, Levi."

Yeah, Jesus. Get a hold of yourself. This is not the way it's supposed to go.

Fuck. His control was usually way better than this. He had to stick with the plan, not let her make him crazy like she always used to, damn her.

He gave a low, slightly feral-sounding laugh and released her, raising his hands in surrender and stepping back. "Nothing's going on. Just saying hi."

Rachel's chin was lifted, fury gleaming in her eyes. Her arms were at her sides, hands curled into fists like she was ready to throw a punch. Spots of color glowed on her cheeks and she was looking at him like he was the devil himself.

Fair enough. As far as she was concerned, he was.

Gideon had come up beside them, giving Rachel a look before glancing back at Levi. "I don't want this shit in my garage, I already told you that. I know you two have issues, but—"

"Issues?" Levi interrupted, unable to help himself. "What issues? Oh, right, you mean the fact that she never visited me in the whole eight years I was inside? Not once? Or even how she fucked off when it was time to deliver her statement to the police and—"

"*Enough.*"

It had been a long time since Levi had obeyed anyone who wasn't a guard, and he wasn't about to start now, especially since he was free. But years of respect and trust had ensured Gideon a certain amount of loyalty so Levi made himself stop and shut the fuck up. Probably a good thing anyway since clearly he needed to get himself back under control again.

Rachel had said nothing, but as he watched, he could see a fine tremble shaking her, almost imperceptible, like a subtle earthquake.

Anger. Definitely anger.

Gideon looked at her. "You okay?"

Levi fought down the instinctive burst of irritation that went through him. Christ, as if he'd ever hurt her. Put the fear of God into her, sure, and maybe scare her. Make her suffer in a very specific way, definitely. But no, he'd never hurt her and Gideon should know that.

Then again, Gideon knew how angry Levi was. How Levi used to ask him where Rachel was every time Gideon came to visit. And how bitter the answer "she decided not to come" was, especially when Zee and Zoe had also made the effort.

But not Rachel. Never Rachel.

She would pay for that, too.

Rachel gave a stiff nod, glancing away from him at last. One hand lifted to rub her arm, a familiar, nervous gesture from years ago.

He found his gaze following the movement of her fingers, noticing for the first time her tattoos, a full-length sleeve of deep red roses and other flowers amid dark leaves spilling down over her skin. The drooping head of a rose hung over her shoulder, too, scattering a fall of red petals like drops of blood over her chest.

It was a beautiful design. Beautiful work. And familiar. She'd used to draw stuff like that in the notebooks she constantly lugged around with her. Was it one of her own designs?

Gideon cursed under his breath. "Look, I get that this is difficult. But if you two can't be in the same room without wanting to kill each other, maybe it would be better if Rachel went home."

"It's fine, Gideon," Levi said.

"Is it?" The other man's dark eyes were sharp. "Because it sure as hell doesn't look fine to me."

Levi crushed his anger flat. Made himself hard and cold, the way he'd been for the past eight years. The only way he'd managed to survive. "I appreciate you coming for me, Gideon. I appreciate everything you've offered me since I got back. But what's between Rachel and me is none of your fucking business."

"What's between us?" Rachel's voice was hoarse and a little thick. "There's *nothing* between us. Nothing at all."

Levi shifted his gaze back to her. He didn't speak, just held her dark eyes with his, because they both knew exactly how much bullshit that was.

Her mouth set in a hard line, and he remembered that, her stubborn will. Like him, she hated backing down. On anything.

Well, this week she would. He'd make her.

Gideon sighed. "Okay, fine. Rip each other to shreds, see if I care. But don't do it here, okay? Blood is very difficult to get out of concrete."

Rachel said nothing, staring at Levi for one angry second.

Then abruptly she turned on her heel and strode out of the garage.

Oh, shit no. She wasn't leaving that easily, not when he hadn't said what he wanted to say.

Levi stepped forward after her, only to find one of Gideon's large, powerful hands gripping his shoulder, stopping him.

"Levi," Gideon said in a low voice. "Let her go."

He stiffened.

No. This is Gideon, remember? Not Mace or any of his hench-assholes. Or one of the guards. So maybe relax and not break his fucking arm.

Levi let out a long, silent breath, making his muscles loosen. Then he glanced at his friend.

In the car on the long drive from the Central Michigan Correctional Facility in St. Louis back to Detroit, Gideon hadn't mentioned Rachel, keeping the conversation firmly about what was happening with Zoe and Zee, and the garage. Filling him in on how Zee had been revealed as big, bad Joshua Chase's long-lost son and his engagement to the daughter of one of Detroit's most wealthy families. And then telling him that Levi had a job he could come back to and could crash on Gideon's sofa until he found himself a place to live.

It was all typical Gideon, generous to a fault. But the guy was operating on the assumption that Levi was the same man who'd gone to prison on manslaughter charges eight years earlier.

And he wasn't.

The Levi who'd gone into prison was a boy compared to the man he was now. A much harder man. A man who knew what he wanted and had put in place meticulous plans on how to get it.

After all, he'd had a lot of time to think about it.

Levi smiled at his friend and gently pulled Gideon's hand off his shoulder.

Then he strode straight out the door after Rachel.